REINCARNATED AS A DRAGON HATCHLING

NOVEL 7

WRITTEN BY
Necoco

ILLUSTRATED BY
NAJI Yanagida

Airship

Seven Seas Entertainment

LITHOVAR TRIBE

BELA
Priestess of the anti-Dragon God Faction and Hibi's younger sister. Took over after her older sister passed away in the Lithovar Tribe crisis and worked with Illusia.

ALLO
A young Lithovar girl who was sacrificed to the Manticore. She was brought back to life with the Ouroboros's skills and has regained her body due to evolution.

HUNGRY HUNTERS

VALON
The man who protected Hibi. An adept warrior, but his face betrays his emotions.

TOLEMANN
A noble from Ardesia. He led his private army, the Hungry Hunters, to the forest in search of the mythical beast Carbuncle who is said to live there.

NOAH'S FOREST

MELTIA
A swordswoman from the Royal Capital. Brought Myria along on her journey after the two met in the village.

MYRIA
A kindhearted girl who named our hero. Traveling with Meltia after meeting her in the village.

BLACK LIZARD
A trusted companion of our hero. Master of poison attacks.

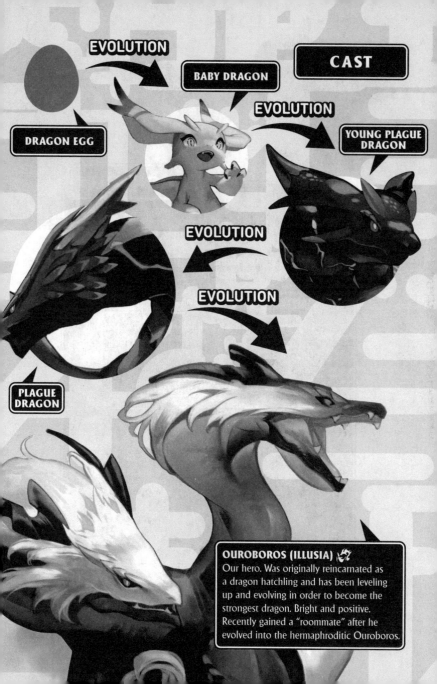

EVOLUTION

DRAGON EGG

BABY DRAGON

CAST

EVOLUTION

YOUNG PLAGUE DRAGON

EVOLUTION

EVOLUTION

PLAGUE DRAGON

OUROBOROS (ILLUSIA)
Our hero. Was originally reincarnated as a dragon hatchling and has been leveling up and evolving in order to become the strongest dragon. Bright and positive. Recently gained a "roommate" after he evolved into the hermaphroditic Ouroboros.

CONTENTS

Our hero, Illusia, has now made friends with the Lithovar tribe, who have dubbed him "Dragon King." After defeating the avyssos that had been terrorizing the tribe for a long time, he heads back to the village, only to find that a large number of its residents have fallen victim to mysterious poison and paralysis status effects. He's also saddened to hear that Hibi, the tribe's priestess and the only one Illusia was able to speak to via Telepathy, has been killed outside the village. It turns out that the villagers' strange status conditions are being caused by a spell cast on the nearby river that the tribe relies on for drinking water. Once Illusia realizes this was the work of an outsider, he asks the Anti-Dragon God faction for their aid and then unites with both factions of the Lithovar tribe to take the fight to the intruders.

Meanwhile, the aristocrat Tolemann and his mercenary group, the Hungry Hunters, have come to the forest to hunt the legendary magical beast, Carbuncle. When they come across the forest-dwelling Lithovar tribe, they suspect the tribe knows about the Carbuncle, so they attempt to massacre the tribe while gathering information. Unfortunately for the Hungry Hunters, the Lithovar tribe has our Ouroboros hero Illusia on their side. Backed into a corner, Tolemann sets fire to the forest, angering the larans, who serve as the forest's guardians. They fuse together to face Tolemann as Laragwolf—more commonly known as the mythical Carbuncle.

The forest is saved by the power of Laragwolf and Ouroboros, and the friction between the two Lithovar factions is resolved. However, sensing that his presence may bring danger to the Lithovarians, Illusia decides to leave the forest behind.

Tensei Sitara Dragon no Tamago datta-
Saikyo Igai Mezasane Volume 7
© Necoco/Naji Yanagida 2018
Originally published in Japan in 2018
by EARTH STAR Entertainment, Tokyo.
English translation rights arranged with
EARTH STAR Entertainment, Tokyo,
through TOHAN CORPORATION, Tokyo.

Seven Seas press and purchase enquiries can be sent to
Marketing Manager Lauren Hill at press@gomanga.com.
Information regarding the distribution and purchase of
digital editions is available from Digital Manager CK Russell
at digital@gomanga.com.

Follow Seven Seas Entertainment online at
sevenseasentertainment.com.

TRANSLATION: Jason Muell, Casper Kazor
ADAPTATION: Harry Catlin
LOGO DESIGN: George Panella
COVER DESIGN: H. Qi
INTERIOR LAYOUT & DESIGN: Clay Gardner
COPY EDITOR: Jade Gardner
PROOFREADER: Meg van Huygen
EDITOR: Laurel Ashgrove
PREPRESS TECHNICIAN: Melanie Ujimori, Jules Valera
MANAGING EDITOR: Alyssa Scavetta
EDITOR-IN-CHIEF: Julie Davis
PUBLISHER: Lianne Sentar
VICE PRESIDENT: Adam Arnold
PRESIDENT: Jason DeAngelis

ISBN: 978-1-63858-766-8
Printed in Canada
First Printing: August 2024
10 9 8 7 6 5 4 3 2 1

CHAPTER

1

The Island at the Edge of the World

PART 1

．．．

THE HEADWIND WAS quite pleasant. When I looked back, the forest appeared small and far away; you couldn't even see the Lithovar settlement we'd just left anymore. Now that I thought about it, I realized that this was the first time I'd ever flown so far.

I had fought against Tolemann's army in order to protect the Lithovar tribe and emerged victorious, but I couldn't stay there. At the end of the battle, Tolemann had told me that it was no use running because, no matter how far I went or how strong I'd become, the heroes and saints would one day defeat me. By "saints" I knew he was talking about humans who, like heroes, had been granted a powerful status by the Divine Voice.

As a rank A Ouroboros dragon, if I were to remain in that village, we'd be facing saints sooner or later, and they'd almost certainly be more powerful than Tolemann's private army. Not to mention, I had obtained a skill related to the Divine Voice known as the Human Realm Path. I didn't know much about this skill yet, but I knew it was coveted by heroes, and it might attract the saints as well.

Many of the soldiers in Tolemann's private army managed to escape, and there were also some I willingly spared. The news that they'd run into me would almost certainly reach the saints, wherever they were right now. I couldn't get the Lithovar tribe wrapped up in that drama.

So I decided to leave the forest with some companions: Allo, the undead girl I'd revived; Petit-Nightmare, the spider monster that my partner picked up; and Treant, who I'd made out of a tree.

Having left the Lithovar tribe behind, I had no idea where I was going. The Lithovar tribe didn't know much about the world beyond the forest, and now, in retrospect, I regretted that I hadn't spent more time learning about this world's geography in detail when I had the chance to speak with Adoff.

But at my current flight speed, I could avoid human settlements by flying high above them. *Although that'll make it harder to find a new place to live...*

I hadn't decided where to go just yet, but I *had* decided on one thing: I was going to show myself off to as many human villages as possible as I went. I wanted to keep the Lithovar tribe settlements off the Ouroboros hunters' radar. I'd already told Nell, the demi-human swordsman from the Hungry Hunters, that I wasn't sticking around in the forest, but it was worth erasing all doubt.

We flew above many towns, and I could see little dots—human figures—moving around down below. I couldn't help but wonder what it looked like from their perspective. Were they pointing up at me and screaming?

("Hey, watch it! You're gonna drop him!")

Hearing Partner's cry, I realized my grip on Treant had loosened, causing it to rustle its branches about in my hands. *My bad, my bad. You could be a little nicer about it, though.*

Partner was glowering at Treant, almost as if she was wondering why I'd even brought it along in the first place. I averted my gaze and decided to ignore her for the time being.

Allo, perched atop my head, was able to maintain her grip thanks to the extra lump of earth I'd used to reinforce her hand, making it bigger. She seemed to be holding on okay, so I decided to pick up the speed.

The masked spider, Petit-Nightmare, had created a web around Partner's head, so I figured it was doing fine. I glanced back over at Partner to make sure...but Petit-Nightmare was nowhere to be seen.

Hey, where'd Petit-Nightmare go? Don't tell me you ate it?

Partner jerked her head back. I turned around and followed her gaze—and had to do a double take when I saw Petit-Nightmare shooting through the sky, straight at me! As I looked closer, I noticed a tiny glimmer of light in front of it—it was a shiny, silky thread reflecting in the sunlight.

H-hey! Aren't you scared it's gonna fall? That doesn't seem safe... I guess it's fine if Petit-Nightmare is having fun, but don't you think it's flapping around a bit too much? Don't let me get to where we're going and then realize we lost it along the way.

After several hours of flying, we finally passed a long stretch of cities. With my current abilities, I figured I could easily travel around the whole world all on my own in around a week. But, to be fair, I had no idea how big this world actually was.

I passed the towns and reached a mountain range with the endless sea stretching out beyond. *These mountains might be a good spot for me to land and take a breather,* I thought.

But, no... It would be best to fly a little farther and try to cross the sea. Unless there was some sort of land bridge, there was no way all the Ouroboros drama would've spread across the water. In fact, maybe it'd be best to stay offshore for a bit, to avoid running into any other parties. *Maybe living on a remote island somewhere would work?*

I crossed the mountains and flew far beyond them. After a few hours, I started feeling a little hungry again. It would probably be a good idea to actually get down to business and find a new place to live. If I didn't find anything, then I'd have to turn back. As I mulled over my options, I started to feel a strange sensation.

Or, rather, maybe that strange sensation had been with me the whole time. After all, I hadn't been able to see the horizon clearly up until now, and yet here it was, completely visible. The reason why became clearer as we got closer.

The sea was falling off the edge of a huge cliff. It looked almost like a waterfall, but it was far too large for that. I felt like I needed a new word to describe this phenomenon. Seawater poured down into a huge, mysterious blue void, so deep that I couldn't see the bottom. And the water just kept coming—tons and tons of it pouring down the edge every second... Just looking at it made me feel like I was being sucked in.

For a moment, my mind went blank. Then came the questions. *What's beyond this cliff? How does this endless* supply of water keep flowing down it without the sea level dropping? If this world isn't a sphere, then what's going on with gravity, and the stars?

There was a large island at the edge of the waterfall, with mountains, cliffs, and a huge tree growing in the grasslands. It looked rather out of place. There was no sign of life there. It was a spectacle to behold, this island on the edge of the world.

Should we...be here? Maybe we should turn back. Whatever this is, it looks like bad news. But, I mean, I am rank A, so I can probably handle it...right?

I'd recently been struggling to find prey strong enough to earn me decent experience points, so I'd been thinking it'd be a good idea to move to a place with some better monsters. But this wasn't exactly what I had in mind...

I slowed down and lowered my altitude in preparation to land on the island. *Yeah. It should be fine.* In the worst case, I could always beat a hasty retreat.

PART 2

I MANAGED TO LAND safely and let Petit-Nightmare and Treant off, with Allo perched on my head all the while. I didn't particularly mind if she stayed there, if that's what she preferred.

I heard a low, guttural roar from Partner, who shot me a slightly terrifying glare. *("I'm starving here.")*

Of course, after spending the better part of a day flying around, I was hungry and exhausted too. If I couldn't find anything to eat here, I was a little worried about whether I'd be able to survive the flight back.

I looked around. The area where we'd landed was a meadow filled with strange flowers that had long, iridescent petals, which seemed to perfectly suit the rather fantastical land we'd found. In the distance, a tiny lone tree sprouted up from the ground, surrounded by rainbow-colored flowers. It bore a single large, bright red fruit.

An apple, maybe? The color was strangely vivid, though. Maybe it'd be a good idea to check it out a bit before letting Partner eat it.

I didn't notice any monsters in the area, though I did spot another much bigger tree and cliffs off in the distance. It was honestly a pretty beautiful sight. *There might be some dangerous monsters lurking out in that direction,* I mused.

Looking off in the other direction, I could see the sea being sucked down into that great expanse. No matter how many times I looked at it, it still made my skin prickle. *Ugh... I'm starting to have second thoughts about being here.*

For now, at least, our goal was to secure some food and a place to roost before worrying about leveling up. It wouldn't hurt to bump up Allo and the others' levels too.

After defeating the hero, I'd acquired a mysterious skill called "Human Realm Path." Judging from the fact that the hero's level cap dropped the moment this was removed, it might be something related to evolution. If that's the case, then in the next evolution we could overcome some of the Ouroboros's flaws and turn into a proper dragon...maybe. A long time ago, something that looked like a demi-human had shown up as one of my evolution options. Maybe it was something like that?

In any case, my next level target would be...

ILLUSIA

SPECIES: Ouroboros

STATUS: Normal

LV: 92/125

HP: 2425/2425

MP: 2432/2432

Wow, okay, that's pretty high. Stupidly so, in fact. We'd fought the red ants in the Harunae Desert, fought the heroes, joined the Lithovar tribe in their avyssos hunt, and engaged in all-out war with Hungry Hunters, and yet I was still only about three quarters of the way there. And the higher level you had, the harder each level was to earn—it was definitely going to take some time.

I usually ended up fighting rank C monsters, around two ranks lower than me. There weren't all that many rank B monsters out there. It was possible that I was already the strongest thing there was in this world. Considering the descriptions of the other evolutionary branches, I felt like the world would've been destroyed ten times over by now if there were a bunch of rank A monsters roaming about. If an Ouroboros were to go to war with some nation and really threw themselves into the fight, it could mean the complete decimation of an entire country. It was a good thing the only Ouroboros we had to worry about was me.

Now that I'd seen the edge of the ocean, I was starting to think that maybe the world wasn't as big as I originally thought.

I still don't have my Final Evolution skill, though. And is the one responsible for the Divine Voice stuff really trying to make me destroy the world?

NAME: **Allo**
SPECIES: **Levana Low Liche**
STATUS: **Cursed**
LV: **59/65**
HP: **362/362**
MP: **381/381**

Allo had gotten much stronger lately. I could tell it was only a matter of time until she evolved. She was currently a rank C+, so she'd probably evolve into a B or B+. Although she had high HP and MP, I was a little worried about her movement speed compared to the others. While I was mulling that over, I noticed that Treant was trying to catch my eye.

Honestly, I was just hoping that Treant would do its best and grow at its own pace. Then again, it seemed like it'd done pretty well fighting alongside Allo in their battle against the Hungry Hunters. *Maybe it'll evolve again soon too.*

SPECIES: **Lesser Treant**
STATUS: **Cursed**

> LV: **14/25**
> HP: **86/86**
> MP: **74/74**

I started to feel a bit overwhelmed, so I gently averted my gaze.

Let's see, so Treant is rank D, right? It hasn't evolved even once since we met in the forest near the Lithovar tribe village, so I guess that makes sense. I'm kinda shocked it's only gained thirteen levels after everything that happened, though.

When Treant joined the party, Allo was still just a pile of bones. Why was it falling so far behind?

Maybe we'll just have to work together and help it level up.

Next up, Petit-Nightmare.

> SPECIES: **Petit-Nightmare**
> STATUS: **Normal**
> LV: **37/45**
> HP: **163/163**
> MP: **155/155**

Petit-Nightmare glanced briefly at me before turning toward Treant and shooting out what looked like a lump of thread, which landed in a clump in front of Treant.

"Grooooo!"

Hey now, Treant's got more seniority than you! Don't expect me to forgive you if you try doing something like that again! I got so worked up that I growled out loud.

Petit-Nightmare turned to face Partner, almost as if disappointed. After being comforted by Partner, Petit-Nightmare shot me another glare. *Seriously, Partner, you were all annoyed at Petit-Nightmare's behavior earlier, and now you're comforting it? Hmph.*

I turned my attention back to Treant. *I won't let anyone bully you, buddy.*

I went to rub my cheek affectionately against Treant, but it moved back a step.

Oh, right. Sorry about that.

Ah well. I needed to try and pick my mood up a bit, find some monsters, and figure out how dangerous this place was. *Keep an eye on Allo for me, okay?*

I looked around at our surroundings and heard Partner snort. She lowered her head and took a big mouthful of the rainbow flowers growing on the ground nearby. Soil poured out between her teeth as she chewed and spat out a big clod of dirt.

("Mm, delicious.")

She sounded satisfied. The whole thing seemed rather silly to me, but I opened my mouth wide to expose my fangs and reached down to munch on a flower, tearing it to pieces. I thought I wouldn't be able to tell from just one, but I could actually taste a gentle sweetness spreading throughout my mouth, and the sweet scent even made its way up to my nasal cavities. It was so good that I felt like I could take a nap right there.

Pretty good. What kind of flower is it?

Reigula: Value A-. A beautiful flower with rainbow-colored petals.
Though it does not wither with age, it is said to take one hundred years to bloom. It is very delicate and difficult to grow. It adds a pleasant sweetness to any meal and causes sleepiness, but certainly there's no one stupid enough to use such an incredibly expensive flower for such purposes.

One...one hundred years?

I glanced over to my side, where Partner was innocently munching away. *What are you doing?*

Hmm, I haven't fallen asleep yet, I thought. *Then again, I am a giant dragon.*

The A– valued flowers were all clustered together in a small area. *If I were a human, I'd want to take them home with me and become a millionaire. But they're apparently quite difficult to grow, and besides, who the heck would spend a hundred years to grow a flower like this? I'm amazed there are so many out here just growing naturally.*

Or maybe there was some sort of bug or monster that took care of the reigula?

Suddenly, Partner jerked her head up, a stern glare on her face. The flower she'd been munching on fell from her mouth. *Did she see something?* I followed her line of sight and saw someone running toward us from a tree that looked like it had apples growing from it.

The figure was running straight toward us, and it appeared to be human—a muscular and nude human. Oddly enough, I couldn't sense its presence, almost as if it had a high-level skill that let it conceal itself.

What was a human doing in a place like this? Were they from a tribe who had been living here for a long time, maybe?

More to the point, though, why was this figure naked? And why weren't they afraid of me? They were running straight toward a rank A Ouroboros dragon! I tilted my head to the side and, as the naked figure approached, I suddenly realized something terrifying.

The figure had no neck. I couldn't spot any sign of injury, so it didn't seem like its neck had been cut off—the skin between its shoulders was terrifyingly smooth. Not only that, but it sported an enlarged humanlike face, stretching from its chest to its abdomen. Alarm bells rang in my head. *This is a bad guy.*

The figure gradually increased its pace as it approached. It wasn't much at first, but it quickly got so fast that I felt a sense of danger. Judging by his speed, this was no weakling.

He had the face of an older gentleman with a beard. However, his expression remained fixed and unchanging—he was quite creepy.

PART 3

A S THE NAKED, headless figure ran straight for me, I briefly considered trying to make a quick escape. The monster was clearly not a normal animal; on the other hand, I was a rank A monster.

I needed to calm down and think rationally. I hadn't ever encountered another rank A monster. Even out here

in this strange place, it seemed unlikely that I'd run into one right off the bat. This was probably just a monster with an incredibly high-speed stat.

I took a step back and took in the sight of the headless human once again.

SPECIES: Adam

STATUS: Normal

LV: 73/100

HP: 833/833

MP: 452/452

ATTACK: 652

DEFENSE: 561

MAGIC: 592

AGILITY: 691

RANK: A-

SPECIAL SKILLS:

   AUTOMATIC HP RECOVERY: Lv 6

   PSYCHIC SENSE: Lv 7

   STEALTH: Lv 7

RESISTANCE SKILLS:

   PHYSICAL RESISTANCE: Lv 4

   HUNGER RESISTANCE: Lv 7

   POISON RESISTANCE: Lv 4

PARALYSIS RESISTANCE: Lv 4

ILLUSION RESISTANCE: Lv 2

CURSE RESISTANCE: Lv 3

CONFUSION RESISTANCE: Lv 5

NORMAL SKILLS:

CLAY: Lv 4

DISEASED BREATH: Lv 5

CURSE: Lv 5

DEATH: Lv 6

GARDENING: Lv 5

GRAVIDON: Lv MAX

POWER FIST: Lv 5

METEOR KICK: Lv 4

HIGH JUMP: Lv 6

TITLE SKILLS:

FINAL EVOLUTION: Lv —

DENIZEN OF THE EDGE OF THE WORLD: Lv —

GRAVITY SHOOTER: Lv —

SORCERER: Lv 6

GARDENER OF THE EDGE OF THE WORLD: Lv —

TENACIOUS: Lv 9

Well, this was definitely going to be a problematic enemy.

Its stats were completely broken. It far surpassed Mother, who still held the top spot of all the enemies I'd fought so far. One wrong step and I could be in for a pretty painful beating from this guy. *Who is this Adam, anyway? You're clearly not the first human, not without having a head and all. Did you drop it somewhere or something?*

Adam: Rank A− Monster. A strange-looking monster that lives in the outermost lands. He has an aggressive personality and once kicked a group of heroes who happened to visit the island to death before they had a chance to mount a defense. In addition to his overwhelming physical strength, he can also use other indirect methods such as curses to kill strong opponents he finds difficult to beat normally. He is the main reason why people are afraid of strange monsters who live on the other side of the sea. Though he attacks animals with an unbelievable tenacity, he has a softer side that adores nature.

I had casually landed here only to suddenly find myself confronted by some kind of secret boss. *Wait a sec, isn't this kinda weird? He's some sort of homicidal creature...yet a lover of nature. If that's not a personality clash, I don't know what is.*

I hurriedly called out to Allo where she sat atop my head, then raised my upper body and grabbed Treant. Petit-Nightmare, just as quick to respond as usual, launched out more silky threads and attached itself to Partner's head.

I kicked off from the ground and leaped up into the air, beating my wings.

Adam passed right under me, then stopped to stare up at me with the same unchanging expression still fixed on his face. He then stamped his foot against the ground with a loud bang several times. I felt fear wash over me. There was something terrifying about watching him express his anger through his physical movements while his expression betrayed nothing. I never thought that the time would come when I would be frightened by a monster smaller than myself. The impact of Adam's foot sent dirt flying up in the air, forming a cloud of dust and causing Adam himself to disappear.

I turned my head to look out past the edge of the island.

I needed to think things over. If we intended to live here, we'd need to get rid of Adam. If I maintained my distance, I should be able to launch long-range attacks at him from here. Or perhaps I should withdraw temporarily and hope we could catch him off guard?

Then again, I was kinda huge—I'd have a hard time hiding myself. If I did something stupid like transforming into a human, with my incredibly low stats, I'd risk just getting kicked to death immediately. Alas, I didn't think Allo, Petit-Nightmare, or Treant would be much help in a fight.

Partner growled. *("Hey, it looks like he's doing something?")*

At Partner's warning, I returned my gaze to Adam. I could see Adam's cloud of dust gathering in the center in a strange spiral. Suddenly the dust cleared, almost as if it had been swallowed up by a whirlpool, and left a glowing black sphere in its place, floating in front of Adam. The black sphere not only sucked up the dust in the air but the chunks of ground around it as well.

This was the gravity magic, Gravidon. From what I'd seen, Gravidon was a powerful attack that could cause more damage than the monster's stats would typically allow. What's more, Adam's MP was way higher than any monster I'd run into before, so I had no idea how powerful this attack would be.

With a bang, a black orb shot out from Adam's mouth. It was difficult to dodge the approaching attack due to its tremendous speed, so I immediately guarded with my wings. The black sphere gouged a chunk out of my wing and exploded with a shockwave. A sharp pain ran through me. My wing bones felt broken, and their feathers fluttered, causing me to lose my balance in the air.

That attack boasted both incredible speed and power. I wasn't sure how many shots I could take. My thoughts were interrupted again, though, as I saw the black light gathering in Adam's mouth once more.

Whoa, that's not fair! Shouldn't there be some sort of cooldown timer on such a powerful attack? Or is this what Gravidon is like at the highest skill level?

I finally lost my balance and began tumbling back to the earth, so I flapped my wings desperately to launch a Whirlwind Slash. Adam deftly dodged left and right to avoid the blades of wind as they slammed hard into the ground in a straight line, sending violent plumes of dust up into the air.

Adam fired a second Gravidon. I once again pulled my wings forward to guard, but the damage was even greater than before. The black sphere embedded in my wing and shook my entire body violently. I could feel the bones in my wings shatter, and I quickly lost altitude.

Damn it, was it a mistake to make a quick escape and take to the air? I knew that he could use Gravidon, but

I didn't expect it to be so accurate and powerful. At this distance, I was at a complete disadvantage. On top of that, with Treant in my hand and Allo on my head, it was hard to make any big movements. Should I close the distance and take him head-on? Still, his exceptionally high offensive power was making me cautious about melee combat—not to mention that story about what happened to the heroes.

Adam looked up at me with his disinterested expression as I tumbled to the ground. As usual, only his feet moved around as he stomped aggressively on the ground.

I used Regenerate as I fell to repair my broken wings. Instead of getting better, the pain got even worse, but somehow the angle of the distorted wings improved, and it finally regained its original shape.

("Watch out, this creep's pretty tough! What're you gonna do about it?!")

Honestly, I'd kind of figured I'd have a little more room to work with against this monster due to the difference between his level and rank. Ouroboros, however, was inherently better suited for long, protracted battles. When it came to fighting a monster of the same rank class, endurance was going to be an issue.

I could still recover if I was attacked, and I still could make my endurance abilities work to my advantage, but

I had to be careful about getting hit since I had Allo, Petit-Nightmare, and Treant to watch after.

Luckily, in terms of offensive power, I had the upper hand. When it came to speed, however, he was superior. If I took this down to close combat, there was a high possibility Allo or the others would get hit, so that wasn't an option.

Adam repeatedly bent his knees and stretched back up. Considering his skills, it seemed like he was preparing for High Jump. He'd stopped with his Gravidon volley, so it looked as if he planned to use High Jump to defeat me in close combat instead.

This was one hell of an opponent. I'd never expected to run into a monster with enough strength to single-handedly take down Ouroboros. On the other hand, though, this was a great opportunity to level up. I didn't exactly have the luxury of choosing easier means—nor was he going to give me the option of carefully choosing how I'd counterattack.

Adam bent down low once again before thrusting back up.

Come and get it! I threw my fist up into the air the moment his feet left the ground.

I threw Treant high into the air. I could see it looking down at me with a dumbfounded expression. Partner also wasn't sure what was going on, looking up in wide-eyed surprise as Treant was suddenly launched into the air.

I spread my wings to slow my fall, then I shook my head and sent Allo flying straight up into the air. Then I looked up and opened my mouth.

"M-Master Dragon!" Allo hurriedly stretched out her body to try and climb onto my nose, but I opened my mouth up again and sucked her in.

Much to my surprise, though she felt like she was covered with human skin, when my saliva touched her body, it felt as if she had melted and turned to mud...

But this wasn't the time to think about it. *Hey, Partner, is Petit-Nightmare's spider web anywhere near you?* I grabbed a strand of it and pulled Petit-Nightmare into my mouth. Petit-Nightmare quickly cut off the thread it was hanging on to and fell down. Apparently, it wasn't keen on being eaten...

It's only for a moment, okay! It's too dangerous outside!

Petit-Nightmare slowly flew away from me as the wind caught hold of the thread. I had no idea it could do that.

Well, now Allo was sheltered in my mouth and Petit-Nightmare was now hopefully a safe distance away. With Treant out of the way as well, I could fight Adam hand-to-hand without having to worry about them.

Adam was leaping right toward me.

I had to admit, his High Jump skill was terrifying. I thought it was just a plain skill when that cow had used it, but it seemed to be surprisingly useful. Not that I needed it myself when I had Flying.

Adam's attack power was high, and he moved fast, with good melee skills to boot. He was also confident, so he must've challenged a dragon like me to melee combat in the past. Even if you were able to dodge any of his other attacks, all he had to do was land a kick on you and you'd be done for. However, I also knew I had skills which could very likely counteract his own.

I threw my head forward and rolled hard in the air as I fell toward Adam, using my Roll skill. Even if my opponent was a master of close combat, he shouldn't be able to slip through this one.

Adam froze in the air for a moment, then pulled his leg around and unleashed his kick. However, Adam's leg bounced off my fast-spinning scales, snapping it in an unnatural direction. Still Rolling, I stretched my tail and pursued Adam as he fell defenselessly. My tail slammed directly into him, sending him crashing to the ground.

Even with how closely matched our stats were, View Status gave me a big advantage. If he could've anticipated that I was going to Roll, he wouldn't have acted recklessly.

Adam hit the ground on his back and bounced into the air. I charged right at him, rotating at high speed. A massive crater was smashed into the ground on impact, and I heard a tremendous scream as Adam stretched out his arms in front of him. "Waaaaaaaugh!"

Gained 4,672 Experience Points.
Title Skill "Walking Egg" Lv — activated: gained 4,672 Experience Points.
Ouroboros Lv 92 has become Lv 96.

Is...is he dead?

I had to admit, an A– monster was pretty impressive and yielded a ridiculous amount of experience points. I didn't think that the time would come when I could raise four levels at once.

The eyes of Adam's corpse were also wide open, staring at my face. It was just plain creepy. *He's not going to get up later, right?* Adam's body was scraped up in a few places and covered in blood, but still mostly intact.

Anyway, I was glad that Roll had scored a clean hit. If the difference in our speed and physique had let him dodge, it was possible I could've been beaten down by one of his powerful attacks.

I looked up at the sky and saw Treant just beginning to fall, so I stretched out my wings to catch it. I bent my wings to reduce the impact, and it rolled down them to the ground before shooting me an angry glare.

Hey, there was nothing I could do about that! That was my only choice to take out the monster!

That reminded me, though. I opened my mouth and stretched out my tongue. Slowly, Allo crawled out of my mouth. My saliva clung to her body, causing it to partially melt, and she was still crawling on the ground, her head titled upward to glare at me. I quietly closed my eyes and bowed my head deeply.

Petit-Nightmare, who had narrowly escaped being eaten, also returned to my side.

I had to admit that this monster was really, truly amazing. However, with him out of the way, it would be pretty easy to live on this far-flung island. It was hard to imagine that there were many other monsters like Adam out there, after all. If I cast Fake Life on his corpse, then I could turn him into quite a powerful monster, though I didn't feel like doing that. Instead, just to be on the safe side, I decided to bury it somewhere nearby. The only question was, where should the corpse go?

When I looked to the side, I saw something flesh-colored sticking out of Partner's mouth.

("This is surprisingly tasty!")

What do you think you're doing?! I know you were hungry. But there are things you can and can't do! Hey! Spit it out! I definitely don't want to digest that humanoid thing!

("You're really annoying, you know that?")

With a grumpy expression, Partner spat it out. All that remained was the leg below the knee.

("Listen, that's mine.")

Who wants to eat that?! There's no way I could eat such a disgusting creature!

PART 4

P ETIT-NIGHTMARE WENT TO WORK on Adam's leg. The spider monster wrapped it in thread and then sat on top of it, sticking out its fangs to suck out his blood. I couldn't believe that Partner and Petit-Nightmare could just chow down on something like that. But then again, it did make a certain amount of sense considering they were both simply monsters and Adam's body didn't look all that disgusting. In a sense, it wasn't much different from a cow with a face on its belly... Though, to tell the truth, I wouldn't eat that either.

I approached the nearby apple-like tree that Adam had been guarding and brought my face close to the single bright red fruit that was growing there. Looking carefully, I could see that part of the skin was sort of hollowed out, resembling the shape of a face with an anguished expression. When my eyes met it, I instinctively turned away.

It was pretty clear this wasn't an ordinary apple, but I wasn't sure what the bizarre fruit was.

Fruit of Wisdom: Value L (Legendary). A fruit made by God that granted the first humans wisdom and allowed them to develop language, civilization, magic, technology, and war. This language and power was passed down by word of mouth and by blood, and still exists within all humans.

The Fruit Tree of Wisdom was burned to the ground by the angels once it had served its purpose. Now there is only one left in the far-flung land where no one ventures.

What the heck was it talking about? I wasn't too sure, but its value was "L"? No way!

Rank L (Legendary)
Rank L (Legendary) indicates the rank above A.

Most monsters and items worthy of this rank have already been lost to time. The only monsters that can claim this rank are those who have gained the attention of the gods.

I'd never heard of such a rank! There was a rank higher than A??

Adam was the first other rank A monster I'd ever encountered, and I'd only seen a few items with that rank such as the Hero's Sword. What was rank Legendary? How many monsters with that rank were there in this world?

It seemed like everything on this island was inflated. Why were there flowers with a value of A− just growing like weeds and legendary fruits sprouting from the trees?

I figured it was best to just ignore the fruit for now; somehow, it just seemed too dangerous. I had the feeling that an upset stomach would be the least of my worries if I ate it.

There was only one Fruit of Wisdom on the tree, but I couldn't help but wonder how many years it took for one to grow. Did Adam eat a lot of them? I didn't think so, but I couldn't help but wonder whether, if you ate it, you'd lose your head too and form a face on your stomach, joining Adam's ranks...

("If you're not gonna eat it, then give it to me.") Partner stretched out her neck and sank her fangs into the Fruit of Wisdom. I hurriedly pulled her head back with my front legs and got in the way.

"Grrrooowwl."

Partner's neck swayed. With the fruit caught on her fangs, the branch bearing the Fruit of Wisdom bent. When the fruit came off her fangs, the branch rebounded, and the force of the impact caused the fruit to snap off the branch and soar through the air.

("Hey! What're you doin'?!")

This was getting ridiculous. *Stop trying to put everything in your mouth! Are you some kind of baby?! If you eat it, it's my stomach that's going to end up digesting it! Didn't you see the message from the Divine Voice just now?!*

("I did! It's a fruit you rarely get a chance to eat!")

So you did see it?? And that's the first thing that came to mind?

The Fruit of Wisdom flew into the air...toward Treant, who just so happened to be yawning at the time. The fruit landed straight in its mouth (hole?).

Partner and I both yelped out growls of surprise as we watched as Treant's mouth-shaped hole closed and its entire body began to glow faintly. Partner, Allo, me, and even Petit-Nightmare were staring at Treant in a daze, but Treant itself looked curiously back at us, twisting its trunk slightly and looking around. Before long, the faint light enveloping its body disappeared.

Are you okay, Treant? It doesn't look like anything's changed.

Partner looked like she was about to say something, but no words came out. *Did you have something to say, Partner?*

"Hm? What're you talking about?"

Huh? Wait... That wasn't Partner. Oh no!

SPECIES: **Lesser Treant**

STATUS: **Cursed**

LV: **14/25**

HP: **86/86**

MP: **74/74**

ATTACK: **28**

DEFENSE: **76**

MAGIC: **65**

AGILITY: **33**

SPECIAL SKILLS:

   DARK TYPE: **Lv —**

   GRECIAN LANGUAGE: **Lv 2**

RESISTANCE SKILLS:

PHYSICAL RESISTANCE: Lv 3

TAKE ROOT: Lv 4

CLAY: Lv 2

REST: Lv 2

FIRE SPHERE: Lv 1

AQUA SPHERE: Lv 1

CLAY SPHERE: Lv 1

WIND SPHERE: Lv 1

TELEPATHY: Lv 1

GRAVITY: Lv 1

TITLE SKILLS:

EVIL DRAGON'S SERVANT: Lv —

DEVOURER OF THE FRUIT OF WISDOM: Lv —

Jeez, its language skills and magic skills had increased. Was that due to the effects of the Fruit of Wisdom? All that after eating one piece of fruit? *I kinda wish I ate it too... But hey, what's this?*

WIND SPHERE: Lv 1

TELEPATHY: Lv 1

GRAVITY: Lv 1

Telepathy?! No way!

I wish someone had told me about this first, then I could've eaten it myself!

("Aaah, if only you hadn't stopped me from eating it, Partner.")

Hey, I didn't know about that! Hey, Treant, do you think you can spit it out? Even if it's only a small chunk?

Treant gently shook its trunk.

It definitely didn't need the Telepathy skill. I sighed and stared at the tree that bore the Fruit of Wisdom. How long would it be till the next fruit?

However, I had a bad feeling about this.

Fruit of Wisdom: Value L (Legendary). A fruit made by God that granted the first humans wisdom and allowed them to develop language, civilization, magic, technology, and war. The language and power were passed down by word of mouth and by blood, and still exist within all humans.

The Fruit Tree of Wisdom was burned to the ground by the angels once it had served its purpose. Now there is only one left in the far-flung land where no one ventures.

I hoped that this was just a legend arbitrarily passed down from generation to generation, but with the mention of gods and angels, the whole thing made me uncomfortable. Was this the same God as the Divine Voice? The way it was all written down made it sound like it was something completely separate...

CHAPTER

2

The Ruins Underneath the Great Tree

PART 1

I STRETCHED OUT MY NECK as I basked in the sunlight. When I looked to the side, I saw Partner sleeping peacefully with her cheeks smooshed against the ground and her nostrils puffed out. Her eyes were closed, but her mouth was still moving, chomping on reigula, the A– valued, rainbow-colored flower that grew here. *There goes one hundred years of Adam's hard work...*

Well, it was fine. No matter how the world saw it, for us, it was just a beautiful, sweet little flower. I seriously doubted humans would ever come this far, so Partner could go ahead and eat it.

Finally, morning had come. Yesterday, I was exhausted from making such a long flight and then immediately launching into a fierce battle with a naked headless man, so I'd decided to take a nap.

I'd lain down to sleep with my body arranged in a big circle and my tail tucked under my chin, making a space for Allo and the others to climb inside. I figured that as long as I was in this defensive position, I probably wouldn't be attacked. Just to be on the safe side, though, Partner and I took turns sleeping.

"Gaaaaaaaaa...gaaaaaaa..."

So much for sleeping in shifts. Left to her own devices, it seemed as if Partner had eaten more of the reigula and fallen victim to its sleep-inducing effect. I stretched my neck further to look inside the circle, where I found Allo lying down in a rainbow-colored flower garden, Petit-Nightmare stretching threads around my body, and Treant resting with its roots in the ground.

Once we were all awake, we decided to head for the great tree on the west side of the island—the most suspicious-looking thing here. If it turned out there were no big monsters living there, we could assume that the island was generally safe. Besides, I wanted to secure a source of food. With all the exertion I'd gone through yesterday, the nutrition I received from Partner eating Adam's body was already being put to use.

I could go a few days without eating anything, but it wasn't like I didn't need food at all. If you were hungry, your HP and MP would recover much more slowly, and you'd get tired more easily.

When I was around the Lithovar tribe settlements, I kept my hunting to a minimum so that I didn't affect the people's livelihoods. My body was too big; if I ate until I was satisfied, it could have caused a minor disaster for them. Here, on the other hand, it shouldn't be a problem if I messed up the ecosystem a little. I wanted to eat my fill and keep my body in tip-top shape.

The great tree seemed to be perched on a cliff. Just how many meters tall was that thing? Even I felt small in its presence. This tree had to be at least three hundred... no, four hundred meters tall. The closer I got, the more overwhelming its size seemed. If it suddenly fell on me, there was no way I'd survive the impact.

I wondered if Treant had any thoughts about the tree, as it was holding its body stock-still. Then again, it was bad practice to compare the two, even if they were both trees. Not that there was anything to compare—they were just too different.

Sure enough, I didn't see that many monsters. In fact, I didn't find any at all, which made me wonder if Adam had gone on a killing spree in the area. I thought there might be some near the base of the tree, but it was just so huge that I couldn't even get a good look at the base of its trunk.

When I looked toward the coast, I noticed several birds fluttering about. At first, I wondered if I could eat them...but then I noticed that from the neck up, they had women's heads.

> **Siren: Rank B Monster.**
> **A monster with the head of a human woman and the body of a bird. A siren's singing voice gently lures other creatures to their death. It often inhabits the sea near land and has an appetite for human flesh. They curse sailors to their death using their songs and peck at the flesh of the corpses.**
> **If you find a mountain of human bones piled up on the beach, it is a siren hunting ground.**

That'll be a no thanks! Is this island full of creatures like this?

Rank B would put them on the same level as Manticore or Mother, right? Do each of those little bird women have the power of a Manticore hidden within them? Things might get a bit dicey if I got swarmed by a flock of them.

I took a quick look up and down the coastline, but I couldn't see any piles of human bones. Well, to be fair, humans rarely came to this area. But why were there so many creepy creatures here? First headless humans, now human-headed birds! Hopefully that great tree, or at least its appearance, wouldn't be too disturbing.

When I looked up at the big tree, I spotted a round pink head peeking out from a large hole near the top of the tree. It let out an excited snort that sounded like it was meant to provoke me. It seemed very interested at the sight of new visitors.

A snake? Lizard, maybe? It didn't have any wings, but could it be a dragon? I thought for a moment that maybe I could eat it...but since I was a dragon too, would that make me a cannibal? Whatever it was, it didn't look very big, maybe three meters at most. For now, I decided to check its stats. I'd learned by now to always check the strength of the creatures inhabiting this island.

Gyva: Rank B‾ Monster.
A dragon with a slender pink body. It specializes in quickly crawling around the ground and up and down walls and using magic to unleash ice to toy with its enemies.

Was every monster on this island ranked B− or higher? Anywhere other than this island, that skinny little guy would be one of the strongest monsters you could find.

Gyva is hermaphroditic, and it can give birth to off-spring from both male and female dragons of other species. It is fecund almost year-round, and if it sees a dragon it likes, it will approach it and try to bring it into its nest.

I lifted my neck up in surprise. The Gyva let out another wild snort, swinging its tail from side to side and slamming it into the floor of its den. I gently averted my gaze. I was starting to have second thoughts about coming so close to this big tree. Why weren't there any decent monsters on the island? I didn't care much if they were a little stronger than usual, as long as they were on the safer side...

I stopped to stand atop a small hill.

From here, I could see the base of the great tree. It looked as if the ground itself had cracked open there, leaving the tree's roots mostly exposed. Hidden in the base of the tree was a large stone entrance. It looked as if some kind of building had been carved right into the tree. Clearly some kind of artifact.

It seemed quite old, but were there really people here a long time ago? Perhaps they were still here, just in hiding.

PART 2

THE ENTRANCE LED to a huge building under the tree. The right door was still attached while the left side was crumbling away, and I could see what looked like the wreckage of a stone door mixed together among the roots. I was a little hesitant, but my curiosity got the better of me and I decided to approach the door.

Partner and I bit at the roots blocking our path and tore them out of the way until we finally reached the entryway. There, I noticed something like a picture etched into the surface of the collapsed door.

I rubbed it with my forefoot to brush off the dirt that had collected on the surface and in the indentations. While I was clearing it away, I finally noticed that these were letters rather than a picture. There was still a fair amount of dirt, and I couldn't tell what was written, but as I examined the carvings, I noticed that the first letter looked somewhat familiar... Suddenly, I felt something click in my brain.

"あw/g/ntnzえ/ga"

This was a mixture of both Japanese and Latin characters. There were places where the characters were broken and illegible, though, and several other mysterious characters that resembled Japanese but weren't an exact match.

What *was* this? It looked pretty old. Did this mean someone from Earth had come here a long time ago? And it was this strange arrangement of letters too. If I entered the building, would I find the answers somewhere inside? I felt as if this building might have something to do with who I was.

I had no memories from before I became a dragon, so I didn't have a strong attachment to my previous world. There was no point in dwelling on what I couldn't remember, so I never thought deeply about what had brought me here. But I could hardly ignore something like this now that I'd found it... Honestly, I was curious.

Partner cast a suspicious look at me as I tried to pass through the door.

(*"You're not seriously going in there, are you? I've got a bad feeling about this."*)

As did I. But I might find the answers about my origins there. If that was the case, I'd risk my life to figure it out.

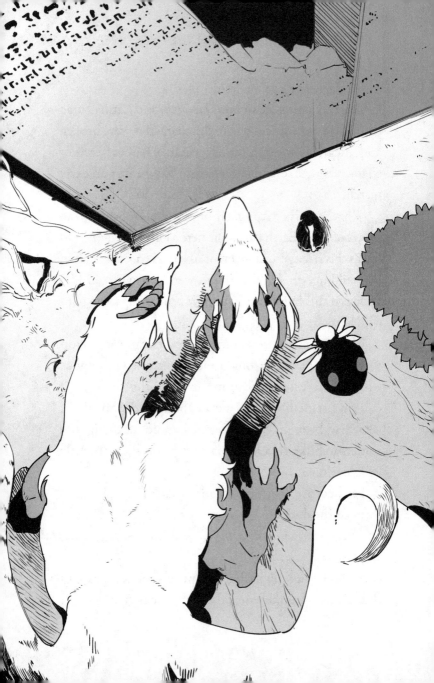

But it was a bit different to have Allo, Treant, Petit-Nightmare, and Partner here with me. Even if I left them out here alone, there was the very real risk that they would be wiped out if a monster attacked.

(*"Do whatever you want. If you're gonna go in, I guess I'm coming along for the ride."*) Partner looked down at our body. (*"If you find anything that looks tasty, I call first dibs. After all, I'm the one doing the walking here."*)

Ah, Partner...never change.

Allo jumped off my head and landed gracefully with her wind magic Gale before puffing her chest out in pride. Petit-Nightmare was standing right beside her.

Aww, you guys!

Treant dashed past Allo and Petit-Nightmare to stand right in front of the doorway, and then jutted its head up and sniffed. Things were kind of dangerous inside, so it might be best to leave Treant here... It wouldn't exactly draw much attention to leave a stick out here among the trees. At any rate, there was no reason to stop now. With great anticipation and anxiety, I peeked inside the door.

The space inside was pretty old. The ceiling was full of holes, and light filtered down through the branches above, leaving the room much brighter than I expected. It was as if spears of light were raining down on the ruins, making the atmosphere somewhat solemn.

Maybe that was just the writing from my past life I'd found outside, though, making me look at all this a certain way.

I used Presence detection and took a step forward into the vast room. It was so large in here that a huge dragon like me could easily fit inside, and I still could have if I'd been even bigger. Here and there I spotted huge pillars decorated with carvings of humans that seemed to support the building. The whole place felt like a temple.

From the depths of the vast hall, two human figures appeared. It was so dark inside that I couldn't see their faces very well, but it felt as if they had been anticipating my arrival. When the two of them noticed my presence, they slowly turned toward me. Something was jumping beside them—a pet, maybe?

I swallowed hard. As I was about to take another step forward, I noticed they were undressed—completely naked. And they had no necks or heads, and a face on their belly. They were more Adams.

SPECIES: **Adam**
STATUS: **Normal**
LV: **60/100**

HP: **60/100**
MP: **374/374**

SPECIES: **Adam**
STATUS: **Normal**
LV: **67/100**
HP: **785/785**
MP: **423/423**

The two Adams, with unmoving faces fixed on their bellies, headed toward me with the same gentlemanly expressions as the Adam I'd defeated earlier. I had no idea what kind of curse would cause that, but whatever the reason was, all Adams seemed to have the same face.

As soon as I took a step back, the twin Adams rushed toward me in a fierce dash. Two monsters running side by side with their expressionless faces made for quite a shocking sight—it was like something straight out of a nightmare.

The thing I'd spotted jumping next to the two Adams was a grotesque monster made up of just a thick neck leading up to an almost-human head. In the center of the face was a huge bloodshot eyeball. Its hair was so long that the tips dragged across the ground and its lips, nose, and other facial features gave it a somewhat feminine appearance.

> SPECIES: **Eve**
> STATUS: **Normal**
> LV: **70/100**
> HP: **476/476**
> MP: **598/660**

No way, no way, no way, no way! Absolutely not! This is bad, super bad!

Their levels were lower than the one I fought before, but this was still out of the question. Three rank A–enemies was no laughing matter. And why did Adam and Eve have to look so creepy? Was this some kind of crime of impersonation or something??

No, this was impossible. I had come in here thinking I was ready, but this was beyond belief. This was like some kind of sick joke, like I'd stumbled into a lair of Adams. *You can't just casually send these monsters up against me like this!*

I could try it, but the inevitable outcome was easy to imagine: I'd be surrounded in no time and beaten to a pulp. I spun around, took Allo into my mouth, grabbed Treant in my hands, and made a dash for the exit. In a split second, Petit-Nightmare was already on Partner's head.

The moment I cleared the exit, I kicked off the ground and took off. Of course, I risked being struck by Gravidon while in the air, so once I was airborne, I circled around the great tree, hoping to lose them.

There was simply no way I could enter those ruins until I was stronger. If not me, then perhaps we could do it if Allo and the rest were strong enough to hold the Adams back. Then we might have a chance.

REINCARNATED AS A
DRAGON
HATCHLING

CHAPTER 3

Compound Monsters

PART 1

I LOOKED DOWN at the ground from my perch on a great tree branch. I couldn't make out any sign of the decapitated woman or the headless man, so it didn't seem like they were chasing after me. Did I somehow manage to get away from the original lovers, Adam and Eve?

When I stretched out my tongue, a round sphere of what looked like hardened soil rolled out of my mouth. *What is this?* As I looked at it in confusion, the sphere cracked and Allo emerged from inside. She must have made a dirt shield with Clay when I put her into my mouth. I guess she didn't care for being in there too much. Then again, my mouth smelled like a dragon.

For the time being, I figured I should leave here for a relatively safe place. I knew Adam could jump up high in the air, but they didn't seem to want to climb trees. With that in mind, I thought maybe I should stay in the tree.

I suddenly had the faint sense that something was approaching me—it seemed even the tree might not be safe. I looked over my shoulder at the source of the feeling, but I couldn't spot anything in particular. Once I was convinced there was nothing there and turned my gaze back in another direction, Partner suddenly stretched her neck toward me to bonk my head with hers.

("Pay attention!")

I turned back to look closer. There was something strange about the branch, like the space was slightly distorted. Somehow, the spot was a darker shade of brown, almost unnaturally so. I spit out some of my dragon saliva and it appeared to land in thin air. Something seemed to have changed the color of its body and blended into the background.

"Shliiick."

It crawled around the thick branches, exposing its emerald skin. It looked like a snake—but with the upper body of a human.

The face was clearly human. He had three additional eyes near his left one, bright red in color, and his mouth was dripping with saliva. His hair was long and dark purple. The left side of his skull was split, revealing what appeared to be the pink meat of his brain inside. A ragged wing protruded from his shoulder.

Chimera Liche: Rank B Monster.
A magus who disobeyed the laws of God in pursuit of immortality and transformed himself into a monster. He may have once been a celebrated hero among men, but now he turns his sword against his past comrades. Driven to madness, he no longer possesses his past wisdom and no longer fears death as he once did. However, the monster blood flowing through his veins drives him to consume human flesh.

DIZZY TETROM
SPECIES: Chimera Liche
STATUS: Cursed
LV: 67/80
HP: 295/295
MP: 326/326
ATTACK: 307
DEFENSE: 358
MAGIC: 411
AGILITY: 420
RANK: B

SPECIAL SKILLS:

MAGE: Lv 8

GRECIAN LANGUAGE: Lv 1

UNDEAD: Lv —

AUTOMATIC MP RECOVERY: Lv 7

TENTACLES: Lv 2

CHANGE COLOR: Lv —

UNDERCOVER: Lv 4

PSYCHIC SENSE: Lv 4

FLY: Lv 2

DARK TYPE: Lv —

RESISTANCE SKILLS:

DEBUFF IMMUNITY: Lv —

NORMAL SKILLS:

HI-REST: Lv 6

CARE: Lv 5

HI-POWER: Lv 5

DARK REST: Lv 4

DARK SPHERE: Lv 7

DISEASED BREATH: Lv 3

TITLE SKILLS:

WHITE MAGE: Lv 7

BLACK MAGE: Lv 7

FALLEN FROM GRACE: Lv —

Yet another strange monster had come our way, but it seemed he still possessed his name from his past life. Well, he might've been a rank B monster, but he stood no chance against me. If he chose to attack, I could take him out in a flash.

Actually, wait a second. Maybe it'd be possible to leave this to Allo and the others. They could do something about this, right? After all it's not like Allo, at rank C+, or a Petit-Nightmare or a Lesser Treant could join me in the ruins.

I decided to focus on playing a support role. The chimera liche's level and rank were high, but his HP seemed a little low. As long as they chose their attacks carefully, Allo and the others should be able to defeat him.

This was an opportunity. If they succeeded, they should all gain at least one level. All three were close to their level cap, so it was possible that they could even reach a full evolution. If everyone reached B or C+ and they worked well as a team, they might even be able to take on Adam with my support. Then, if these guys could hold the Adams back, I'd have a chance to check out the ruins.

Nonetheless, all three of them had particularly low speed stats, which were essential. Unfortunately, Petit-Nightmare's poison thread wouldn't work either, as the chimera liche was immune.

"Grooowl!"

At my roar, Allo leaped onto my head, Treant took a spot in front of me and to the side, and Petit-Nightmare hung from a large, overhanging branch close to Partner's face. It was best to have someone waiting nearby in the case of an emergency so the whole party wasn't wiped out all at once.

Allo put her hands on my head and used her Mana Drain skill. Black light seeped out of my body and surrounded Allo. Her MP should be at maximum now, but just by absorbing my MP, she could increase the power of her magic attacks. This should hit the rank B chimera liche pretty hard.

Come on, Allo! Hit it while we still have the initiative!

Allo raised her hand toward the chimera liche. In the same moment, a brown light gathered in front of Treant's face, forming into a dirt sphere and flying toward the chimera liche. This was probably the Clay Sphere skill that it'd gained from the Fruit of Wisdom.

The chimera liche didn't even flinch. The earthen sphere lost momentum on the way and fell to the chimera liche's feet. Allo looked at Treant, dumbfounded.

Treant's magical power was 65 while the chimera liche's defense was 358. Even if it hit, it was unlikely that he'd even suffer any damage. *I know you wanted to try out your new skill, Treant. Trust me, I know that feeling.*

Treant turned around to look at us, almost as if attempting to apologize. *There's no time for that! Face forward! Now!*

Swoooooosh!

The chimera liche flew toward the branch we were on with that single wing spread fully open. He opened his mouth wide and swung his long-clawed hand down at me—but he suddenly stopped in midair, and I spotted a faint red line in front of him. It seemed that Petit-Nightmare had stretched out some threads in the way and continued spitting more threads at the chimera liche, holding him firmly in place.

Alas, this only lasted for several moments. While Allo began to adjust her aim, the chimera liche forcefully snapped out of the threads and leaped forward again. Was he really just too strong for them?

I smacked the chimera liche away with my front leg, sending his body slamming into the branch with a heavy thud and a bounce. He quickly recovered and put some distance between us and him before lowering his posture and glaring at me.

At this rate, it was going to be hard to land an attack. If I wasn't too careful, he would quickly notice the difference in our abilities and probably run away, so I decided it would be best if I didn't take any action or contribute to the battle unless it was absolutely necessary.

PART 2

T HE CHIMERA LICHE flapped his single wing and floated into the air, his long snake body swaying strangely. As he raised his arms, a black light gathered above his body. He was definitely using Dark Sphere... but he was aiming it at me? He seemed to think I was the only threat.

In fact, if it weren't for me, the chimera liche would probably be able to crush all three of my companions without even using his skills. He was making the correct choice in targeting me, and to an extent I was grateful he was doing it.

"Gale!" Allo pointed her hand at the chimera liche from her perch atop my head and cast a spell. A tornado appeared ahead of us and shot toward the chimera liche. He swooped in circles to avoid the tornado, which ultimately hit a branch and gouged a vertical slice right out of it.

As expected, the chimera liche was fast.

Gale had a wide attack range and great speed. However, the chimera liche was a speed type and able to move in three dimensions. With the difference in rank on top of that, it was a bit difficult for Allo to land a proper hit.

The chimera liche flew up to my side and swung his arm, releasing a sphere of black magic from his hand.

Swoooooosh!

A spiraling mass of black light spun at me.

It was pretty simple to avoid, but since I was built like a brick house, I wasn't exactly agile. If I wasn't careful, Treant could be blown away by the missed attack.

Not only was there a difference in rank between the chimera liche and me, but I also had a ton of HP—it was nothing for me to just take the blow. I stretched out my front legs to catch the mass of magic and crushed it. Fragments of black magic scattered from the gaps between my claws, and some of the skin on my palms tore away, sending splashes of blood flying.

Ow! As I expected, I was able to take the blow. Luckily for me, I could easily regenerate my hand, but I wouldn't want to take a blast like that head-on.

The chimera liche landed on another tall branch and drew magic into his hands once again, black light pooling around them. Another Dark Sphere? The target was... me. Again.

"Clay!" shouted Allo, and two giant needlelike clumps of dirt sprung up. However, the activation of the technique was much slower than usual. When I checked Allo's status, I saw that she'd used a significant amount of MP. Normally, her magic used the soil on the ground, so it usually consumed much less MP. Up here in this tree, however, there was no dirt nearby, so she had to create it with magic before she could manipulate it.

Using Gale and Clay probably put Allo at a disadvantage. It might be a bit rough for her to take on a higher-ranked opponent up here.

As Allo lowered her arm, the two giant earthen needles went flying. At the same time, the chimera liche unleashed a Dark Sphere brimming with magical energy. The sphere of black light smashed straight through the two dirt needles.

Fragments of the needles fell onto the branches and shattered, sending soil flying about. The sphere of black light didn't show any signs of losing momentum even after blasting through the two needles. In fact, it stayed right on its trajectory, heading straight for me.

I stretched out my hand to take the attack head-on when the black light suddenly picked up speed and shot straight through my hand to hit my chest and explode.

"Graw!"

Ugh. I'd let my guard down! All my attention was focused on Allo and the others, and I had neglected my own defenses. I didn't expect to be hit by such a small trick. The chimera liche was probably still aiming at me, but I couldn't take my attention away from protecting Allo. It was fine if I got hit, but if Allo and the others were hit by the chimera liche's Dark Sphere, they'll be wiped out in a single shot, so I didn't have a lot of options available to me.

Blood was dripping from my chest. Should I use Regenerate? No, I decided to leave it alone until the battle ended. Curing all the damage could discourage the Chimera liche and cause it to give up and run away. Besides, the chimera liche's MP wasn't inexhaustible either. If he realized that his Dark Sphere was no use against me, he'd probably opt for a quick escape.

Even without recovering the damage, I could endure twenty more direct hits, so I might as well leave it alone.

"Shaaatch!"

A dirt cannonball hit the chimera liche's exposed brain and broke up into clods of dirt upon impact. He clicked his tongue in annoyance and brushed the dirt off his hair with his hand.

That was Treant's Clay Sphere. Treant stuck out its lower lip and glanced back at Allo with a triumphant look, almost as if challenging her to press the attack with her Gale.

Allo glared silently back at Treant. It was unusual for her to be angry, but this wasn't the pouty look she shot me from time to time—she looked truly annoyed.

C'mon, guys, keep your cool. Can't we all just be friends here? Don't ruin your pretty face with an expression like that. Besides, if Petit-Nightmare, Partner, and even Allo ganged up on Treant, I had no idea what I'd do.

All the same, the enemy was quite cautious and managed to avoid Allo's Gale. The attack was simply too powerful for him to ignore, so he had to dodge out of the way. Treant had only managed to hit his weak point with Clay Sphere because he hadn't been paying attention, but even then it only did a point or two of damage.

However, we were just going back and forth here, with neither our side nor the chimera liche ever quite managing to hit a decisive blow. Maybe he was wary of me because I'd knocked him down and was trying to avoid coming closer. If I got a little closer, we might have a chance, but...at this distance, he could easily avoid Allo's magic attacks with time to spare.

Maybe I should use Whirlwind Slash to get rid of its wing. As it was, things were looking like most of the experience points would be lost.

While I was hesitating over my next plan of action, Allo got off my head and jumped forward.

Hey! It's too dangerous for you to head out that far alone! I was probably the one the chimera liche was actually wary of, but the next biggest threat would be Allo, who had become something of a magical cannon. After all, since I'd just been standing by, it's possible that the chimera liche assumed I didn't have any long-range attacks. With the difference in their stats, and being strengthened by absorbing my magic power, Allo's magic attack had a good chance of killing the chimera liche if she could only get a proper hit. Once she was further away from me, it was easy to imagine that the chimera liche would set his sights on her.

Allo looked back at me and nodded.

Fine, I understand. You're going to lure the chimera liche closer to me. After all, you can't increase your level unless you take risks.

PART 3

THE CHIMERA LICHE paused for a moment before turning his gaze to Allo as she stepped out in front of him. As I expected, he seemed to have decided to come and kill her now that she'd left my guard because her long-range magic attacks posed a threat to him.

Everything thus far had gone according to plan, but it wasn't going to continue that way.

The chimera liche bent down, spread his single wing, and pushed off his branch straight for Allo. He seemed to be avoiding using Dark Sphere—probably worried about conserving MP.

As he stretched out his large, clawed arm, Allo used Body Transformation to bloat her left arm. The additional weight made her lower her posture. It seemed she was making her arm larger than usual—was she planning to use her bloated arm as a shield to prevent damage from making it to her body? But even if she blocked it like that, she'd probably still lose nearly all of her HP.

Did she seriously want to take the chimera liche on in melee combat? They were both the same rank, but Allo's attack power and speed were quite low. What's more, the chimera liche's HP was high, hardly making him an opponent to take on in melee combat.

I prepared Whirlwind Slash just in case.

A thick fog gathered around Allo before the chimera liche could reach her. Fog of the Dead? It became hard to see—which made it hard for me to help.

"Shaaatch!"

Through the shadows of the fog, I could see the chimera liche trying to slam his arm into Allo.

Oh no. Now I had no choice. I hurriedly aimed at the chimera liche's back and geared up to fire Whirlwind Slash...but there was something about the sight of Allo that made me hesitate. I stopped at the last minute.

But then, as I watched, Allo's head and bloated arm were lopped off. *No, no!* Could that have been a dummy made of Clay? Wait...the reason she'd made her arms so bloated was probably to make a distinctive silhouette that was easier for her enemy to confuse with a substitute!

"Shaaa... Shaaaaatch?"

Allo's shattered dummy transformed into a myriad of arms which clung to the chimera liche's arm. The fog began to recede, and I was able to see Allo making a foothold with Clay and put both hands right on the chimera liche's exposed brain. It seemed like she intended to hit its weak point with a magic attack directly.

"Shacka shacka..."

The chimera liche's body was shaking. If you looked closely, you could see that it wasn't just his arm she had secured in place: His entire body was being held down by numerous earthen arms.

This was the soil that had scattered on the branches when she made the dirt needles using Clay. At the time, it'd looked like she was wasting a lot of Clay, but it seemed as if that was merely a stepping stone to make full use of Clay on trees without needing soil underfoot.

If something took time and effort to make, it was best to prepare it first and use it later. The monster was held down by multiple arms and then wrapped in many layers of spider webs. Taking advantage of the fog, Petit-Nightmare seemed to have set up a trap of its own.

"Shaaaaaaaaatch!"

Due to the difference in stats, if the chimera liche continued to struggle, the spider webs would soon loosen, and it would break free of the dirt arms. Still, Allo should be able to use her magic before that became a problem... or at least that was what I thought until the chimera liche's abdomen split open vertically, revealing countless long, reddish-black internal organs.

This was one of the chimera liche's unique skills: Tentacle. Though I'd known about this ability, I never imagined that the tentacles in question would tear out of its stomach. Holding the arms and body down wouldn't be enough.

One tentacle stretched toward Allo's chest.

A circle of black light spread rapidly around Treant.

The light expanded quickly, and in no time, the chimera liche and I were within its range. This was one of the skills that Treant learned with the Fruit of Wisdom: Gravity. I'd seen it a few times before. It was a highly versatile skill that held down anything within the target range.

Treant's magic might not be a big deal to the chimera liche, but it still served as a third weight on its body along with the spider webs and arms of dirt. The chimera liche's torso lowered as Gravity held it down. The tentacles that were aimed at Allo also lost their trajectory and only managed to grab the robe that she was wearing.

"Shi... Shiiii... Shiick..."

Awesome! Great assist, Treant! You're all doing great!

"Uuungh..." Allo was in range of the Gravity attack too, and it was making her hunker down. But all the same, I felt Treant really saved the day.

Allo once again put her hand on the chimera liche's head, and cried, "Gale!" A small, compressed mass of wind hit the bare spot in the monster's head. The chimera liche's body swayed as if it had been spun around and then began to wobble and shake strangely. Allo had landed a proper blow. Green blood flowed from the wound on the chimera liche's head.

"Ah... Aaaaaa!"

However, it seemed that they were not yet finished—his defense was too high. The chimera liche's four eerie eyes glared at Allo. Then, the bundle of threads wrapped around the chimera liche's neck was lifted, pulling the chimera liche's head up.

"Ungh!"

The chimera liche pulled his neck down and tore through the threads, but a faint red line remained on his neck.

"Shhhh... A, ah..."

The chimera liche touched his neck as if it stung. *Looks like you got in a good hit there, Petit-Nightmare.*

Treant stood in front of the chimera liche, as if it was finally its turn to enter the fray. Alas, Treant's stats were still a bit too weak, so I would've preferred if it stopped there... Treant closed its eyes, though, and a gentle light began to envelop the chimera liche.

Huh? Rest?

"Aaaaaaaaaugh! Aaaugh!"

A look of anguish crossed the chimera liche's face, and his scream turned hoarse. Then his shoulders drooped to the ground, and he stopped moving as all the energy left his body.

It seemed that Rest, a skill he was weak to, was the decisive blow. Good job, Treant, for knowing that healing magic would damage the undead.

Allo shot a dissatisfied look at the proud Treant, who apologetically looked away from her. W-wait, did you accidentally use Rest on Allo... No, I'm not gonna read into that look...

> Gained 469 Experience Points.
> Title Skill "Walking Egg" Lv — activated: gained 469 Experience Points.

Oops... Did I absorb a quarter of the experience points? Well, even if I didn't take any action in the battle, I still managed to play a role in drawing the enemy's attacks, so I guess it made sense. The real question was how much Allo's level had risen.

PART 4

I DECIDED TO CHECK the levels of Allo and the others right away. When I looked up, I saw

Petit-Nightmare sitting near the chimera liche's neck with a red string. It seemed to notice my gaze but ignored it and concentrated on sipping the chimera liche's bodily fluids. I couldn't help but wonder if it was rotten...

Sure enough, it didn't seem terribly interested in leveling up. *Ah well, we'll start with Petit-Nightmare, then.* I used View Status as I watched it do its thing.

SPECIES: **Petit-Nightmare**
STATUS: **Normal**
LV: **45/45 (MAX)**
HP: **163/190**
MP: **18/177**

Whoa, eight levels in one go!

Maybe it'd been storing nutrients in preparation for evolving. If all went well, the next evolution would be Nightmare? I was worried that it'd be even harder to control if it got too big, but I definitely couldn't leave it to its own devices.

Now that I thought about it, I wondered whether it was a good idea to raise Petit-Nightmare's level at all.

This could only go poorly. It was all too easy to imagine it attacking travelers if I took my eyes off it a moment too long...

Next up was Allo's level...or at least that's what I intended, but then Treant started moving about, trying to catch my attention. It was hard to believe just how different these two were in terms of personality.

Treant, I sometimes wonder if you're some type of angel. You've got Telepathy, y'know? You could try using it more.

I kind of regretted the fact that *I* didn't have Telepathy. I didn't need attack magic when I could rely on Whirlwind Slash, but if I had Telepathy, I'd be able to communicate my intentions to Allo and the others way more efficiently, and depending on the situation, I could avoid some monster battles. I could do it myself or even ask for help. And it went without saying that it would be convenient for communicating with humans.

Gravity seemed to have various applications too. If someone like me, who specialized in magical power, released it, it should be able to stop the movements of the surrounding monsters in a split second...

Well, I couldn't do anything about the past, so it wasn't worth thinking about. Ultimately, I was the one who stopped Partner from eating that fruit.

SPECIES: **Lesser Treant**
STATUS: **Cursed**
LV: **25/25 (MAX)**
HP: **86/141**
MP: **3/92**

All right! Eleven levels!

Treant's level was so low to begin with, it was pretty easy for it to level up compared to the others. But this was great. *Treant, I'm so happy for you. Maybe people won't make fun of you anymore for not being evolved.*

It'd been a long road. I'd never imagined that gaining twenty-four levels would be so hard. I really owed it to that Fruit of Wisdom. Good, I was really glad Treant ate it. Or at least I was glad that I didn't eat it. I was always worried that I would have a Lesser Treant for the rest of my life.

For some reason, Treant looked at me with a complicated expression. *What's wrong? Can't you just be happy for yourself?*

Last up was Allo. She'd been working so hard, so she should've reached her max level, no doubt. She had fought so well against that rank B opponent, after all.

If anything, it might've been a bit of a waste of experience points because she was close to maximum level.

"Master Dragon!"

Allo ran up to me, waving her hands, and hugged my face. *Hey, hey, I can't check your level if you're that close. Wait a moment...huh?*

NAME: Allo
SPECIES: Levana Low Liche
STATUS: Cursed
LV: 63/65
HP: 362/378
MP: 88/397

She only gained four levels?? Is that all? I was expecting her to have earned at least half of the experience. What was going on?

I must've overestimated it since I had the Experience Doubler skill. It certainly became harder and harder to level up after you reached level 50.

"Hm?"

Allo stared at me with a puzzled look on her face. I quickly averted my eyes, but Allo tilted her head and followed, stepping in front of my face. My heart ached for poor Allo. It looked like it wasn't enough. Well, at this rate, the next time we hunted monsters, I could easily make up for it. Right? Right?

Allo seemed to have figured out how it'd gone from my expression and lowered her head, dejected. Treant used its branch to tap Allo on the shoulder, but she only looked back at it with an indescribable face.

If Treant or I tried to encourage her now, it would only have the opposite effect. Petit-Nightmare, hanging from a string, threw itself at me as if to tell me to get a better sense for those around me. Treant flipped over in place and made a loud noise.

I knew how they were feeling, but there was such a massive difference between my level and theirs that they really didn't want to take me on.

Allo didn't seem interested in Petit-Nightmare and Treant's flirting with disaster, instead slumping down and wallowing in her disappointment. But since she was already completely human-looking, she didn't really need to be in such a hurry, right? Also, if you thought about it, maybe it was better that she didn't develop any monster-like features.

Allo whispered quietly, "I thought I could finally become strong enough to be useful to you."

I felt a wave of guilt wash over me.

You can do it! It's just a measly two levels, Allo! Next time! Next time for sure!

PART 5

PETIT-NIGHTMARE MUNCHED on the chimera liche for a bit before it finally crawled off the monster's neck, its spider belly swollen. Then it spit out a red string from its mouth and covered its own body. Finally, before Petit-Nightmare's head was completely hidden, the little spider glanced at me and waved its arm.

Huh?

When I nodded back, it spat a red string out onto the ground. It looked like it was waving at Partner specifically. *C'mon, now you're just going to annoy me.* Now I understood how Treant felt about Petit-Nightmare's treatment.

Partner yawned and stretched her neck under the branches of the great tree. She certainly seemed comfortable with her popularity.

Petit-Nightmare's head was quickly hidden beneath the thread as it completed a red cocoon more than twice the size of the spider within—big enough to hold a person. It seemed as if it was ready to evolve—the question was what kind of evolution awaited.

It would likely emerge at around rank C+, placing it alongside Allo. Allo would probably evolve to rank B in no time, though. With a rank C+ and B on the party, things would definitely get easier.

To be frank, among the three, the only one who could attack properly was Allo, who was still ranked C+. She was specialized in magic and could suck up MP from me with Mana Drain. Allo was good with long-distance, Treant was a tank, and Petit-Nightmare was specialized in short-range. If each one of them expanded on their unique traits through evolution, we should have a nicely rounded team. In that case, they might even be able to defeat even chimera liche-class monsters without my support.

If that happened, their levels would start rocketing up even faster. If we just looked around a bit, we should be able to find a bunch more rank A monsters like Adam and Eve, and then we could finally enter the ruins.

I was excited for Petit-Nightmare to come out. Judging by the pattern established so far, it shouldn't take that long. Besides, the cocoon was already pulsating. Combined with the fact that the thread was red, it actually looked quite similar to a heart. Petit-Nightmare was about to crawl out of it at any moment.

Suddenly, I felt someone staring at me from behind, so I turned around. Treant was looking at me as if it wanted to say something.

What is it? Ah, maybe because it was a monster created using Fake Life, it needed Fake Life to evolve, like Allo.

Treant had never evolved before, so it'd never occurred to me. *Hey, Partner, stop scoffing at me for a second and use Fake Life—and put as much magic into it as you can while you're at it! Good luck, Treant, I'm looking forward to your future form.*

Partner shot me an irritated look and let out a snort of annoyance. A black light covered Mr. Treant—Fake Life.

It wasn't exactly the most elegant magic, but hey, hopefully Treant was going to evolve properly. Did it work?

A single tree branch stretched out of the black light. Or, rather, it was merely the tip of a tree branch, which was split into five. It looked just like an arm. When the black light faded away, a somewhat larger Treant appeared. The bark of the tree was rather dark and tough, and the leaves were more bluish than green. What's more, the surface of his body looked a little stiffer than before.

I wondered if I could really hold out hope here. Just what kind of monster was this?

Magical Tree: Rank C+ Monster.
A Treant who is gifted at magic.
Treant takes advantage of its unique resilience and fights with the help of magic. Many adventurers try to slay it due to the unique magical powers of its leaves. However, because of its annoying fighting style, many people give up and leave after fighting for half a day.

All right! C+! Now that's quite a success! I thought for sure that he would be ranked C-, but apparently I had nothing to fear. This was all thanks to the Fruit of Wisdom!

Hmm. It seemed like the notes about the new species were kinda rude, though...

SPECIES: **Magical Tree**

STATUS: Cursed

LV: 1/60

HP: 161/161

MP: 3/110

ATTACK: 43

DEFENSE: 85

MAGIC: 113

AGILITY: 56

RANK: C+

SPECIAL SKILLS:
  DARK TYPE: Lv —
  GRECIAN LANGUAGE: Lv 2
  HARDEN: Lv 2
  AUTOMATIC MP RECOVERY: Lv 1
RESISTANCE SKILLS:
  PHYSICAL RESISTANCE: Lv 4
NORMAL SKILLS:
  TAKE ROOT: Lv 4
  CLAY: Lv 2
  REST: Lv 2
  FIRE SPHERE: Lv 2
  AQUA SPHERE: Lv 2
  CLAY SPHERE: Lv 2
  WIND SPHERE: Lv 2
  ANTI-POWER: Lv 2
TITLE SKILLS:
  EVIL DRAGON'S SERVANT: Lv —
  DEVOURER OF THE FRUIT OF WISDOM: Lv —
  WHITE MAGE: Lv 3
  BLACK MAGE: Lv 2

Whoa! Looks like you've gained a ton of new skills, and your skill levels have shot up too! I definitely had high hopes for future success!

Hmm... Petrify, huh? That'd be nice. Poison Cloud, Physical Barrier, Anti-Power... Yeah, I could see how people would find that annoying.

Power was magic that increased attack power. I wondered if Anti-Power would lower it instead. If Anti-Power lowered the opponent's attack power, Physical Barrier strengthened Treant's own defense, and then Rest recovered HP while Poison Cloud slowly sapped away its enemy's HP as they were looking for an opening... It looked like Treant could possibly attack with sphere-type magic.

That sounded about right, and if so, this was a particularly nasty configuration. If this were a fighting game, that kind of skill combination could make me rage quit.

Treant looked at its branch—or rather, its hand—and hopped around happily before showing it off to me. Well, that was good at least.

However, it was a happy miscalculation that Treant got a rank C+. I'd really appreciate it if it could do something to reduce Adam's ridiculously high attack power. I needed to raise my own skill level too if I wanted to hold my own, seeing as the Adams still had an incredibly powerful long-range magic in Gravidon.

Treant's new form seemed very strong against physical attacks, but what about magical attacks? Usually, you gained new resistance skills and normal skills as you leveled up, so it would be nice if it'd gained something like that.

Treant was finally running out of steam with its little celebration, and behind it, I could see Petit-Nightmare's red cocoon swaying slightly. Before I knew it, the cocoon, which had been a bundle of soft threads, had hardened. It looked like it would hatch soon.

As I stared intently at it, the cocoon eventually cracked, and something like a black feeler pushed out from inside. I watched, temporarily stunned, as a white face appeared after the feelers and looked around. The crack in the red cocoon spread, and a large spider emerged from inside.

Petit-Nightmare was two times...no, three times bigger than before. It was no longer petit. The red cocoon must've been under a considerable amount of pressure holding it in. It was about two meters long, just a little larger than a grown human. While it'd been quite cute up until now, that cuteness had been replaced with a terrifying sight.

It must be stronger than Treant, right? I guess I'd have to see its status first.

Nightmare: Rank C+ Monster.

The rare final form of evolution, in which an individual has grown up in a harsh environment and was manipulated by strong magical powers. Its appearance, along with its abilities to hide in the dark and slay its enemies, makes it truly worthy of the name Nightmare. In regions where Nightmares appear, there are many legends saying that if you encounter a white-faced monster, you should run away immediately. However, by the time the Nightmare shows itself, you're already caught in its trap.

SPECIES: Nightmare
STATUS: Normal
LV: 1/70
HP: 122/122
MP: 18/115
ATTACK: 111
DEFENSE: 69
MAGIC: 118
AGILITY: 97
RANK: C+

SPECIAL SKILLS:

DARK TYPE: Lv —

AUTOMATIC HP RECOVERY: Lv 3

POISON BELT: Lv 5

PSYCHIC SENSE: Lv 3

ONE HUNDRED FACES: Lv —

STEALTH: Lv 5

RESISTANCE SKILLS:

PHYSICAL RESISTANCE: Lv 3

MAGIC RESISTANCE: Lv 2

POISON RESISTANCE: Lv 4

CURSE RESISTANCE: Lv 4

NORMAL SKILLS:

VENOM FANGS: Lv 3

SPIDERSILK: Lv 5

CALL ALLIES: Lv 1

SILK SPOOL: Lv 3

POISON WEB: Lv 3

HANGING THREAD: Lv 3

SNEAK ATTACK: Lv 3

CURSE: Lv 2

HUMAN TRANSFORMATION: Lv 3

REGENERATE: Lv 1

DARK SPHERE: Lv 1

CLAY: Lv 1

TITLE SKILLS:

EVIL DRAGON'S PET: Lv —

MASTER SPINNER: Lv 5

MEANIE: Lv —

MUTATION: Lv —

TENACIOUS: Lv 5

CUNNING: Lv 4

AVYSSOS EATER: Lv 2

ASSASSIN: Lv 3

FINAL EVOLUTION: Lv —

Well, well, the stats were all pretty high. It kind of made Treant look pathetic in comparison, especially considering they were the same rank. The only place Treant excelled was in defense. Nightmare's skills were all impressive too. Stealth and Psychic Sense were both great skills that would make it easier to not only avoid danger but to hunt as well, once we got used to them. And if what I saw from the chimera liche was any indication, Dark Sphere was strong also. Having Regenerate was good since it meant we didn't have to worry about the loss of limbs. This would all make a huge difference.

Then there was Human Transformation and the Special Skill One Hundred Faces. I'd never heard of that before.

Special Skill "One Hundred Faces"
Taking on the form of another monster or human does
not cost MP.

This sounded just like Manticore's Nekomata! Human Transformation took a ridiculous amount of MP, so I was definitely glad to see that. Jealous, even.

How come you and Treant are getting all these skills I wanted??

Well, now I knew there were other skills like this besides Nekomata, so I could hope that maybe someday I'd be able to acquire them too. Human Transformation was such a wasted skill, after all, so there might be more support skills that could make up for it.

But what did it mean that Final Evolution was added to Nightmare's title skills? Was C+ the cap for Nightmare? Or maybe normal monsters were just like that? Relatively speaking, C+ was a fairly high rank, so it was possible. But if Treant reached rank B, these two would completely swap positions. I decided not to worry about that, though. Part of me wanted to see that happen, though another part felt guilty. Maybe Allo would be the next to reach her final evolution.

Nightmare looked at Partner, wondering what was going on. Partner immediately dropped her gaze, so

Nightmare looked at me instead. I couldn't stand it either and quickly averted my eyes.

If Treant were to evolve, Nightmare would become a burden on the party. I didn't know much about the upper limits of evolution, though—maybe there was a way to remove the upper limit. Maybe. After all, I'd had more evolution options appear in my Title Skills. It was too early to be pessimistic.

Anyway, what was important was that Allo, Treant, and Nightmare had all reached C+. Their skills had gotten stronger, with the exception of Allo, and I could see how to fight properly with them. Surprisingly, we might be able to easily explore the ruins. Well, they'd only just finished evolving, so I decided to try setting up a base here in this tree for the time being. Adams didn't seem to climb trees, so it was a good place to rest. If we were attacked by anything like a chimera liche, I could take it on with no issue. However, I really would like to avoid dealing with an attack from an Adam while I was sleeping. Adam and Eve were the worst looking monsters I'd ever seen—both in stats and appearance.

While I was looking for a suitable hole in the great tree, I heard a monster's cry off in the distance. Looking over, I spotted a slender pink dragon with its tail whipping back and forth—the Gyva dragon in heat.

Oops, looks like it found me, a guy in the tree! I should've set up a higher base camp. In any case, I decided to withdraw from the area—not that I couldn't beat the Gyva, I just didn't really want to fight it. It wasn't showing any hostility, after all, which made it kind of hard to attack...

"Stay back."

Allo silently raised her hand toward the Gyva, and green light gathered in her hand.

"Wind magic, Ga..."

I lowered my head toward Allo, extended my tongue, and quickly slurped her into my mouth. Allo struggled around between my jaws. I understood that she really wanted to level up and evolve, but that was out of the question right now—we should only fight against monsters who viewed us as enemies.

As usual, I held Treant in my hand and kicked off of the branches. Nightmare spit out a red string toward the tip of my tail and hung on in midair.

Let's go up a little higher. As I gained altitude, the Gyva arced its neck and gazed at me with regret.

"Quooooon! Kuoooooon! Quon! Kuoooon!"

I heard a pitiful, high-pitched cry from the Gyva, different from the sound it had made before. When that didn't work, it turned its belly up and hopped around on the branches.

You can keep that up for as long as you want—you're not gonna win me over that way!

CHAPTER 4

Basilisk's Evil Eye

PART 1

I USED WHIRLWIND SLASH to scrape off a chunk of the great tree's thick trunk and dug a nest hole. The blade of wind cut through the trunk. In between resting and waiting for Automatic MP Recovery to take effect, I patiently enlarged the hole. It took a bit of work, but finally it was big enough that I could fit in there with some space to spare. It felt about as big as the shrine of the Dragon God, a memory that felt rather nostalgic.

Well, Adams wouldn't come up here. After we leveled up, we'd enter the Adams' shrine at the base of the great tree.

I noticed that Nightmare was wrapped up in a huge spider web stretched between the branches. Maybe it was more comfortable among its webs outside the hole.

If Allo had tried to sleep outside, I would've stopped her, but I figured Nightmare would do whatever it pleased. If it seemed like things were getting too dangerous, it'd come back here. Besides, it could act like a security guard this way—although I doubted that any monsters living in a place like this would be caught by its web.

I'd assumed that Treant would need to be exposed to sunlight, but there it was at the deepest part of the burrow, with its trunk bent low, snoring loudly from its mouthlike hole. *There's no way you'd survive out in the wilderness alone,* I thought.

I was hungry, so I decided to let Allo rest in the den and go out for a little hunt. It would be no good if other monsters attacked while I was away, so I checked everything with Psychic Sense but didn't feel any particularly strong signs. Still, just in case, I didn't plan on going too far. I'd be back in about fifteen minutes.

I kicked off a branch and flew around the great tree. When I moved a little, I saw a huge white bird in the air. It was around four meters in length, I figured, with a long, sharp, pointed beak that covered its face like a mask.

Masked Bird: Rank C+ Monster.
A large bird monster that flies in a remote place. The beak is deformed and protects the head like a mask. In

addition to boasting overwhelming flight performance, it is also good at magic. Its powerful close-range attacks can easily penetrate armor.

Perfect, I'd found just the right monster!

I left the great tree to pursue the masked bird. The monster caught sight of me and quickly turned in the air to flee. I immediately took chase, bypassing it easily, and stopped in its path to wait for it. Surprised, the masked bird suddenly flapped itself to a halt and took off in the opposite direction, lowering its altitude. Too bad. It was probably confident in its flying prowess, but alas, it couldn't overcome our stat difference.

As I trailed close behind, the masked bird opened its beak wide and stared at me.

"Caaaaw!" A pair of tornadoes shot at me from its wings.

Wind magic, huh? It was similar to Allo's Gale, but this skill was called Twin Gale, suggesting that it always used two in parallel. I could probably take them head-on, but I slowed down and hovered in the air. Then, taking aim at the two approaching tornadoes, I unleashed Whirlwind Slash. It tore through the tornadoes to rip diagonally across the back of the fleeing masked bird.

"Caaaaaaaaaaw!" The bird's body bent at an extreme angle, and its feathers flew up into the air. Eyes closed,

its body fell powerlessly. Ruptured by Whirlwind Slash, the shapes of the tornadoes collapsed and scattered into the air.

I flew toward the falling masked bird and stretched out my front legs to grab it—but the masked bird's eyes suddenly opened wide, and it twisted its neck to take aim at mine, thrusting its beak forward for a close-range strike. I swiped at the masked bird's beak with my front claw, and the sheer force of the blow shattered it down to the base.

Pretending to be dead? Sorry, but I couldn't afford to take any further risks after seeing it move. I'd already seen its skills using View Status. I knocked off the bird's head with my claw.

Gained 246 Experience Points.
Title Skill "Walking Egg" Lv — activated: gained 246 Experience Points.

With my other claw, I pierced the masked bird's back and flipped it upside down to drain its blood on the flight back. I was glad to score such a big catch. However, I'd gone quite a bit farther than I'd intended. It wouldn't take too long to get back, but hopefully some rank B monsters hadn't shown up in the meantime.

I held onto the carcass of the masked bird with my front legs and returned straight to the burrow. I landed on the branch in front, leaving the masked bird there while I checked things out. To my surprise, when I turned to look at Nightmare's nest near the entrance, there was a monster caught in the web. I never thought there would be monsters in this land that would fall for a trap like that.

The monster was writhing about, already managing to shake off the threads. Once the restraints were loosened, it landed on the branch, rolled its body back and forth to remove the remaining threads, and then licked its whole body with its tongue.

It seemed to be about the same size as Nightmare, but my spider companion remained cautious and kept its distance.

The monster had a long, snake-like body with small legs. The head sported two horns and a fin-like crest. It had a rather cute appearance, but considering it had easily broken out of Nightmare's thread, it had to be around rank B or so. The monster tilted its neck up and glared angrily at Nightmare before turning around to look at me. Its gaze instantly softened, and it let out a gentle cry.

"Quon! Quooooon!"

Yup... It was a Gyva, the pink dragon with raging hormones. How did it get all the way up here without wings?! Gyva once against twisted its body around to show its belly. *Listen, I'm not interested!*

"*Qu...*"

"Gale!"

A tornado emerged from the burrow and whirled toward the Gyva, scraping bark from the branch as it went. Nightmare scurried up its threads into the overhanging branches to escape the attack as the tornado blew the gyrating Gyva right off the branch.

"*Kuoooooooooooooo?!*"

Obviously, it didn't stand a chance like that. The Gyva twisted its body around in midair, coiled its arms, shifted its center of gravity, extended its neck, and managed to hook its mouth on the end of the branches. A string of Nightmare's web was still stuck to its head.

"*Quo?*"

Pulled by the thread, the Gyva's body lifted slightly. Its mouth now empty, the Gyva was mercilessly hit by yet another tornado and thrown off the great tree.

"*Kuuuuuuuuuuuuuuuuuuuuuuuuuuuuuuuuuuuuuuuuuuuu uuuuuuuuuuuuuuuuuuuuuuuuuuuuuuuuuuuuuuuuuuuuuuuuuuuu uuuuuuuuuuuuuuuuuuuuuuuuuuuuuuuuuuuuuuuuuu!*"

The Gyva's body slammed against multiple branches on its way down before falling out of sight.

Well, it didn't seem to be dead, in spite of its rank. Of course, it would've been done for if it'd fallen straight to the ground all this way, but the branches on the way down broke its fall. In any case, it wouldn't be coming back up here for a while.

As I settled my claws on the branch and watched where the Gyva fell, Allo stood next to me and leaned against my body. I turned my head to find Allo also staring after the Gyva, her face blank. When she noticed my gaze, she turned to face me and smiled proudly.

I don't think those things are malicious, so just try to act in moderation, okay? Considering we're both dragons, I don't know how I feel about eating it.

PART 2

ALLO SAT IN SILENCE, her arms outstretched. At the tips of her fingers, a large lump of dirt slowly changed shape.

I had asked her to use Clay to make an earthen hearth. I wanted to grill the masked bird, but it would be a catastrophe if I did something wrong and set our base on fire, so I asked Allo to coat a part of the branch in front of the nest with her Clay soil. A spot at the opening to our burrow was as good a place as any for a hearth. After all, an oven was indispensable in any home, as well as for living a comfortable dragon life.

The masked bird's slender, fleshless body hung from the roof, suspended by Nightmare's threads. It had already been disemboweled, cleaned, plucked, and had the meat cut from its thighs. We were making a hearth big enough for a super-large dragon, so the masked bird should fit in perfectly.

Allo gently reached out to me. "Master dragon, I don't seem to have enough power." Her complexion was getting worse, evidence that the magical power used to maintain her body was decreasing. I could see the fatigue worsen the more magic she used.

She didn't need to ask for my permission; she could take my magic from me whenever she needed it. But perhaps it would be better to just take a break from time to time. The scale of the magic used was much greater in battle, but since this also required precise adjustments, it seemed to be taking more out of her than usual.

When I urged her to rest, she merely puffed out her cheeks and shook her head.

Listen, I'm glad you're doing this, but…

Partner glared at the unfinished hearth and then at me, looking rather annoyed. (*"Food, food! C'mon, what the hell do you think you're doing?! I'm not gonna eat it raw. At this rate, it'd probably be faster for me to just find a cave of my own somewhere to cook it!"*)

Listen, we've gotta cook this thing properly and let the fire heat it all evenly. You can have the organs if you want, but otherwise you've gotta wait.

Partner reluctantly stretched out her neck, scooped up the innards with her tongue, and lapped them up into her mouth. I was reluctant to eat that stuff myself, but she seemed to enjoy it.

Allo stretched out her arms to me, as if to cling to my body. "Tail. Please lend me your tail."

Hmm, I really felt like I should let her rest.

Suddenly a tree—or rather, Treant—came over to her. As Allo eyed it suspiciously, Treant turned its face toward the hearth and slowly closed its eyes. The half-finished part of the hearth began to glow, and dirt appeared out of nowhere.

"No, it's okay. I'll do it." Allo's voice was hollow as she stopped Treant. She approached the hearth and held the part Treant had just made with Clay. The hardened soil crumbled away. As expected, Treant looked dejected, its trunk drooping slightly, and it returned to the burrow.

Well, I guess I wouldn't like it if someone changed something I was in the middle of working on either. I understood how she felt. Besides, Allo's Clay skill was level 6, while Treant's was only level 2. I doubted they could work with the same precision. Allo didn't expect Treant to be that despondent, and she looked a little apologetically at its back as it left.

She watched after it for a bit, but it turned around and put out its arm as if to urge her on.

This was a tough situation. I knew she was tired and needed to take a break. Of course, I could give her more magic to make up for her lack of energy, but then she would probably continue working. I didn't want to force her to stop, but at the same time, it seemed wrong not to. Hmph...

("Food! I want food!")

Did that idiot already finish eating all the innards? Allo shook her head and looked at the obnoxious Partner before turning back to me.

Sorry about that. I extended my tail, and Allo quickly hugged it tight, using Mana Drain to absorb MP from me.

After a while, the giant hearth was completed. Unlike the furnace, the work of coating the kitchen floor with

Clay to prevent it from burning didn't require that much precision, so it was taken care of in no time, though I still had to really hold myself back to just heat up the hearth using Scorching Breath. After a few minutes of continuous heating, I lowered the suspended masked bird, pushed it inside the hearth, and closed the lid.

After waiting a few minutes, I lifted the lid and took out the roasted bird. The fat on its body gave it a glossy sheen—apparently it was quite a fatty creature. I had to admit, this thing was a lot bigger than I originally thought!

At my current size, it was rare for me to get the opportunity to consume all the food I needed. After flying for so long with neither food nor drink, I was grateful to be able to eat my fill of meat. What's more, it was deliciously greasy.

The smell of the roasted bird filled my nostrils, causing saliva to well up in my mouth and wet my tongue. I grabbed a thigh with my front claws and forcibly tore it off. Just as I was about to sink my teeth in, Partner suddenly stretched out her neck, bit down, and snatched it out of my hand.

Why, you...!

Partner turned her head upward, bent her neck, threw the masked bird meat lightly into the air, and bit down, deftly downing the meat in a single gulp. A happy expression settled onto her face as meat juices sprayed out between her lips.

I guess I can't be mad if you're enjoying the food that much.

Well, there was still plenty of roasted meat left. My turn eventually came around, and I decided to savor it slowly to tease Partner. As soon as I took a bite, the meat's hot juices filled my mouth. It was absolutely delicious. It'd been a long time since I ate something so amazing. If I had any complaint, it was that it could really use some salt. There *was* an ocean nearby, so maybe it wouldn't be a bad idea to make some to keep on hand.

After sucking the meat off the bones and spitting them out, I gazed out at the island spread out beneath the great tree. From my current height, even the vast forest looked tiny enough to pick up with my fingertips.

However, it was still huge, and overwhelmingly so. In the distance, I could see the line of the huge waterfall. It looked just like the edge of the world, as if the sea had been cut away in a straight line. From there, there was absolutely nothing as far as the eye could see.

I'd had mixed feelings about this place since the first time I encountered an Adam, but life here wasn't so bad.

PART 3

I WOKE UP TO THE SUN shining through the entrance to our burrow. *Is it already morning?* I stretched my neck and felt my bones creak. As I stretched, Allo woke from where she was sleeping next to me. I wondered if I had woken her up; however, Allo merely shook her head in confusion.

"I don't get sleepy," she said.

Is that so? She always closed her eyes and stayed still when we went to bed, so I figured she'd definitely been asleep, but it seemed that she would stay awake the entire time and merely rest her body. Allo certainly looked awake now, with her eyes wide open despite the early morning.

I squinted to look over at Treant, only to find it bent over and snoring. With that, I left the burrow.

Partner shot me an annoyed glare. *("I don't really care when you want to wake up, but you don't need to start moving around so early.")*

I never really felt particularly sleepy in this body, but I couldn't help but wonder if Partner had a different experience. For me, just sitting still with my eyes open was enough to help me recover from fatigue, so that's what I often did. However, it seemed that Partner was not satisfied unless she got a full night's rest. Honestly, it seemed more like a matter of personality rather than physical constitution.

The branches just above the burrow were covered with Nightmare's spider webs. Nightmare came on down when it noticed us; it gave me an indifferent look before offering Partner a smile. Sure, we had very different personalities, but I couldn't fathom why Nightmare treated us so differently.

Partner yawned and looked down at the base of the great tree before noticing Nightmare approaching. She turned to smile back at our visitor. These two certainly got along well. At the beginning, I didn't really care for being tied to Partner, since I couldn't exactly get away from her, but she'd grown on me. Her rough-and-tumble personality reminded me of the children of the Lithovar tribe.

Partner welcomed Nightmare, who hopped playfully on over, only to be swallowed up by Partner's gaping mouth. I could spy a single spider leg slightly protruding from Partner's mouth, trembling weakly as if asking for help.

Unsure of what just happened, I opened my mouth wide. Allo, who was walking beside me, was staring at Partner's mouth with a pale face, just like me.

("Now that's a big piece of chicken!")

Reading Partner's thoughts, I finally figured it out. She was still half-asleep and thinking about the roasted masked bird we ate the night before, so she must still be dreaming of eating something. I quickly bent my neck around and headbutted the back of Partner's neck from below, causing her to spit out a drool-covered Nightmare, who slammed upside down into a nearby branch.

Now that was a close one. If Nightmare wasn't more careful, it could've easily been one-shot KO'd over that stunt. Fortunately, it made it out unharmed.

Nightmare spit out a thread and attached it to the branch above to regain its balance, then glared at me. *What? Are you complaining about something? If I didn't help you, you would've been eaten!*

Nightmare bowed its head slightly toward me and approached Partner cautiously. *Well, you're surprisingly simpleminded, I see. Even though you were nearly eaten, you still haven't learned your lesson.*

("The meat's back!")

Partner stretched out her neck and bit into Nightmare, then raised her face skyward. I bent my neck down again and rammed my head into the back of Partner's neck even harder than before.

After Partner had regained consciousness, I took Allo, Nightmare, and Treant down from the great tree and walked around the forest at its base. Once again, Allo made a large bucket-shaped jar with Clay and hooked the handle over Treant's branch. I used View Status to identify herbs and edible nuts, and then threw them into the jar.

> **Leol Fruit: Value E+**
> **Beadberry Fruit: Value D−**
> **Harbel Grass: Value D**
> **Red Hot Grass: Value E−**

I gathered some items that looked like they could be used as seasonings, and others that simply caught my eye as well as some items I thought might be high in value.

The leol fruit was yellow and round with orange spots. It seemed to be a citrus fruit, akin to a lemon, judging from the status description. Beadberry fruit was somewhat elastic and rich in nutrients. It came together as a single bunch, kind of like grapes. Harbel grass was a fragrant herb with a weak sleep-inducing effect. Red hot grass was a grass that turned red before it sowed seeds, and the red part was said to be ridiculously painful. These could be defense mechanisms to keep them from being eaten by animals, but, if you were careful with the amount you used, they could make for good seasonings.

All in all, it was a fruitful trip. After that, we headed to the seaside and picked up some salt on the beach. I began to feel like we could live a pretty fulfilling life out here.

I was a little worried, however, about the way Treant's branches creaked under the weight. He didn't complain about it, though, and he maintained his composure. *You don't need to play the tough guy, y'know.*

Partner shook her head about wildly and cried out. *("Bird! I wanna eat some bird!")*

There weren't any large birds anywhere close by. Even looking up at the sky, I didn't see any flying about. Occasionally I spotted some weird giant fly-like bugs, but that was about it. I did see a flock of human-headed sirens in the ocean, but I had no desire to get involved with them, never mind eat them. I'd sooner starve to death than eat Adam, Eve, or the sirens. If push came to shove, I'd sooner eat humans.

In my ranking of food from another world that I definitely didn't want to eat, siren was third, Adam was second, and Eve came in first. When I first encountered an Adam, I thought I'd never see a more messed up monster than that, but Eve easily claimed that spot. Nope, no thanks.

Sorry, Partner, but masked birds are pretty hard to find.

Even I was willing to give up and eat *some* less desirable monsters—compromise was important. After all, the first thing I ate in this world was a caterpillar that was bigger than myself. I felt sorry for human beings, as I was simply not going to let myself be so picky.

When I looked around, I noticed a stone statue of a bipedal, muscular cowman standing calmly between two trees. A cloth was wrapped around his waist, and he gripped a long club in his thick hands. The statue stood around three meters tall; it was quite impressive. It would probably make for a nice decoration back at our burrow. It didn't seem that old. Did Adam make it?

("Hey, Partner! Look down at the ground, would ya?!")

Down? I scraped the ground with my forefoot. In the grass, there was what looked like the footprint of a giant bird.

It must be nearby.

I searched frantically for a trace of the unseen bird along the way.

As we walked on, we passed more strange stone statues. There was a giant wolf statue, a caterpillar with a human face on its head, and a giant three-headed turtle with creepy grins on its faces. I couldn't help thinking that whoever made these had kind of a weird sense of aesthetics.

It must've been an Adam, right? It would make sense that their taste would be a little strange. However, as I continued to hunt the birds, a part of me worried that I might run into the sculptor. Was this really such a wise idea?

Hey, Partner, what do you think?

("Bird meat! I want bird meat!")

Is food all you ever think about?

It looked like she wouldn't be of any help here.

PART 4

OUR LEISURELY WALK through the forest finally brought us to the creature that had left those footprints. It stood about four meters long, and its body was covered in pure white feathers and stood atop long, thin yellow legs. It resembled a gigantic, slightly skinny chicken.

However, close to the tail, the feathers gave way to green scales. The tail was clearly longer than that of a normal chicken, and the tip of the tail, which rose up close to the chicken's head, had eyes and a mouth. It looked like an ominous serpent.

That was fine by me. I had no qualms with eating a chicken with a snake tail. In this world, it was just a different kind of normal.

From the neck up, though, the creature looked like a wrinkled old man with bright red eyes. The old man's hair was as white as the feathers on his chicken body. There wasn't even a hint of black in his pupils, just an eerie red glint. There was something creepy about his elongated neck too.

("Chicken! I want chicken!")

Are you really going to eat that thing?? No matter how you looked at it, it was awfully similar to Adam. Or maybe it was related to the sirens?

Fangs jutted out of the corners of the old man's mouth, and there was something about the sight that struck me as incredibly disgusting. If this had been the first monster I laid eyes on after coming to this world, I would have been prepared to die the moment I saw it.

Basilisk: Rank B+ Monster.

A monster with the tail of a snake and the body of a chicken. The Final Evolution of the Cockatrice line.

Its red eyes emit a powerful petrification curse. The flesh of its body has a strong poison, and anyone who dares get too close to it risks paralysis.

I think we're missing a pretty critical detail here, right?? Sure, it's got the tail of a snake and the body of a chicken, but it really feels like this description of the basilisk is omitting a pretty important detail regarding its head.

What was with this island?! There were simply too many monsters that should've never existed! There was something altogether sinister about how their bodies were designed.

Then again, I was really glad I hadn't come to this island alone. If I wandered out here on my own and encountered a bird with a human head and a man with a face on his belly, I would've definitely lost my mind. I may have even ended up befriending Gyva just because she didn't look so messed up.

The old chicken man—the basilisk—stood next to a black leopard with its limbs turned to stone, which was desperately rolling around. The bird man held its paws in place and bit into its underbelly, pulling the black panther's guts out of its stomach and letting them hang loosely between his teeth. The leopard jerked and convulsed, but the basilisk merely swallowed the viscera he had yanked free from the creature's body.

The basilisk twirled his neck, then turned to face his own tail, the serpent, beside him. The snake turned toward me as if to make its presence known.

The old man then turned his expressionless face straight at me. His eyes were cold. The head was shaped like a person's, but even if that was the only part you could see, you'd still be able to tell it wasn't human. There was something simply too frigid about his expression. I involuntarily crouched down and avoided his gaze.

("*Chicken! Give me chicken!*")

Is that all you think about?! I thought about the strange stone statues we'd seen on our way here and realized that maybe they were the result of his petrification abilities. Judging by what I'd witnessed just now, this could've been a way of preserving food. When he got hungry, he would transform the monster back and then feast.

But for now, it was time to check his stats.

SPECIES: **Basilisk**
STATUS: **Normal**
LV: **88/88 (MAX)**
HP: **655/655**
MP: **233/245**
ATTACK: **440**
DEFENSE: **555**

MAGIC: **450**

AGILITY: **550**

RANK: B+

SPECIAL SKILLS:

TWINHEADS: Lv —

SPLIT PERSONALITY: Lv —

MUTUAL UNDERSTANDING: Lv 2

DARK TYPE: Lv —

FLY: Lv 1

AUTOMATIC HP RECOVERY: Lv 6

HEAT SENSOR: Lv 7

STEALTH: Lv 7

POISON BELT: Lv 8

PETRIFYING GAZE: Lv —

INSTANT DEATH TYPE: Lv 8

TWO-TONGUED: Lv —

DEATH SCREAM: Lv —

RESISTANCE SKILLS:

POISON IMMUNITY: Lv —

PARALYSIS RESISTANCE: Lv 8

PETRIFY IMMUNITY: Lv —

INSTANT DEATH RESISTANCE: Lv 8

CURSE RESISTANCE: Lv 7

CONFUSION RESISTANCE: Lv 4

NORMAL SKILLS:

    PECK: Lv 7

    FILTHY TONGUE: Lv 8

    DOUBLE POISON: Lv 8

    HI-QUICK: Lv 6

    HI-REST: Lv 6

    DEATH: Lv 6

    HI-SLOW: Lv 4

    SINISTER VOICE: Lv 5

    SHRIEK: Lv 6

TITLE SKILLS:

    FINAL EVOLUTION: Lv —

    TENACIOUS: Lv 6

    POISON MASTER: Lv 7

    SYMBOL OF MISFORTUNE: Lv —

Level B+, huh? Well, even so, he had pretty modest stats. Attack power and magic power were both pretty low; it would have a hard time landing a killing blow against monsters of the same rank. I couldn't let my guard down, though—he had too many skills to worry about. In fact, it might've been better to just not get involved at all.

("Hey, that's my chicken over there!")

Is it even edible?? Even if we killed the thing, he's still full of poison! He even has the Poison skill!

"Hiissss!"

The serpent on the basilisk's tail made its presence known. The white feathers glowed briefly before the light was absorbed by the basilisk's body.

Was that Hi-Quick?? Or maybe it was about to use its magic. If he boosted his stats with magic, then there was no way I'd be able to catch up. I felt kind of bad for Partner, but I thought it was probably best to get out of here.

I looked at Allo, who shrugged in response before setting her shoulders in resignation and closing her eyes tightly. A wave of guilt washed over me as I quickly gulped her up. Next up, Treant.

Wait, what was Treant doing? For some reason, it stepped forward and spread out its branches as if to challenge the monster to come closer. *What're you doing?! I understand that you're happy to have evolved, but if you take that guy's attack head-on, you'll be crushed!*

I panicked and tried to grab Treant, but the basilisk—the old man's head, at least—roared and then ran toward me.

"Gyaaaaaaaah!"

His harsh voice struck a chord of fear inside me. He was also fast, incredibly fast. The body of a slightly skinny gigantic chicken, accompanied by the head of an old man, rushed at us with tremendous speed. In spite of the difference in our physiques, I was frightened. It was a fatal mistake.

Treant's body changed from wood to stone. It shook its branches, but in no time flat, Treant had turned into a stone statue. *Treant, no!*

While I was at a loss, the basilisk gradually closed the distance.

"Hyah!"

At Partner's command, Treant was bathed in a gentle glow—Holy magic. However, there was no change in Treant—it was still a stone statue.

("Hmph, that's no good. This is bad.")

Partner's head slumped down, seemingly regretting having brought us out here for her chicken cravings.

However, it was my fault for hesitating to escape. What should I do? There was no way that they'd just stay this way forever. After all, the basilisk treated his petrified collection as preserved food. That meant that he also had the power to return them to their original state. The only way to save Treant was to disable the basilisk and force him to use his power.

PART 5

"*G*YAAAAAAAAAAAAAAAAAAAAAAAAH!*"*

The basilisk's old man head lunged at me, shrieking loudly. His glittering, red eyes looked demonic. A chill ran through my body as I looked straight into the basilisk's eyes. Evil Eye of Petrification.

Fortunately, I was conscious of the flow of magic power flowing through my body and quickly countered it, preventing any change in my body. Because of the significant difference in magic power between us, I was saved from the status ailment. The basilisk's gaze trembled in surprise.

I tried to catch the basilisk with my front claws, but he spread his wings and jumped back quickly to dodge. I couldn't afford to underestimate my opponent. Not only did he have the body of a chicken, but he also had magic-enhanced speed. With my offensive power, though, I should be able to take him out with a single blow.

Spreading my wings, I used Whirlwind Slash to shoot a blade of wind. I chased after the blade of wind and closed the distance between me and the basilisk.

"Gyah!"

The basilisk jumped to the left and avoided the blade of wind. I was running right behind the attack and kicked the monster up into the air.

Now's my chance! I just need to punch him in the face as hard as I can!

The basilisk's wrinkled face puffed up. I kept the basilisk's skill set at the forefront of my mind and tried to anticipate his next action.

No mistake, Double Poison was next!

I stopped on a dime and froze on the spot.

"Gyuuh!"

As expected, a black liquid spewed forth from the basilisk's narrow mouth.

Here it comes! Basilisk's Poison Belt skill was level 8, and so was its Double Poison skill. This was a ridiculously deadly poison attack. But if I dodged now, I wouldn't have another chance.

"Groooooowl!"

I swung my arms and slammed my front leg straight through the basilisk's venom. My vision was blocked, so I couldn't see well, but I could tell that my front leg hit the basilisk.

In any case, it worked. However, since he had High Rest, I needed to make sure he depleted his MP entirely if I wanted to kill him. Until then, I couldn't afford to play around with the monster. In order to cure Treant's petrification, I would need to break his leg before he could recover.

The poison splashed on me. It was absolutely dreadful, but fortunately I had Poison Resistance: level 6, and high vitality. Ouroboros could handle the pain.

I felt a sharp, burning pain on my scales. In particular, it felt as if the front leg that directly covered my face had been pierced by a needle. I looked at my arm and my body froze in an instant: The old man's face was biting into my arm and injecting venom. A mouthful of teeth embedded in my scales.

Thinking about it, the basilisk probably had the Heat Sensor skill. Even if I was able to get out of sight, he would still be able to find me.

My blow seemed to have landed on the basilisk's face, though he was left with little more than a bruise. I had just thrown out my hand and wasn't able to land a direct blow.

"Gyaaah..."

Next, a lukewarm sensation ran through my arm. A ragged bluish-purple tongue emerged from between the basilisk's teeth and licked my scales. A chill ran through me, and I felt my front legs weaken.

Just what is this guy?!

I tried to hold the basilisk down with my forefeet, but I couldn't help but tremble. This guy had the skill Defiled

Tongue. That seemed to have added some kind of status ailment. I tried to slam the basilisk's head on the ground with my front leg, but I noticed that the serpent's eye was staring at me with its neck raised.

"Hiiissssss!"

The moment the snake stretched out and hissed, a black light shone from the tip of its mouth.

Ah, was that Hi-Slow?! It was a magic that reduced speed. I had good memories of that magic. Even if all it did was slow you down, it could really put a wrench in your plans.

I hit the basilisk with my tail, and with the recoil I flew back to avoid the Hi-Slow magic. This thing really was quite dangerous. Even though I was able to keep my distance, the monster quickly closed back in. I decided to take another look.

ILLUSIA
SPECIES: Ouroboros
STATUS: Poison, Magic Resistance
Down, Petrify (Slight)
LV: 96/125
HP: 2304/2517
MP: 2496/2520

He's certainly got a medicine cabinet full of status ailments! Luckily, he didn't have Slow, but he did have access to decreased magic resistance and petrification. Was the resistance reduction added when he licked me with his tongue? And petrification would explain how heavy my front legs felt.

I dropped my gaze to the front leg that had been bitten by the basilisk. The tips of my forelegs had turned gray and hardened; however, the hardened area was gradually expanding.

No, I got hit?! Because of my petrified front legs, my speed suddenly decreased.

I wouldn't be able to catch the basilisk if that happened. And more importantly, at this rate, I'd turn to stone. With my body transforming like this, it was likely that the basilisk would press the attack.

As expected, his level was only as high as it needed to be to survive on this island. He was fighting pretty dirty.

Maybe I could just cut my limb off and regenerate it? No, it would take a lot of time, magic, and concentration to completely repair my front legs. There was no doubt that the basilisk would target me while I was vulnerable. So what should I do?

At that moment, I heard a loud noise behind me. I turned around to see Nightmare looking at me from between the trees, and when our eyes met, it quickly moved its head. *Come over here,* it seemed to be saying.

Shortly thereafter, Nightmare disappeared behind the trees. *Hey, wait! Nightmare...!*

I thought it had just completely fallen out of sight, but perhaps it'd been busy making traps? But there was enough of a difference in stats and physique between the basilisk and Nightmare that I doubted there was much it could do with mere threads. No, Nightmare had set many traps for enemies before. It must've already thought of something.

I staggered back down, glaring at the basilisk. The basilisk charged at me. I retreated to where Nightmare was, and once I'd attracted the basilisk, I turned around and started running.

When I glanced back to confirm the basilisk's position, I noticed the petrified figure of Treant at the edge of my vision.

Wait for me, Treant, I'll definitely save you!

PART 6

....

THE INTERVAL BETWEEN my footsteps as the basilisk chased me felt disgustingly short. With my petrified front legs, I couldn't run as fast as I wanted. I twisted the upper half of my body around and shot out a Whirlwind Slash, but the basilisk calmly avoided the wind blade by bending his back. The old man's withered face distorted as he laughed.

Gah! That bastard managed to dodge the attack so easily! I was just trying to buy some time, and yet he still managed to close the distance.

I dodged around the tree where Nightmare was hiding and slowed down, guiding the basilisk to pass through there. When the basilisk rushed in, ultra-thin red lines reflected light around the basilisk's body: Numerous threads of spider silk were stretched between the trees. But could the basilisk really be stopped with that many threads? No, Nightmare had to have something else in mind.

The petrification in my arm was gradually expanding, so I didn't have much time. I made a sharp turn and charged at the basilisk.

"Gyauugh?"

The basilisk tore through the red thread as if it wasn't even there. He might've slowed down for a moment, but that was about it. He glared at a nearby tree. Nightmare had been hiding above that tree, and now it appeared and spat out clumps of red thread.

"Ptaa!"

Black saliva flew from the basilisk's mouth. It was much smaller than what it used on me, but it still appeared to be the Double Poison skill. Nightmare's poisonous red thread ball withered in the spray of the basilisk's saliva and fell to the ground as the droplets that made it through struck Nightmare, sending it to the ground, legs writhing in pain.

Nightmare?! Nightmare dealt with poison, so it was highly resistant to it. Thanks to that, the damage seemed to have been suppressed... But even so, the rank between the two was too different, which explained why Nightmare was left breathless.

The basilisk showed no further interest in Nightmare and immediately returned his gaze to me.

"Groooooowl!"

I was about to shoot another Whirlwind Slash when I saw the snake on the basilisk's tail slamming its body against the ground in an attempt to unravel the threads wrapped around it.

The basilisk's tail was much slimmer than his body, and snakes didn't have limbs to throw off the threads. It seemed like he couldn't deal with the threads that wrapped around his snake appendage.

With the snake stuck, now was my chance!

Between Hi-Quick, Hi-Slow, and Hi-Rest, the monster had a lot of powerful magic at its disposal. However, these were all used by the snake—it was similar to how my own magic skills worked. If I managed to lop off the snake tail, the basilisk wouldn't be able to keep up the fight. On top of not being able to reapply Hi-Quick—an important lifeline to this creature—if Hi-Rest was gone too, it would be a lot easier for me to capture him.

The basilisk's eyelids twitched, slowing down as he ran toward me. His bright red eyes were focused on my wings, and the basilisk curled his tail snake behind himself, as if to hide it from me.

Huh, did it sense what I planned on doing? Since the tail was his lifeline, it made sense that he would be more cautious. What I needed to do was to somehow distract the basilisk.

Suddenly, I became aware of a certain feeling rolling across my tongue. Ah, yes, Allo!

"Grooowl!" I opened my mouth while calling out to Allo within.

"Gale!" Allo's scream came out of my open mouth.

The basilisk opened his eyes. As expected, this attack took him by surprise. Even Heat Sensor wouldn't have been able to discern Allo's position against the background warmth of my mouth. Her tornado scraped along the ground as it closed the distance and collided with the basilisk's face.

The tornado quickly dispersed, but it clearly had done some damage. Allo was a mage who relied on sheer firepower to strike back at enemies with high HP. What's more, she was also able to absorb my MP to power up her magic, easily allowing her to attack higher-ranked opponents.

The basilisk skidded to a halt, his front end pushed back by the power of the tornado. The basilisk realized he had an opening, though, and quickly took the opportunity to flee. If he hadn't moved, I could've easily aimed at his body; unfortunately, my timing was off, and I was still physically injured. However, this gave me an opportunity to recover with Hi-Rest. Escaping was his biggest mistake.

I shot a Whirlwind Slash at the serpent tail. The basilisk had turned his back to me in a desperate bid to get his tail free from the spider silk.

"Hng!"

The snake twitched and trembled. It seemed that he sensed the wind blade directed at him and stretched out his body to avoid the strike. But alas, it was too little, too late. Whirlwind Slash's blade was the size of the basilisk's entire body. Though he attempted to evade the strike, his tail was lifted up in an instant.

"Hiiisssss?!"

The snake screamed as the wind blade cleanly cut off its head. The headless snake body moved about wildly, but it was only for a short time. Reddish-purple blood immediately spurted out like a hose from the cut, and at the same time, it lost momentum and drooped down to the ground, motionless. The severed snake head turned black and motionless.

"Gyaaa!"

The basilisk spread his wings, kicked off the ground, and sprang up into the air as if he intended to fly away and escape. However, his speed was plummeting. It seemed that the effect of Hi-Quick had finally worn off.

I immediately spread my wings and soared into the air to circle around in front of the basilisk, then I swung my petrified arm down on the basilisk's head like a hammer. It felt like bone shattered under my claws. Did I overdo it? This arm was more powerful than I thought.

Gained Resistance Skill "Petrify Resistance" Lv 1.

Oh, I got a new skill. Come to think of it, this was the first time I'd received this status ailment.

The basilisk plummeted straight to the ground, its jaw hanging slack. I landed next to the basilisk's head. Partner looked around restlessly and let out a cry of relief when she spotted Nightmare on our back. The light of Hi-Rest enveloped Nightmare, and in a few seconds, it abruptly stopped wriggling its legs and stood up. It looked like it was fine.

The basilisk lay on the ground, his entire body convulsing as poison dripped from his mouth. Only his bright red eyeballs moved around, finally settling on me and fixing me with a glare.

Now, let's get my Treant back. I wasn't too worried about my legs. I could always cut them off and regenerate them later.

I felt something wriggling in my mouth—Allo. *Just in case, it would be best to keep you hidden a little longer.*

"I can't handle this anymore. What's going on?" Allo's feeble voice called out from within my mouth. Well, that basilisk couldn't do anything now... I let Partner keep an eye on the basilisk while I lowered my neck down in the opposite direction, opened my mouth, and stretched my tongue out. Allo, covered in saliva, rolled down my tongue. Her expression instantly relaxed. She stunk of dragon.

"Master Dragon!"

I quickly turned to face the basilisk.

Let's get Treant back already! Something told me that this thing wasn't going to be edible no matter how long we boiled or cooked it. Besides, there was plenty of better food out there.

Having realized that he was doomed, the basilisk raised his head as if he'd made up his mind, glared at me again, and then turned his face to the sky.

"Gyaaaaaaaaaaaaaaaaaaugh!"

An agonized voice erupted from the old man's crushed face. It was an eerie voice that gave me chills. His voice was imbued with magic—could it be that skill Ominous Voice? Well, I didn't think he was going to do anything yet. There were no indications of abnormal conditions in his body.

The face of the basilisk smiled at me, which I found quite suspicious. Although the old man's face was crushed, he wore a kind expression.

When I turned my gaze to look off in the distance, I noticed that Treant's body had regained its color. It stayed frozen in place for a while, but when it noticed me looking at it, Treant moved its eyes and rotated its branch as if just now noticing it'd been reverted, and then twisted its trunk slightly. It seemed that Treant was a bit late to notice that it could move again.

That basilisk is really something else!

How odd that, at the end of his life, he would go out of his way to heal Treant. Though he may have been an enemy, I couldn't help but respect him.

What should I do? He was a pretty dangerous enemy, so I was definitely going to kill him, but I somehow felt reluctant to do so. Maybe we could bring him with us? But no, try as I might, I just couldn't imagine traveling together with him. Not that I was one to discriminate based on appearances, but this was something different entirely.

("Hey! He's doing something!")

Partner pulled me out of my reverie, and I turned back to see the basilisk wrinkling its distorted face to show an ugly, evil smile. I felt the magical power of the basilisk increasing rapidly, and, terrified, I reflexively swung my claws as hard as I could, swiftly decapitating him. Fresh blood spouted everywhere, and the basilisk's head fell to the ground.

I was glad I was able to crush him before something happened—I always got caught by this kind of surprise attack. Thanks to Partner calling out to me, I was able to avoid getting hurt.

"Aaaaaaugh! Waaaaugh! Waaaaaaaaaaaaugh!"

A loud cry erupted from the basilisk's head, then his face relaxed, turned black, and flattened in exhaustion.

It was an unpleasant voice, as if I had struck his brain directly. Well, I didn't expect that decapitating him would produce such an unnerving noise.

> **Gained 3,168 Experience Points.**
> **Title Skill "Walking Egg" Lv — activated: gained 3,168**
> **Experience Points.**
> **Ouroboros Lv 96 has become Lv 97.**

I was happy about the level up, but...my vision began to blur, probably because of the strange scream. I wasn't sure, but I was certainly annoyed.

"Gaaa! Aaaaaaa!" Partner was roaring like crazy.

Oh no, it looked like he did give us some kind of bad status after all. I breathed slowly and tried to calm myself down.

"Gaaaaaa!" Partner pointed her fangs at me, so for the time being I shoved my head right into her mouth.

"Hnngh!" My headbutt bent Partner's head back.

("S-sorry about that. I guess I was confused there for a moment.")

It seemed that she was better now, but I was still a little dizzy. The basilisk's dying scream probably had the effect of the Screech skill, which included the status effects of Illusion, Confusion, and Berserk. The skill was ridiculous.

What the decapitated head had cried out was probably the Special Skill, Death Scream. Even after dying, he still got one last jab in. What an annoying skill.

And yet, he'd still healed Treant. I turned to look for Treant and saw it moving toward me. In any case, I was glad it was okay. Or at least I thought so at first—but it seemed that Treant had actually been hit by the status effects too. It lunged at me with a branch sticking out in front of it. I thought the front of its mouth was glowing, and the moment I noticed it, a red ball of light flew at me: Treant's Fire Sphere skill.

Oh no, you've been affected too!

"Gale!" Allo's voice echoed out.

A raging tornado wiped out the fireball, shaking Treant's body and causing its leaves to fall. Allo then swung her left hand, bloated with dirt, and punched through the upper part of Treant. It fell forward at her feet.

Allo!

Allo had a great resistance that gave her immunity to status effects, thus she was left unaffected. High-ranked undead really were something else.

Ha, basilisk. If you thought that Treant could hunt me down, you're too naive. If you want to beat me, you'd need at least fifty Treants.

"Shck! Shck!"

Now Nightmare ran excitedly to me. This was obviously different from its usual behavior. It seemed that it had also been hit by the basilisk's status effects. Its eyes were locked on Partner.

It was finally time to punish this cocky Nightmare. Should I poke its head lightly and bring it back to its senses? Just a light little tap. If I put all my strength into it, I'd risk knocking it out with a single blow.

From behind Nightmare, a new kind of monster, a large bipedal cow, was heading for us, as well as a monstrous three-headed turtle. These were the ones who'd been petrified by the basilisk.

Among the swarm of monsters, I also spotted an Adam.

Hey, how the hell did you get petrified by a low-ranking basilisk?! What a disgrace for a rank A– monster! This has to be some kind of joke!

Having all regained their ability to move at once, they seemed intent on killing one another due to the wide-ranging status effect that had been inflicted upon them. I initially wondered why that attack had removed their petrification status, but it all made sense now. When the other monsters heard the basilisk's voice, they would all come rushing to crush whatever had killed it. It was a hell of a combo.

Partner calmly put the approaching Nightmare in her mouth and urged me on with her eyes. I nodded back and swallowed Allo up, grabbed Treant with my front claws and lifted it up, and then kicked off the ground and started flying at a low altitude.

Partner wistfully looked behind us.

(*"All that chicken... All that fruit..."*)

Just give it up! You can't eat that, and we don't have time to go grab our jar!

But Nightmare poked its head out of Partner's mouth and spit out a thread toward the jar that lay discarded on the ground and around the basilisk's upper torso. Pulled by the string, the basilisk's body and the pot were both dragged along behind us.

Nightmare was as handy as ever. Apparently, its confusion cleared up once it was sucked into Partner's mouth. I figured things would've played out differently if it were me, but Nightmare seemed to really like Partner, and I was sure being in her mouth helped. Kinda perverted, if you thought about it.

Nightmare, who was still sticking its head out of Partner's mouth, glared at me. I turned my face forward.

Anyway, once I got away from the monsters, I needed to sort myself out a bit. And after all that, Allo should've been close to evolving.

PART 7

S OMEHOW, I MANAGED TO ESCAPE from the basilisk's hunters by flying at a low altitude. They were just beasts in a state of excitement and derangement, after all. If I kept my distance, they'd just focus on killing one another instead of chasing after me.

It seemed that the basilisk wanted to get me involved in that melee, but fortunately, the huge gap between our magic power levels was enough to keep me from suffering any severe status ailment.

When I looked over my shoulder, I could see the monsters fighting to the death and screaming off in the distance. The Adam I'd noticed among them shot a Gravidon into the monsters around him before landing a few flawless blows with his feet. Adam was an attacker type that specialized in attack and speed, so I didn't think there'd be any opening for monsters below his rank to take advantage of. Then again, he was turned into a stone by the lower ranked basilisk...

After I'd put some distance between us, I finally landed. Nightmare had managed to carry the jar with a thread, but it was a bit careless in how it grabbed onto the jar, and all the contents had gotten mixed together.

The basilisk that Partner had wanted to eat was also tattered, with its feathers peeled off and its flesh gouged up. It couldn't be helped, seeing as it'd been dragged along on the ground and all, but the sight was still pretty vulgar. It almost looked like it'd suffered a brutal execution.

What's more, the basilisk's Poison Belt seemed pretty potent, as it left behind a trail of reddish-purple bodily fluids, each droplet scorching the soil below and leaving the ground smoking.

This thing definitely shouldn't be eaten. Partner, do you really want to eat it? I'm always in your debt and grateful for everything you've done for me, so if you really want to, I won't stop you—I doubt it would be too much for our stomach to handle anyway. But still, I really can't recommend it. If you just wait a minute, I'm confident I could prepare something even better.

Once we landed, I put Treant down, rested my chin on the ground, and extended my tongue, sending Allo rolling out. Being covered in my saliva made the dirt stick to her. Oops. But once she got up, Allo nodded to let me know that she didn't care. I nodded back in turn, but I didn't dare speak my thoughts.

That's right! More importantly, evolution, evolution! With this, Allo should've finally entered the next evolutionary stage.

> NAME: **Allo**
> SPECIES: **Levana Low Liche**
> STATUS: **Cursed**
> LV: **65/65 (MAX)**
> HP: **382/382**
> MP: **368/405**

Here we come! This would be Allo's fourth evolution.

Allo was brushing her muddy body dejectedly, but she seemed to have guessed from my face that she had reached the level cap, and she immediately brightened up and waved her hands up and down happily.

Let's also take a look at Nightmare and Treant's stats. These guys might've gone up quite a bit too. I turned my gaze to Nightmare as she popped out of Partner's mouth.

> SPECIES: **Nightmare**
> STATUS: **Normal**
> LV: **14/70**
> HP: **122/174**
> MP: **84/163**

As expected, Nightmare was knocking it out of the park! It'd really helped out back there. Sure, it was relatively easy to level up in the early stages, but this was still quite a feat.

Nightmare didn't seem particularly happy to be praised by me; in fact, she merely averted her gaze and spit some silk up onto Partner's neck to climb up. Partner frowned a little at the sight of her saliva-covered Nightmare climbing over her.

I know that feeling.

Finally, Treant. It approached me with a look of anticipation. *Don't you worry, buddy, I'll take a good look at it.*

> SPECIES: **Magical Tree**
> STATUS: **Cursed**
> LV: **1/60**
> HP: **161/161**
> MP: **87/110**

I quickly looked away.

Hey, Partner! I want you to use Soul Addition (Fake Life) on Allo so she can evolve!

Treant was staring at me with its eyes fixed, expressionless, but I couldn't meet its gaze. Allo approached me, carefully avoiding Treant, as if to be considerate of me.

"Grah!"

Partner let out a growl and black light clung to Allo. Eventually the black light disappeared, and Allo reappeared in its place. She just stood there with her eyes closed. Was this her next evolution?

The mud that was clinging to her had fallen cleanly off. However, even though she had evolved, she didn't seem to have changed much in terms of appearance. Allo had already regained much of her appearance when she re-evolved into a Levana Low Liche, so this might just be natural.

If anything had changed, it was that she had grown a little taller and her face had become prettier somehow. Before, I would've said she looked like she was about ten years old, but she must've grown by about three years.

Levana Liche: Rank B+ Monster. A top-ranked undead of the Levana lineage that freely manipulates soil and cloaks its body in it. An undead, with its strong attachment to the living, has finally succeeded in creating a perfect, ideal body from a mere lump of earth. Its beauty will captivate even the adventurers who seek to subjugate it.

B+?! That puts you about on par with the Mother of the avyssos, who gave me such a tough time back in the woods near the Lithovar tribe settlement! I can't believe how far you've come! Allo was a magic attack type, and if by any chance she got really angry, even I might take a lot of damage.

Seemed like I was going to have to stop carrying her around in my mouth so much.

NAME: Allo

SPECIES: Levana Liche

STATUS: Cursed

LV: 1/85

HP: 164/164

MP: 179/179

ATTACK: 121

DEFENSE: 101

MAGIC: 260

AGILITY: 88

RANK: B+

SPECIAL SKILLS:

GRECIAN LANGUAGE: Lv 4

UNDEAD: Lv —

DARK TYPE: Lv —

BODY MORPH: Lv 7

PRIVILEGE OF THE DEAD: Lv —

MASTER OF THE EARTH: Lv —

EVIL EYE: Lv —

UNDEAD MAKER: Lv —

RESISTANCE SKILLS:

DEBUFF IMMUNITY: Lv —

PHYSICAL RESISTANCE: Lv 4

MAGIC RESISTANCE: Lv 5

NORMAL SKILLS:

GALE: Lv 7

CURSE: Lv 4

LIFE DRAIN: Lv 5

CLAY: Lv 7

REGENERATE: Lv 5

CLAY DOLL: Lv 6

MANA DRAIN: Lv 6

LINGERING ROPE: Lv 4

FOG OF THE DEAD: Lv 4

CHARM: Lv 1

WIDE DRAIN: Lv 1

DARK SPHERE: Lv 1

TITLE SKILLS:

EVIL DRAGON'S MINION: Lv —

HOLLOW MAGE: Lv 7

EVERLASTING BODY: Lv —

FINAL EVOLUTION: Lv —

UNDEAD QUEEN: Lv —

Let's see here, it looked like her Evil Eye skill had increased too? I'd never seen it used before, but I wondered what kind of effect it would have. The only newly added Special Skill she had was Undead Maker. It sounded kind of disturbing.

Under Normal Skills, she gained Charm, Wide Drain, Dark Sphere... *Hmm, I wonder what Charm does?* Wide Drain sounded like a wide-range energy draining attack. It didn't exactly say, so I couldn't tell if it was HP, MP, or both.

And then...the new Title Skills were Final Evolution and Undead Queen. Hmm.

Was this Allo's final evolution? Nightmare had also stayed at C+, so that might be it. Treant was the only one who didn't have Final Evolution yet. Over time, Treant might actually become the strongest of them all.

Well, Treant, Nightmare, and Allo had all finally evolved... C+, C+, and B+.

It looked like it would take a little longer for me to evolve, so I'd put it off for later, but if I leveled up a bit, I might be able to head to the temple located under the great tree.

That place must have something to do with me.

Now that I knew about the relationship between this world and the world I came from, I didn't think it was

any of my concern. There were too many things important here that were important to me, and above all, while
I had knowledge of my previous life, I didn't have any
episodic memories. Frankly speaking, I had absolutely no
attachment to the idea of returning to my original world.

And yet, I still wanted to know.

PART 8

....

AFTER RETURNING TO THE BURROW, we hung
the basilisk up by its legs and laid out the fruits
and herbs that we'd collected during the search.

Was the basilisk actually edible? It was only natural to
think something that looked like a big chicken could be
eaten, but the old white-haired man with bright red eyes
part really gave me second thoughts.

("There a problem?")

Well, yes. It may look fine, but its body is full of poison.

Despite how it looked, the poison remained a problem. Partner would still probably eat it without a second
thought, though, and after all the effort we'd made to
bring it back with us, I figured we might as well cook
it. If the vaporized deadly poison floated in the air, even

Partner might have second thoughts, but if she didn't give in, I certainly would.

My Ouroboros body was huge, but I'd never been able to completely eat my fill. The masked bird had a reasonable amount of meat, but I still felt like I hadn't consumed enough calories. I was definitely still running low on energy from the trip over here. We'd bagged ourselves a massive monster this time, and one that looked like a chicken at that. It seemed like a good idea to try and keep myself well nourished.

Besides, there weren't many decent monsters here anyway, right? Between Eve, the sirens, and the basilisk, what was with all these human heads? Of course, Adam didn't have a human head, he just had everything else.

I plucked the feathers off the basilisk and cut off the tips of its legs, exposing the light reddish-purple meat. Then I split its belly vertically with my nails, sending red-purple blood flowing out.

When I touched the poisonous blood with my front paw, pain shot through me. The surface of the scales on my forelegs melted a little. I shook my front leg and lightly scattered the basilisk's poisonous blood.

I put my front claws in the crack, felt around inside the basilisk's body, and pulled out the internal organs. There was a deep purple, water balloon-like organ, so I tore it apart, grabbed it with my forepaws, and brought my face closer. It had a strong odor. A poison sac? It was like the poison made here was mixed with the blood throughout its body. When I held it in my hand, poison poured out. I threw the poison sack off the branch where I was perched. Just how dangerous was that poison, really? Would it be bad if we touched it? Or even ate it?

Suddenly, Partner approached me. With a light growl, she used Hi-Rest, and a gentle light enveloped my forefoot. *Thanks, Partner.*

(*"Now hurry up."*) She shook her head in annoyance. Ah, she was just upset that I had stopped. *You really are a stubborn one.*

I had Nightmare hang the basilisk on the upper branch, draining its body of its poisonous blood. I felt a bit better as I watched the poison leave its body.

Among the items we'd collected, there were a few medicinal herbs that could cure poison. Maybe I should mash them up and fill the basilisk's cavities with it?

With Allo's help, I lined up the various medicinal herbs I'd collected and checked them one by one. I decided we'd use the Poisoning Herb: Value E, Admirab Mandogora: Value C+, Harbel Grass: Value D, and Red Hot Grass: Value E.

Poisoning herbs were medicinal herbs that had a detoxifying effect. That should somewhat counteract the poison of the basilisk.

Harbel grass was an herb with a soothing effect, and red hot grass was an herb with a pungent taste similar to chili peppers. Since tonight's dinner was kind of a big deal, I felt like we could splurge a bit.

Admirab Mandogora was a pitch-black carrot about the size of a fat puppy, which looked like a human doll. To be honest, it was actually a monster, but since it was a rank E monster, I was able to defeat it without any trouble. According to the Divine Voice, it seemed to be treated as a luxury food because of its unique smell that stimulates appetite. However, since the smell was a little strong, it was said that it should be used sparingly. If you put your nose close to it, you could catch a whiff of garlic. I figured this should be fine.

I asked Allo to dice these plants for me, as they were too small for my talons to cut up.

She quickly shredded the Poisoning Herb, Harbel Grass, Red Hot Grass, and Admirab Mandogora with Gale. It took only a moment for the small tornado to erupt from her fingertips, chopping and mixing the four plants together and leaving them heaped in a single pile.

I was truly amazed. Allo proudly looked back at me while I stood there dumbfounded. Oh, how I wished I also had Gale.

Salt created from the sea water was mixed in with the chopped-up plants. I took down the basilisk, sprinkled the spices Allo had prepared all over its body, and rubbed it in.

As a finishing touch, I stuffed its belly with as many poisoning herbs as possible, which I'd rubbed with salt beforehand. Once I ran out, I decided to go down under the big tree again. Poisoning herbs weren't that rare, so you could find a lot of them just by looking around for a bit.

I heated Allo's homemade hearth with Scorching Breath and tossed the basilisk in. The smell of roasting meat soon mingled with the fragrant scent of Admirab Mandogora.

I followed the smoke coming out of the hearth with my nose. *Oh, that's the stuff!* Admirab Mandogora was even stronger than garlic, which was quite a persistent smell in its own right. I absolutely loved it.

Partner seemed to agree, drooling from between her fangs. I checked the furnace regularly and took it out when the skin started to singe.

The basilisk had turned into a gigantic roast chicken with a beautiful sheen. I took out the poisoning herb stuffing and threw it out onto a branch. Then I buried my nose in the basilisk and inhaled. I was enveloped by a mixture of roasted meat and the scent of Admirab Mandogora. There was grease on the tip of my nose.

Wow, that was perfect. This was no longer a basilisk. No matter what anyone said, it was now a fine roasted chicken.

"Graaa!"

Partner let out a growl before biting into the roasted basilisk. It seemed that we'd finally reached the limit of her patience—but the same could be said for me as well. Not to be outdone, I attacked from the other side.

The fragrant smell of the Admirab Mandogora, the hot meat filling my mouth, and the flavors bursting across my tongue were absolutely divine. I was glad that we brought it home. And thanks to our countermeasures, I didn't detect much poison either.

No matter what, I had to get some more Admirab Mandogora. Sauce oozed from my mouth. It was perfection.

CHAPTER

5

Deadly Beach Birds

PART 1

AFTER ENJOYING THE basilisk roast chicken, I had a good rest and resumed my exploration activities the next day. I took Allo, Nightmare, and Treant down from our burrow in the great tree nest and walked through the forest. Today's goal was to collect more Admirab Mandogora, a spice that surpassed even piperis in my opinion...and raise Allo's level while we were at it.

Since she'd just evolved, Allo's level was quite low, but with my support, we should be able to get her up to one-third of her level cap in no time flat. Once that was done, I figured we could enter the underground ruins.

I didn't find any suitable monsters, but I kept looking around for any buried Mandogora.

After a while, we passed through the forest and arrived at the beach. I straightened my neck and looked around. The ocean was truly beautiful, but I could see the edge of the world in the distance. The whole scene left me feeling a little uneasy, though it was hardly a bad view. There weren't many places you could see something like that, so it was best to appreciate it when the opportunity presented itself.

However, it seemed that there weren't as many monsters around here as there were in the forest. Just as I was thinking about heading back, though, I saw three birds with human heads—sirens—gathering around something on the beach.

The sirens, with their finely chiseled feminine faces, turned their human heads to glare at me, their long hair hanging down to the ground and blood dripping from their mouths. It was a disgusting sight.

Ah, it's these guys again. They all looked the same, but they were all rank B and barely covered with any kind of clothing. I thought for a moment about quickly turning back, but then I caught a glimpse of the skin color of something the sirens had gathered. Suddenly, I recalled the explanation I'd gotten about them earlier.

Siren: Rank B Monster.

A monster with the head of a human woman and the body of a bird. A siren's singing voice gently lures other creatures to their death. It often inhabits the sea near land and prefers to eat human flesh. They curse sailors to their death using their songs and peck at the flesh of the corpses.

If you find a mountain of human bones piled up on the beach, it is a siren hunting ground. Sirens enjoy eating human flesh.

That's when I realized it. The sirens wanted to drag humans down and drown them in the sea. The gathered humans were exhausted and showed no sign of resistance. They could already be dead by now.

I didn't have time to wonder why there were humans here. I quickly fired off a Whirlwind Slash at the sirens. I knew I risked hitting a human if it struck too close, so I aimed it slightly off target. With any luck, this would scare the sirens away—but I wasn't holding my breath.

The expressionless faces of the three sirens all twisted into terrifying, ugly scowls.

"Gwaaaaaaaaooor!"

Looks like they're all coming in! So let's stick together and fight this one out! I let out a roar to attract their attention.

(*"Hey, uh, Partner..."*) Partner turned to me with an anxious and worried expression on her face. I knew exactly what she meant, but even so, I still couldn't just let them go. Even now, a part of me was still human.

Besides, even if I thought about it analytically, this was still the right choice. The fact that there were humans here meant a lot. I wanted to make that clear. Maybe we could learn something new.

(*"No, well, I mean..."*)

Oh, of course sirens were dangerous. They were small but worthy of their rank B—and I wasn't keen on the fact that there were three of them. But they were still only B. If I took things seriously, they shouldn't be able to stand a chance against us. And if we could take them down, that would help with leveling Allo up quickly as well. The most important thing was how many of us got involved in the fight. If we fought all the sirens together, it would be more difficult to level up.

Their attacks would be dangerous for Allo and the others, but Allo was immune to status ailments and I had high magical power, so I should be able to avoid the worst of it. Even if they broke through my defenses, I'd still be able to recover. In that sense, I could act both as a melee attacker and a shield.

"Ahahahahahaha!" The sirens all sounded loudly as they flew in low and split in three directions before rushing in to surround me. Though a bit abnormally high pitched, their voices sounded almost human. Sirens were great at singing, so their voices were clear and beautiful.

All right then, I know you're all rank B monsters, but let's see how you plan on fighting against a rank A like me! The gap between us is vast, so I'll show you a thing or two!

("Hey, look at that.")

What, what was that just now? I looked in the direction Partner indicated with her chin. The siren flew away and the gathered humans fell down, completely covered in blood. Most damningly, everything from the neck up was missing. Just as I'd thought, it was too late, but we could still take a moment to mourn the corpses.

Just as I was thinking that, however, I noticed that there was no blood coming out from the necks.

Buffeted by the waves, the human corpses rolled on the sand. They had rather dapper faces on their bellies. Even though he was almost certainly dead, Adam wore the same flat expression on his face as when he was alive.

Oh, wow! I'll show you A rank! Yesterday, I was partially turned to stone by a basilisk, so today I guess we're eating siren for dinner!

I shouldn't have gotten involved. I was glad they'd left us alone. *Don't you guys like humans? There's no need to settle for lookalike monsters!*

Treant was too heavy to flee quickly, so I had no choice but to pick it up. As long as I could keep an eye on the sirens, I didn't need to worry about exposing my back.

Damn! I'd panicked because I thought they were humans! I shot Partner a sidelong glance, but she merely remained expressionless with her mouth open and fangs exposed. *This is bad, real bad.*

PART 2

WITH ALL THE SIRENS flying around, I decided to check the status of the closest one.

I didn't know how intelligent they were, so I couldn't say anything about that, but it seemed that speed was their highest stat. You could tell by how much it differed with a given siren's level. All the same, I decided to find the most powerful one I could.

SPECIES: Siren

STATUS: Normal

LV: 69/80

HP: 359/359

MP: 228/423

ATTACK: 287

DEFENSE: 311

MAGIC: 482

AGILITY: 550

RANK: B

SPECIAL SKILLS:

   FLY: Lv 7

   AUTOMATIC HP RECOVERY: Lv 3

   ENSEMBLE: Lv 8

   AUTOMATIC MP RECOVERY: Lv 5

   STEALTH: Lv 2

RESISTANCE SKILLS:

   MAGIC RESISTANCE: Lv 4

   PARALYSIS RESISTANCE: Lv 5

   PETRIFY RESISTANCE: Lv 5

   INSTANT DEATH RESISTANCE: Lv 3

   CURSE RESISTANCE: Lv 7

   CONFUSION RESISTANCE: Lv 5

   ILLUSION RESISTANCE: Lv 7

POISON RESISTANCE: Lv 5

SLEEP RESISTANCE: Lv 5

NORMAL SKILLS:

LULLABY: Lv 4

SONG OF CONFUSION: Lv 4

SONG OF SERENITY: Lv 4

SONG OF DEATH: Lv 6

SONG OF CHARM: Lv 5

SONG OF RESENTMENT: Lv 7

SONG OF DEMONS: Lv 5

SONG OF ILLUSION: Lv 7

WHIRLWIND SLASH: Lv 4

TITLE SKILLS:

CUNNING: Lv 5

TENACIOUS: Lv 6

SINGER OF THE EDGE OF THE WORLD: Lv —

DEATH CHORUS: Lv —

As expected, I was quite a bit faster than they were thanks to the difference in rank, but it was a bit difficult to actually attack them due to their numbers. It seemed a bit cruel to leave these guys to Allo and the others right now. After all, rank B was fairly strong. I wasn't sure if I could protect Allo, Nightmare, and Treant in a melee.

And besides their speed and numbers, they had many skills that weren't well detailed—and most of all, they fought at long distance. It looked like I'd finally run into someone other than myself who used Whirlwind Slash.

Whirlwind Slash was quite strong. It wasn't as powerful as a striking attack, but its attack power was close to that of a splitting attack. Once you got used to it, you could shoot it at will, and it had quite a long range. The time it took to shoot was quite fast for the magic system. It was also ideal for restrained attacks and hunting weak enemies. Even against equals, depending on the opponent's type, you could still potentially take them down if you kept your distance and fired with reckless abandon.

It used about one-sixth of my MP, which was no small amount for an Ouroboros like me. Sirens had quite a bit of MP themselves, but if they'd just been fighting Adams, these creatures should have lost some of their MP and not yet fully recharged. It would be a bad idea to just recklessly shoot off a Whirlwind Slash, but it was worth considering as an opening attack. If they were to fire Whirlwind Slash at Allo and the others, then I would have no choice but to defend them.

Anyway, I figured it was best for me to take the lead. I stiffened my wings and began to flap to generate some magic-imbued wind. Then I channeled the power through my arms and out through my toes before sending out a Whirlwind Slash toward the leading siren.

At that time, the tone of the sirens changed. The three cries were aligned, and their voices rose together in harmony. The sound was beautiful, a stark contrast with their unpleasant appearance. The Whirlwind Slash hit...or so I thought. I felt a bit dizzy trying to track the leading siren, watching it split into two and fly left and right. Those two sirens divided further into two more sirens each. They each formed a pair and flew side by side in the sky.

What is this? They... They shouldn't be able to do that.

No, no. I had experienced a similar situation before in the Harunae Desert. This was the hallucination skill, Mirage.

The Song of Illusion probably used their singing voices to produce the same effect as Mirage. There was no way a rank B monster could suddenly split itself in two like that. This made the battle all the less desirable. I wasn't interested in fighting illusory enemies. I prayed hard, trying to shake off the hallucination—but all that happened was that the illusions started to appear slightly shaky, likely as a result of all three of them using their power at once.

It would be practically impossible to miss them if I just confirmed them using View Status, but it was almost impossible to do when they were flying side by side.

Damn! That was even after sending out three attacks!

The six sirens looked down at me with disgusting smiles on their faces, as if mocking me. Confusion, impatience, and hesitation washed across my face.

The two sirens in the lead slowed down a bit and joined the other two groups in gaining altitude. Then, they hovered in the air diagonally above me for a moment, moved their wings a bit, and shot a Whirlwind Slash.

Between the real sirens and the illusions, a total of six Whirlwind Slashes rained down on us.

Oh no, that was just way too many. Though I knew that half of them were illusions, if I made one wrong move, I could put Allo and the others in danger. I had no choice but to go on the defensive. But if I kept up what I was doing, I'd run out of choices fast. Since I wasn't willing to gamble on which ones were real, I had no choice but to take the safest route.

Suddenly Allo landed on my shoulder.

"Curse!"

From Allo's hand, three sinister lights emitted and rose into the sky, trailing a line of black. However, Curse's light was weak and slow. This obviously wouldn't hit the sirens. They had a high curse resistance, anyway, so it wasn't like we could expect much of an effect even if it hit. I hadn't used curses all that much, in any case so I didn't know much about them, but from my experience with Dragon Scale Powder and Demon's Breath, the impression I had was that they were a delayed poison rather than a special healing condition. They weren't of much use in direct combat.

Hey, Allo, stop moving around so much. These guys are seriously dangerous.

Something occurred to me, though: Allo was unique among the undead as she had the skill Nullify Status Abnormality. Hallucinations didn't usually seem to be reflected in status ailments, but there *was* also a skill called Illusion Resistance. Did Allo's Status Abnormality Nullification offer resistance to illusion-type skills?

It was worth a shot.

I focused only on the siren who Allo had shot the Curse at and who attacked us with the Whirlwind Slash. I extended my tail toward Treant and unleashed Whirlwind Slash at one of the sirens. My bold movements startled the sirens, making them tremble. Two Whirlwind Slashes approached me from the front, released by the siren flying in the lead. It was a lot faster than the other two, probably because of the difference in magic power.

I thrust my head forward and caught one of the Whirlwind Slashes head-on. Intense pain slashed across my face, and a gash opened from the top of my forehead to the bottom of my left eyelid. Blue blood dripped into my mouth. Well, I could at least take a single blow.

The other Whirlwind Slash, as Allo had been showing me, was just an illusion: Before it reached me, it became a bubble of light and disappeared. My Whirlwind Slash collided with the siren's own Whirlwind Slash in the air—but my magical power was double theirs. My wind blade smashed straight through the siren's, scattering the enemy's attack, and slammed straight into the siren's chest.

The siren closed her wings and took a defensive posture as the blade of wind collided with her.

"Aaaaaaaugh!"

The siren screamed, and her feathers and crimson blood danced in the air. She spread her wings, marred by several horizontal red wounds, and the lower half of her wings drooped down, revealing a deep red gouge on her abdomen. As I watched, her eyes went white, and she tumbled down to the ground below. The figure of the siren next to the one I'd hit directly with Whirlwind Slash became hazy and disappeared into thin air. The other siren phantoms likewise faded away until there were only the original three sirens remaining.

They'd been flying around so energetically just moments ago, but a single Whirlwind Slash from me put an end to all that? With all their specialization in speed and MP, they didn't have the toughness to fight me. Maybe they shouldn't have gotten so puffed up over beating some Adams. Adams were a weak rank A at that. I was sure they had caught them off guard and made the first move, but if those Adams had seen through it, like Allo did, it would've all been over for them.

> Gained 1,690 Experience Points.
> Title Skill "Walking Egg" Lv — activated: gained 1,690 Experience Points.
> Ouroboros Lv 97 has become Lv 98.

Huh, I leveled up? I guess that last basilisk must've been bigger than I thought, and there was still a bit of experience left over.

I thought we could escape now, but it didn't seem like the remaining sirens had any intention of retreating. In fact, they both looked furious. The pitch of their voices shifted in unison, from the high soprano from before to a dissonant combination of high and low. The sound alone made me feel ill. I'd thought I had the advantage now that I'd taken one of them down, but I'd only had the upper hand due to my superior long range and attack speed. I braced myself as they closed in.

PART 3

MY VISION WAS DISTORTED from the two sirens' cacophony. I started to feel nauseated, and my mind went blank. Judging by the sensation, I figured I'd been afflicted with the Confusion status. Could this be their Song of Confusion skill? While I still had my wits about me, I banged my head against Partner's.

"Gyaugh?!"

Partner screamed, but thanks to that, my own thoughts became a little clearer. Just having a heavy head to bang against didn't help in its own right, but since she specialized in recovery, I could smack against her with all my might to help heal damage.

Allo placed her hand on my head and seemed to be preparing to use her skill, but then she looked at me with a smile and withdrew her hands. Apparently if I hadn't cleared my head on my own, she would have done it for me.

I turned to see how Treant and Nightmare were doing.

Nightmare was crouched on the ground, curled up with its legs bent. I guess it knew that bad things awaited if it wasn't careful. Depending on the situation, not moving at all could be an issue in its own right, but frankly speaking, now that I was thinking clearly thanks to Allo and Partner, it was clear that Nightmare and Treant were having a hard time.

Treant was staggering and wandering away from me.

Dammit, you're just confused! Just try to emulate Nightmare here!

"Gyashaaa!"

Treant let out a roar and a circle of black light spread around it: Gravity. Well, it'd been a long time since I last heard Treant raise his voice like that. It'd been acting much more passive lately. Treant seemed to have put all its MP into that Gravity, and me, Allo, and Nightmare were all within range of the ensuing pressure.

Allo, leaning against my neck, managed to only get hit in one of her knees, but Nightmare, who was already crouching, was struck head-on by the mysterious gravitational wave, and its feet sunk deeper into the ground. It would be bent up onto itself in no time at all.

Dammit, you're a pretty useless ally, but the moment you turn into an enemy, you use your best attacks!

"Groooowl!"

I roared and shot a Whirlwind Slash at one of the remaining sirens, but my vision was blurry, and the Whirlwind Slash flew far below its mark. Damn, I needed to try to aim a little higher.

Another siren launched a Whirlwind Slash from behind

me. I flicked it with the tip of my tail and took the blow directly. The two sirens circled around me, singing a discordant song. With my concentration disturbed, the actions of the sirens were even worse. If I focused on one, I had to neglect the other, leaving them open to try to attack Allo and the others. I tried to think of how to deal with it, but the cacophony kept breaking my concentration.

I tried to not think too much and just focus on one thing at a time. It was the best I could do at the moment, no matter how hard I tried to think about it.

Should I focus exclusively on the sirens for now, then? They shouldn't have much leeway at this point, at least not after their battle with Adam. The sirens could be quite a challenge if they just used their Whirlwind Slash over and over—that was the obvious strategy for a siren in a hurry to win. But if that wasn't an option, then what was the next best thing? Whatever they chose, it had to introduce an even larger gap between us.

I tried to calm myself as much as possible and focused only on dealing with the flying siren and its Whirlwind Slashes.

Allo seemed to be busy creating clumps of sand with Clay, hitting Treant with them to try and get it back to normal. Whenever she had a spare moment, she'd use Gale to create a tornado to keep the two sirens in check.

While Allo continued making her Clay Spheres, I dealt with the two sirens' Whirlwind Slashes as they circled around me. The battle was quickly becoming repetitive. Eventually, the frequency of the sirens' Whirlwind Slashes gradually decreased, and my Confused symptoms seemed to improve. It was about time for them to leave. I took advantage of Allo's Gale and launched more Whirlwind Slashes toward the sirens.

However, either the sirens could read our movements or I hadn't yet perfected the attack, because they evaded Gale with minimal effort and then shifted their speed to dodge my Whirlwind Slash.

By chance, Treant attacked the sirens with a Clay Sphere. The siren, already exhausted from having dodged my previous attacks, seemed to have completely ignored Treant the entire time. It didn't look like the siren it struck took much damage, but it seemed to cause the two of them to give up their current tactic. The hit siren grimaced and shook her head to clear off the dirt. I focused my attention on one of the sirens as they continued to let out that dissonant sound, flying in a whirlpool pattern as they circled in closer on me.

The closer I got, the louder their singing voices became and the sicker I felt. But if we brought this to a melee battle, there was no way I could lose. If they wanted to come at me, I'd destroy them with a single blow. I was just getting tired of the mental attacks that kept making me so sluggish.

The sirens' tune changed. A discordant jumble of highs and lows suddenly transformed into a frightening and intense song. At the same time, my disturbed mind gradually calmed down. I didn't feel like I was suffering from any particular status...but could this be Song of Death? If it was, I would need to end this battle quickly. I quickly pushed off the ground with my front legs.

With a twitch, Nightmare finally stood up, and a ball of black light emerged in front of its body. *This must be Dark Sphere.* Since the Song of Confusion had finished, it had to have figured there was something it could do.

But the sirens were much faster than Nightmare. Even though they'd stopped singing that song, the effects of Confusion still lingered. I wasn't confident that I could aim straight, so what options did I have?

PART 4

I LEANED FORWARD, keeping my eyes trained on one of the two sirens flying around me so as not to let her escape my sight. Partner kept an eye on the other. At times like this, having two heads was convenient—I'd definitely be left with a blind spot if I only had one head.

Perhaps I was still under the influence of the siren's Song of Confusion as I still felt a bit odd, like I had severe motion sickness. I held my breath and prepared for the siren, who slowly turned around and closed in on me.

The sirens didn't seem to have any decent close-combat skills, but the fact that she'd been closing the distance after being cornered meant that there was a high chance that she still had one card up her sleeve. I wasn't affected by the song skills they were singing now, so that didn't seem to be it. Could it be that their current song was a buff for themselves or their allies?

However, if it was a skill like Berserk, it would be a waste of effort. I was confident that even if they hit me with a boosted attack, I could repel it with no difficulty.

The song grew even more intense, and an ominous red light began to surround the two sirens' bodies. The atmosphere around us seemed to have changed.

Still, the song didn't end. The siren opened its mouth wide and sang loudly as the red light grew stronger and stronger. When the light reached its climax, the sirens suddenly closed in and charged toward me in a pincer attack.

This didn't seem like the Berserker status. If it *was* something like that, what was the purpose of closing in at the same time?

I aimed at the siren in front of me and fired three Whirlwind Slashes at the spot I expected her to be. She was so close that, even if she could react in time, it should be difficult to avoid.

The siren opened her eyes wide, flapped her wings, and let loose two Whirlwind Slashes in a row. I dropped and dove. The siren managed to maintain her speed even as she pulled into a tight turn. I was quite impressed by the way she moved, but alas, it was impossible for me to imitate due to my large body and the recoil from the Whirlwind Slash.

"Gale!"

Allo immediately followed up with Gale to restrain the approaching siren, but the sirens cut through the wind and forced their way through. It seemed that she chose to take the attack directly rather than dodging and risking exposing an opening.

As expected, it seemed that the damage from Allo's weak magic attack was negligible. One of the siren's eyelids seemed to have fallen off, though, and her red, bloodshot eyes glared at Allo.

Well, if we were to compare a siren and myself, I was superior in terms of offensive power, and it was a difference that couldn't be covered with some status-raising skills. If we were going to fight at close range, that wasn't exactly bad news for me: In front, I had powerful jaws that could snap up a siren and kill it instantly and, behind me, while my tail might not be strong enough to slay a siren in a single blow, it was still strong enough to do some damage.

The siren in front of me lunged at my face. The bright red light clinging to the siren stretched out in front of the creature, and its tip began to swirl. *No way, it has a magic attack for melee combat?!* I once saw a magician under Tolemann using the Demon Hand magic skill. The user's magic power was among that of the top class of humans, but that was at best that of a rank C monster, and his skill level was low too, so he didn't seem to be able to use it properly despite boasting a great deal of power.

If I remembered correctly, that Demon Hand skill had also shown a swirling red light before taking effect. Could this be the Song of Demons skill? It wasn't a support skill or an obstruction skill, so maybe I'd misread it.

I was right: The light that escaped from the siren's body turned into a huge, reddish-black arm that swiped right at me.

("They're coming from behind too! Watch out! It looks like they've put a lot of MP into it!")

It seemed like the enemy was doing something special—or rather, this was their all-or-nothing attack. Since Allo and the others were nearby and I couldn't dodge them, I had no choice but to get my companions away from me.

"Kyaa!"

I shook my body to throw Allo off. Things were getting dangerous. At Allo's level, it was okay to keep her around when I had things under control, but her level was still too low for her to stick around when it got dangerous.

"Groooooooowl!"

"Gyaaaaaugh!"

Partner and I roared in tandem at the sirens as they glared at us. With Partner keeping watch at the rear, I followed her lead and extended my tail behind me, covered my front with both wings, and entered a guard position against the siren's attack that rushed in from the front. Arms of reddish-black light seized my wings and tore them apart.

Hnng!

At practically the same instant, pain shot through my tail, and I lost all sense of the tip, as if I'd been paralyzed. Did she rip it off?

But it wasn't for nothing. As I lowered my torn wings, I raised my head and bit into the dark red arm now that it had lost momentum. My mouth seethed with burning pain, but I forcibly held the arm down with my fangs and dragged it to the ground. When I slammed the reddish-black arm into the earth, it evaporated away.

I aimed at the siren who was at the base of the demon's arm and swung my front leg over it. The siren shot a Whirlwind Slash at me and used the recoil to gain some distance, but I pushed my shoulder forward and scored my talons across the siren's face.

Fresh blood scattered into the air between me and the siren. The siren spread her wings, trying to dampen the impact of a backward bounce, but she slammed her back into the ground violently, threw herself up, and flew back into the air.

How did she survive? She had to be dying, but she clearly wasn't dead yet. And what happened to the other one? When I turned back to look, I saw the second siren had fallen to the ground and was lying there with the whites of her eyes showing. Her wings were gone, and her body was twitching like a beached fish.

When I looked at my partner, blue blood was dripping from the gaps in her fangs and a siren's feather was stuck between her black teeth. When Partner told me to swing my tail before, the siren had been forced to change its trajectory—only to end up being caught in Partner's teeth.

Wow, no way.

"Gyaugh."

("I ate it. It was pretty painful.")

Yeah. I held it down with my fangs, but I certainly didn't go that far. I mean, I didn't have the courage to do something like that—or even think of doing it, for that matter.

It seemed that devouring the magical devil arm whole had led to the siren's wings being bitten off as well. How exciting. I wondered if I could have finished things by doing that too and avoided taking so much damage.

("It kinda disappeared in my mouth.")

That's right. It was just a large mass of magical power, after all. It's not like it melted on your tongue.

Gained 1,411 Experience Points.

Title Skill "Walking Egg" Lv — activated: gained 1,411 Experience Points.

As soon as I heard the Divine Voice, the last siren stopped moving.

"Aaaaaaaugh."

I pushed the siren away, sending her rolling into the distance, and she glared back at me. Looking at her gouged-up face, I involuntarily flinched. Her cheeks were torn, exposing her teeth. Seeing through the layers of skin like that was just too painful. The siren kicked off the ground and jumped up in the opposite direction at a sharp angle. She intended to increase her altitude and escape.

Oops. I clicked my tongue in annoyance and tried to shoot a Whirlwind Slash, only to realize that my wings were torn and couldn't make any wind. Whirlwind Slash was created by manipulating the wind with magical power using my wings, transmitting it through my arms, and releasing it from the tips of my toes. In order to do that, I first needed to use Regenerate to repair my wings.

At that moment, Nightmare flew at the siren with tremendous force. I couldn't believe my eyes at first. Even if Nightmare wasn't as fast as I was, it flew at a relatively low altitude and slid toward the siren. In front of its face was a Dark Sphere, shining black.

What skill is that?

I was confused for a moment, but when I saw Nightmare come from diagonally below the siren, drawing a strange trajectory, I finally realized that it was connected to the siren by a thread. While I'd been holding the demon's arm with my fangs, Nightmare had been attaching threads to the siren's body.

The siren pulled the string as she vigorously leaped up, using the recoil to thrust Nightmare forward.

"Aaagh?!"

The siren raised her voice, neither angry nor screaming. Even I was taken aback for a moment. Just when I was relieved to have escaped, the siren, who had been standing still, suddenly flew into the sky at amazing speed, so I figured she must have been even more surprised than I was.

Nightmare came face-to-face with the siren, who lost her balance in surprise, and shot a Dark Sphere at her face from point-blank range.

"Aaaaaaaaaugh?!"

The siren screamed as black flames engulfed her face and she began to fall. Nightmare rode the siren halfway down before spitting a thread onto a nearby tree branch and swapping to that. As the siren plummeted to the ground, she glared at Nightmare sitting upon its safe perch.

Well, it seemed that she still had some HP left! The siren was on the verge of death, but due to the massive difference in their stats, Nightmare couldn't finish the siren off even with that close range Dark Sphere.

Oh no. They were a pretty long way from me now. If the siren went into a frenzy and attacked Nightmare, it'd have no chance.

Nightmare tried to run away. The siren's body continued to tumble toward the ground, but then it stopped in midair and shook violently, its neck constricting as if it was being squeezed.

"Hng…"

This was the last sound to come out of the siren's mouth. She stretched out her tongue and hung suspended in the air by her neck. I understood immediately: Nightmare had looped a string around its enemy's throat before she escaped. I couldn't bear to look at the disturbing expression the siren's face had taken.

> **Gained 1,738 Experience Points.**
> **Title Skill "Walking Egg" Lv — activated: gained 1,738 Experience Points.**
> **Ouroboros Lv 98 has become Lv 99.**

I was slowly but surely getting close to level 125. Clearly, the best way to level up was to fight groups of monsters one rank below you.

Well, then. I looked down and groaned, circulating magic to my wings. As I used Regenerate, the wounds on my torn and distorted wings closed before my eyes, and they began to regain their shape. Next, I applied my magical powers to the tip of the tail, and it regrew from the severed stump, returning to its original length.

Ahh. That certainly calmed me down.

Allo's level must've risen considerably, I was sure of it. If everything was okay after I checked up on her, perhaps we could start heading out to the ruins.

CHAPTER

6

Lord of the Ruins

PART 1

THE NEXT DAY, I woke up in the burrow. Allo, who'd been sitting on my head, jumped to the floor. When I crawled outside, I came face-to-face with Nightmare, who was sitting among its spider webs on the branches above the burrow. Nightmare climbed down from its web, from branch to branch, to scuttle down the tree's trunk.

I looked down at the ground from the great tree to see a variety of monsters flying around the trunk. One had the head of an eagle and the body of a lion... Was that a griffon? It looked pretty strong. If any of them noticed us, though, they didn't seem to be coming near us, thank goodness.

Turning my attention away from the griffon, I looked at the roots of the gigantic tree. In the underground ruins at the base, something was engraved in the script of the world I used to live in. There had to have been some kind of clue in there about that place. I didn't remember any of it, and I didn't think I'd ever go home either. Allo and the others were much more important now than people I couldn't even remember. If I couldn't have both, then I honestly didn't care if I never got my memories back, even if it meant some things were a little harder.

But that didn't mean that I didn't care about my position in this world. It was only natural to want to chase after something when it was dangling right in front of you.

When I glanced to the side, Allo was standing next to me looking down at the ground as well. After a while, Treant emerged from the depths of the burrow, putting a fingerlike branch to its mouth to suppress a yawn. It seriously didn't look all that reliable.

In any case, Allo's stats had increased significantly after their deadly battle with the sirens.

NAME: Allo
SPECIES: Levana Liche
STATUS: Cursed
LV: 14/85
HP: 324/324
MP: 345/345

She'd jumped up from level 1 to level 14—thirteen levels in one go, quite an achievement. Thanks to her high MP and quick judgment, she'd done quite well for herself as a level 1. At this rate, she'd max out in no time. If she leveled up just a little more, she'd be on par with the big centipede and Mother. I'd been assisting her up until now, but soon she'd be catching up with me. Allo's achievements so far had proven that the high firepower magic in this world could inflict damage on higher-ranked opponents as long as their MP held out. If her level continued to rise steadily, she should be able to use techniques with higher firepower than even mine.

Allo would undoubtedly be the key to breaking through the Adams in the ruins. When I first laid eyes on her, I could've never imagined she would become this strong.

SPECIES: **Nightmare**
STATUS: **Normal**
LV: **18/70**
HP: **190/190**
MP: **183/183**

Nightmare had gained four levels. Both of them had been doing their best, but it's easier to raise levels when in the single digits, so Allo's increase was greater; it probably helped that Allo contributed more too.

Well, increasing four levels in one battle was still impressive. For me, Walking Egg increased my experience points, and Dragon King's Son reduced the amount of experience points I needed to level up. However, I still couldn't level up if I didn't fight directly.

Next up, Treant.

> **SPECIES: Magical Tree**
> **STATUS: Cursed**
> **LV: 5/60**
> **HP: 178/178**
> **MP: 126/126**

Wow, looked like Treant was up by four levels too. That was weird. Even if it was still in single-digit levels, it seemed really odd that it would have gained any levels at all considering how little it did. Not that I was complaining.

"Gao..."

Partner had a rather harsh evaluation of her own regarding the Treant situation: (*"It's probably because it attacked me with magic while it was confused!"*)

Well, you're still doing your best, Treant!

Besides, even though I was about to challenge the world's finest dungeon, I absolutely couldn't take a level 1 monster with me. I was glad that it'd gained some levels, at least.

(*"If it's going to level up just by standing around and doing nothing like that, then I bet even worms crawling around nearby will level up too!"*)

Whoa, calm down there! Why such negativity toward Treant?

Seeing the exchange between me and Partner, Treant just stared back at us with a serious expression. Oh no, it was almost like it was looking forward to the upcoming battle. *But your level is still low, so try to attack from behind for a while!*

According to the Divine Voice, though, the original Magical Tree was a monster that made adventurers cry by increasing its own defenses while continuously using interference magic...but unfortunately, that tactic wouldn't work for Adam.

At the end of the day, Adam was still a rank A monster. In order to block even one hit from those absurdly high-powered attacks, Treant would need at least 700 HP. Even with support magic, Adam was way too much for a rank C+ opponent. A single punch or kick would mean certain death for Treant, even if it was leveled to the max. Maybe if it could use a maximum level Anti-Power, which lowered attack power, and Physical Barrier, which raised the user's own defense, Treant might still be able to survive—but just barely. It still couldn't hope to take on a full-frontal assault. It couldn't even pull any sneaky moves like Nightmare. Unfortunately, as things currently stood, the only role Treant could be expected to play was a super-degraded Allo, relying on its magic skills.

My HP was 2,586, and my defense stat was also an order of magnitude different from Treant's, so even if I took several consecutive attacks from Adam, I could still survive as long as I kept my distance and recovered. At least this would still keep Treant alive. It also helped that I was an endurance type dragon.

What're we going to do with you, Treant? Well, it wasn't like we were going to form our strategy around Treant, but I also didn't expect it to go out of its way to follow me either. From here on out, things were going to get dangerous.

Treant silently stepped forward, crossed its branch arms, and looked down at the ground. It looked like such a strong character. *Oh, I'm really happy that you're going to fight with me, but, uh...don't force yourself, okay?*

PART 2

A LONG WITH ALLO and the others, I landed at the base of the great tree, at the entrance to the ruins. The huge stone doors were breathtaking, and the image of the headless inhabitants lingered in my thoughts. As I prepared myself to enter, I sensed the presence of a monster behind me—it seemed dangerous. The ruins were dangerous, but the rest of the island was full of danger too.

Even though their ranks had risen through evolution, Allo's level was still in the lower range. Her stats improved dramatically with each battle, so it wouldn't be a bad idea to defeat just one more rank B monster around here.

When I turned around to check on Allo, I saw a conspicuous, shockingly pink Gyva. The horned dragon was wriggling its body at a distance from us—it really didn't seem to bear any grudges. Had it forgotten the way Allo mercilessly pushed it down to its death last time?

While Gyva danced, it would occasionally glance at me with its round black eyes. It seemed to be trying to appeal to me... *I'm sorry, but it's really not my thing!*

Allo was staring at it, so I turned to her and nodded. *Blow her away so she doesn't die.*

"Gale!"

The tornado that appeared from Allo's shadowed fingertips rushed straight for Gyva, creating a sandstorm. Gyva noticed halfway and hurriedly regained its posture, but it was already too late: the pink dragon's body was tossed into the air and soared far away.

Gyva's dejected cry echoed in the distance. *"Kuuuuu-uuuuuu!"*

The attack was quite powerful. Evolving into a Levana Liche had given Allo a fairly high increase in magical power, and the Gyva seemed to have taken a decent amount of damage.

Well, it wouldn't kill her, at least. It'd be a pain if other monsters came after us, so we should hurry up and enter the ruins.

I lowered my head to pass through the door of the ruins and stepped into the large room inside. With the light leaking from the gaps in the ceiling to guide me, I took in my surroundings. In the corner of my vision,

I noticed a huge pillar supporting the ceiling, carved into in the form of a human.

When I stopped walking, they appeared.

Two men who looked like naked, neckless masses of muscle, and, hopping between them, the head of a one-eyed woman with one thick leg extending out from her neck: the same group I'd met before. So it looked like this was going to be a set battle. It seemed as if they were the ones guarding the ruins.

Well, here we are again.

SPECIES: Adam
STATUS: Normal
LV: 60/100
HP: 729/729
MP: 374/374

SPECIES: Adam
STATUS: Normal
LV: 67/100
HP: 785/785
MP: 423/423

SPECIES: **Eve**
STATUS: **Normal**
LV: **70/100**
HP: **476/476**
MP: **660/660**

There were three rank A− monsters standing in our way. Just like before, they each had a grotesque appearance and seemed to be filled with malice. Compared to when I first saw them, though, I'd gained quite a bit of tolerance, and I'd already memorized most of Adam's behavior patterns. I wasn't going to get scared and flee like the first time we fought.

The ceiling inside the ruins was low, so I couldn't properly use Flight here, but even if I did try to use it against the Adams, they would just shoot a Gravidon at me. Besides, he suffered the same limitations I did—even Adams couldn't use their High Jump skill here.

Last time, I could only run away from those three figures, but this time Allo, Nightmare, and Treant had evolved one step further. Allo, who was high-ranked and specialized in magic attacks, was probably the only one who'd be able to deal damage from the outset, but Nightmare also was able to pull off some tricky moves with its threads. It was great to have a chance to use those threads to slow down higher-ranking opponents.

And then there was Treant. Well, what was there to say about Treant? Depending on how he used the ability, Gravity could be put to a variety of uses. The last time we encountered it was when he shot it at us, of course.

As soon as the trio spotted us, they rushed toward me, their facial expressions as unchanging as ever. Eve slowed down a little and followed behind the two Adams. It seemed that she wanted to avoid rushing straight into combat if she could, probably due to low HP.

Let's check her skills.

SPECIES: Eve

STATUS: Normal

LV: 70/100

HP: 476/476

MP: 660/660

ATTACK: 360

DEFENSE: 411

MAGIC: 821

AGILITY: 711

RANK: A−

SPECIAL SKILLS:

AUTOMATIC MP RECOVERY: Lv 5

STEALTH: Lv 6

RESISTANCE SKILLS:

PHYSICAL RESISTANCE: Lv 3

MAGIC RESISTANCE: Lv 4

POISON RESISTANCE: Lv 1

PARALYSIS RESISTANCE: Lv 4

ILLUSION RESISTANCE: Lv 1

INSTANT DEATH RESISTANCE: Lv 2

CURSE RESISTANCE: Lv 2

CONFUSION RESISTANCE: Lv 3

NORMAL SKILLS:

WIDE CURSE: Lv 7

DEATH: Lv 7

HI-REST: Lv 8

SLEEPWRACK: Lv 6

HI-CARE: Lv 7

TITLE SKILLS:

FINAL EVOLUTION: Lv —

DENIZEN OF THE EDGE OF THE
WORLD: Lv —

SORCERER: Lv 8

TENACIOUS: Lv 9

As I expected, she was a recovery-specialized type. Her MP was high, and her agility was on par with other spirit classes. It would be a good idea to eliminate Eve first. If I had a straight-up fistfight with the muscle-bound Adams, I could just beat them down over time. But with Eve, who could keep healing them over and over again, they would be nearly unbeatable. These Adams' levels were lower than that of the individual I'd fought before, though, and my level had risen considerably since then.

Eve's HP was extremely low, so if I got a good hit in, I should be able to kill her in one blow. However, her agility was even higher than an Adam's. She was nearly as fast as me, even though her rank was lower than mine. Adam would also surely try to protect Eve.

Her attack power was low, but I couldn't underestimate her: It was still enough to take down Allo and the others.

The question was to what extent the Adams would protect her. They may have come up with a combat strategy with two Adams protecting Eve as a healer. I had to discern the intentions from my opponents' movements and change the way I moved according to their pattern.

Once we were ready to start moving, I might give them an opening to use Eve's Hi-Rest. If that happened, we had no chance of winning. Recovery magic was extremely convenient to use on yourself, but it was really trouble-some when your enemies used it.

There were three possible patterns. Would they all act together, or would one of the Adams stick with Eve? I'd appreciate it if they stuck together—it was easier to fight when your opponents' movements were severely restricted.

First of all, I needed to watch our opponents' approach.

PART 3

As I turned my attention to Adam and Eve, a flash of light emitted from the tip of Treant's nose and headed toward me. For a moment, I was concerned that Treant was under the effects of confusion again, but when it touched me, it spread to cover the surface of my body and seeped into my scales.

> **ILLUSIA**
> **SPECIES:** Ouroboros
> **STATUS:** Physical Barrier (Slight)
> **LV:** 99/125
> **HP:** 2586/2586
> **MP:** 2498/2498

Whoa, it used Physical Barrier—that'll help boost my physical defense!

That was great. Even if Treant's own stats were too low for it to act as a tank, he could use its support magic skills on the rest of us. It was definitely better than nothing.

This is awesome! Keep it up! Treant hadn't had many opportunities to use these skills, what with being turned to stone and then attacked by Confusion so soon after evolving. *Feel free to keep it coming, Treant!*

Perhaps excited at all the praise, Treant puffed out its trunk proudly. After that, it cast Physical Barrier on Allo and Nightmare as well. Even with this buff, though, those two would die immediately if they were hit by Adam, so it almost seemed like a waste of MP. Allo stroked Treant's trunk and praised it for its achievement, but Nightmare only glanced at Treant in annoyance.

The two Adams rushed forward at the same time and picked up speed as they moved away from Eve. *I see.* I'd assumed one of them would stay with Eve, but maybe due to Eve's speed, they deemed her capable of defending herself. My best option was to take advantage of the enemy's tactics and take Eve down. I shot Allo and the others a glance, ordering them to wait.

Allo would be an important force in this battle. However, if she was attacked by an enemy, two shots would be more than enough to take her down. We would need to be careful about the roles each member played.

I jumped forward, stepped in front of the two Adams, and tried to crush them with my front foot. The Adams jumped to the left and right and split into a pincer formation against me.

I fired a Whirlwind Slash at Eve, who was a little farther in front of me. Eve started moving at the initial stage of my attack, moving at high speed on her one leg and dodging the attack completely. My triple Whirlwind Slash made a big crack in the stone floor where it landed.

Eve kept her distance from me, moving in a round-about way. She only stopped when an Adam was between us. *Is that how it's gonna be?* If I targeted her, then she'd run away and move to a position where an Adam was in the way so that the attack blade couldn't reach her.

Meanwhile, the Adams jumped at me from the left and the right. *Partner, you should keep an eye on the Adam on one side and give me instructions.*

"Roooar."

I kept the lunging Adams at bay with a Whirlwind Slash. The two of them kicked off the ground, moving left and right, and closed the distance. Once one of them got close enough, he jumped up toward my face.

(*"Another one's coming from over here too! Use your tail!"*)

I swung my tail to Partner's side and brandished my claws at the Adam on my side. He evaded my talons by a hair's breadth, leaped on top of them, and quickly kicked them to jump one more step and approach my face. The Adam was quick and strong. Opportunities to unilaterally attack against these two did not come easily, but as long as the opponent was engaging me at close range, it was easy to take the chance to attack if I was prepared to take damage.

I flicked my fangs, and the Adam changed his stance in midair. It seemed like he was aiming to kick me straight in the face. But my fangs were merely a feint: I immediately headbutted him in the forehead. His body slammed to the ground with great force, but he used the recoil from being hit to get up quickly. *Gyah.* That guy kneed me in the head! I attacked back while also protecting myself.

("He's jumped back in! They're coming from above!")
Listen, I know.

Apparently, behind me, Partner tried to strike Adam with our tail, but Adam merely kicked the tail upward. I didn't see it, but because we shared the same physical senses, I could feel what happened.

I shot Scorching Breath at the ceiling. The Adam bounced up, ready to kick me, but I jerked my shoulders to stop him. The Adam above me was soon wrapped up in my Scorching Breath, and he disappeared. It should've been impossible to avoid it at this range; there was no possible escape from the fire. Even with Adam's stats, he would still take a lot of damage if struck directly by the attack.

However, the Adam appeared through the scorching heat, riding on a hemispherical lump of dirt. It seemed like he'd immediately deployed an earthen shield with Clay. Huh, so it could be used that way as well? You learn something new every day. Slamming into my front leg, the Adam kicked the earthen shield away and dodged to the floor.

I smashed the earthen shield with a swipe. Before Adam could stand up, I extended my front claws and swung them toward him, though the Adam managed to jump back to escape.

I shook my front legs, rolled my body forward, and hit him in the side with my tail.

This seemed to have caught Adam by surprise; I struck him cleanly in the face on his belly, sending him flying into the wall. Eve rushed over to the staggering Adam. Light spread in a circle around Eve, and the Adam's wound healed.

So that was Hi-Rest. I averted my gaze from that Adam, who was recovering quickly, and received a kick from the other Adam, who was jumping out of my blind spot, leg first. I immediately pursued him with my tail, but the Adam retreated before I could connect and gained some distance.

From the beginning, it seemed that he didn't intend to damage me and was merely trying to keep me in place. The kick was also lighter than before. It didn't seem like he was going to do much on his own.

"Gah!"

Partner used Hi-Rest. The pain in my forehead eased up.

("Hey, are you just going to ignore us over here?! We're going to need to heal if you hope to survive!")

Ah, he was sticking close to the other Adam. Even if I were to approach him, all I could do was some more easily reversible damage. As long as Eve could move around freely, it wouldn't take long for her to heal them, so there was just no way I could close that gap. But I'd wanted to see how they behaved, so I let it go this time.

It turned out that it was just barely possible to take on these two opponents at once. Compared to the previous Adam, these were a lot easier. Clearly, the difference in levels was huge; however, it would do me no good to chase after a fleeing Adam and leave an opening for his partner. As long as Eve was left untouched, the Adams would just take turns dealing damage to their opponents.

However, if I were to aim for Eve, the two Adams would interfere. If I were alone, there would be nothing I could do to break this formation.

("Can't you just wait for the head to use up its MP and then take it out?")

No, I'll focus on killing the two Adams and leave the jumping severed head to Allo and the others.

("Ah?")

Partner glanced at Eve, an eerie, single-eyed, decapitated head, jumping up and down with its tongue dangling sloppily out.

("You're not gonna do anything about that?")

Right, that's all I could do.

I looked at Allo and the others. Allo eyed Eve for a moment, looking uneasy, but she nodded in uncertain agreement. It should be fine. It's not like I wanted to throw her into a match against Eve blindly. *Don't worry about it.*

Treant stood up straight, as if to say to leave it to him. When Treant was full of confidence, I couldn't help but feel anxious. Where did that confidence come from? It was good that he wanted to participate, though.

I decided to have Allo take over the battle with Eve.

Simply put, Eve was the same rank as her. Sure, it would be difficult for Allo and the others to fight even against rank B sirens, even with the three of them, but Eve was a recovery type. She had almost no offensive skills. She seemed to have status ailments and instant death moves, but those skills wouldn't work on Allo. And her attack power was low compared to Adam's. The three of them should be able to take a single blow from her. Most importantly, Allo didn't need to defeat Eve—all she had to do was keep her occupied. That would make it difficult for Eve to use her own agility to rendezvous with an injured Adam and heal him.

Simply losing her secure position would be enough to greatly diminish her function as a healer. All that would be left was for me to quickly hit the two Adams once they'd lost their means of recovery. If even one of them could be taken down, the three opponents would no longer be able to cooperate.

PART 4
TREANT

WELL, WELL, MY MASTER certainly came up with quite the unreasonable order.

When Master took his eyes off me, I unlatched two branches that were connected together and scratched my own bark. In order to keep up with Master's favorite, Ms. Allo, and the cheeky newcomer, Spider Face, I confidently agreed to Master's command. However, from my point of view, it was clear that we were no match for that one-eyed creature.

No wonder Ms. Allo was flustered. In the first place, it was difficult for us to keep that quick-moving eyeball in one place.

What to do? For the time being, let's try shooting gravity waves where it's easy to see so that I can tell Master that I'm doing my best.

Neither Ms. Allo nor Spider Face were very fast—and certainly not me, a tree. I twisted my trunk and stretched my roots to try to follow along, and then Ms. Allo touched me.

"Maybe it's coming here from the other side. It's almost here."

Hmmm, what do you mean? I tried asking her, but Ms. Allo simply silently turned her gaze toward Master. Master withdrew and blocked the humanoid creature's attack with his shoulder.

Huh? Shouldn't he normally be able to avoid that?

"Master Dragon took the blow on purpose."

As if to prove Ms. Allo right, Master quickly bit into the humanoid creature, shook his head up and down, and slammed it into the floor. He swung up again and tried to hit it once more, but the humanoid creature forcibly pried open Master's fangs and slipped out of his mouth. However, half of his body was smeared with his own blood. When the humanoid creature glanced back at us, it immediately ran toward us.

I finally understood what Ms. Allo meant when she said it was coming this way. It seemed that Master, even while fighting the two humanoid creatures, was skillfully narrowing down the opponent's retreat route by making use of the wall and his own body.

In order for the humanoid creature to escape quickly and receive treatment, it needed to reach our position. Using any other route, it would leave his injured body exposed to Master. And since the one-eyed monster couldn't get close to Master, she couldn't get close to the humanoid creature.

One-Eye stared at us. When I turned my attention to her, a sinister feeling came to me, telling me to leave.

I could pick up other people's intentions and, conversely, convey my own. This was a skill Master referred to as Telepathy. When I got it, my master was visibly disappointed. I was afraid Ms. Allo would get mad at me for thinking it, but honestly, it was a little comforting to see our mighty master envy me for the power I'd gained.

However, I tried not to use it much because I didn't want to invite any negative attention. If he saw that I was mastering it, he might get so frustrated that he'd treat me more sloppily than he does now. So, I decided to hide my Telepathy.

One-Eye jumped toward me, her disheveled hair flying. *Kill!*

Her intent came through strongly—she planned to kill us all. Her speed clearly showed the difference in our stats.

I can't run away first; we have to do it in turns. Okay, so I'll let Spider Face run away first. Spider Face understood when to withdraw. I couldn't go wrong if I just followed her lead. Ms. Allo, who always put Master ahead of herself, would probably try to stay until the end, but I knew she'd give up if I just explained to her that her loss would sadden the master.

We didn't need to concern ourselves with One-Eye—she wouldn't dare chase after us if we ran away.

Ms. Allo leaned forward and touched where the floor was chipped and the dirt exposed. I thought she was about to use her earth magic, Clay, but that didn't seem to be the case.

The soil rose and formed into two hills. It took on the shape of a human being, and soon it looked exactly like Ms.

Allo. The two earthen Ms. Allos had one bloated arm each. This was the shape of Ms. Allo's close combat form.

The surfaces of the earthen Ms. Allos were covered with magical brilliance and immediately took on a realistic color. In this way, two copies appeared in front of the real Ms. Allo.

"Clay doll."

The scale and precision were different from when she was making rabbits before. It must have been a power gained through evolution. If we suffered a poorly timed attack, it would lead to instant death, but with the clay dolls standing in front of us, they could provide a massed attack and allow us to keep our distance.

"Treant..."

Hmm? What is it, Ms. Allo?

"Try to hit that monster with attack power reduction magic."

Hmmm, Anti-Power? I didn't feel like that would work, so I was thinking of using Gravity, which seemed doable, but... *Well, let's try it. If for no reason other than that Ms. Allo asked me to.*

Ms. Allo smiled.

I'm sorry, but whether or not it works is another story.

Ms. Allo's expression tensed as she raised her hand to the sky. Now, a thick fog spread around us, and visibility grew worse. I truly envied Ms. Allo for her various talents. I didn't know what she was planning, but she must've had something on her mind.

Luckily, the sound of One-Eye's were unique and stood out, so it wouldn't be difficult to narrow down her position even with limited visibility.

I wandered about for a bit, but once I heard her strange footsteps, I turned toward the sound, my nerves on edge.

There were four shadows: two bodies were facing one another and another two standing in between them. It was probably Ms. Allo, the two copies of Ms. Allo, and One-Eye.

One-Eye approached the two copies of Ms. Allo with strange, jerky movements, but incredibly fast. At this rate, I figured she'd reach them in a matter of moments, but when Copy Ms. Allo tilted her body, One-Eye suddenly slowed down. It seemed that Spider Face had stretched a thread between the two copies of Ms. Allo. *Hmmm, I see.* Now, even in this space with few obstacles, we could still operate with ease and catch our target.

I cast Anti-Power magic, and a black light drifted out and hit the back of the one-eyed creature—or rather, the back of her head. I wanted to believe that it worked, but would my magic be effective against such a monster? I really needed to relax.

The first thing I noticed was that One-Eye had moved to look back at me. My whole body shook, and I moved away from her.

I felt relieved once I put some distance between us. I didn't hear her characteristic footsteps coming toward me either. I risked a glance back and saw that the one-eyed creature seemed to have lost interest in me. She was squirming about in an attempt to unravel the spider silk and jumped up and over the head of one of the clay dolls. The clay doll tried to hold up her bloated arm like a shield, but it was too late. One-Eye's leg crashed through Ms. Allo's arm and deeply gouged her from her shoulder to her heart, and the clay doll of Ms. Allo was thrown back, its body torn apart and neck broken. Such a simple kick was incredibly powerful. Was it really safe for us to be involved in this battle?

But I was grateful to not be the target.

As I tried to keep my distance, I suddenly worried that some other magic might hit me. I quietly turned back, accumulated my MP, and prepared to release a Clay Sphere. However, as soon as it was released, One-Eye pierced the other clay doll's belly with her heel. Were they destroyed already? The clay dolls seemed much more fragile than Ms. Allo. Anyway, now Ms. Allo's shield was gone, so I hoped she would retreat soon. Staying in the fight any longer would be dangerous.

I wondered if using Anti-Power on One-Eye had actually been effective or not, but the arm of the clay doll that had been pierced straight through its abdomen reached out and touched the monster's large eye.

Huh? It's still moving? Maybe it's stronger than the first doll, or the magic affected it differently...? In any case, it seemed strange.

"G-Gale."

Wind magic shot out and slammed into One-Eye's weak point at close range.

"Aaaaaaaaaaaugh!"

An ominous scream rose, and One-Eye went flying back and rolled on the floor. At the same time, the fog caught in the wind cleared. Did the clay doll chant a spell?

No, it couldn't be—it was the real Ms. Allo who had just been pierced through the stomach. The Ms. Allo standing behind me had been but a clay doll.

Allo had probably made her arms bloat, setting up a trap by using the obvious silhouette it would create even in the fog to trick the enemy into targeting the wrong Allo. After showing this shape, she hid in the mist and changed the shape of her arm again.

Considering I was likely to get hit, I wanted to lower the enemy's offensive ability, even if it'd have little impact.

In order to catch an opponent with such great advantage in speed, you had to create a situation where you could get close enough and the opponent was off guard. It was a good tactic. The power of Ms. Allo's magic attacks was tremendous. No matter how superior her enemy was, if their weak point was attacked from close range, they wouldn't be able to withstand the blow.

A single bright red eye glared at Ms. Allo. The monster was clearly pissed off. Light surrounded the body of the one-eyed creature and her injuries seemed to heal in the blink of an eye. It seemed to be some kind of recovery magic. Were Ms. Allo's daring attacks for naught?

Ms. Allo was crouching in place, clutching the large hole in her abdomen. Both her HP and MP seemed to be close to their limits.

One-Eye slowly approached Ms. Allo. *No!* I gathered MP into the Clay Sphere and shot it at the creature. The sphere of hardened soil suddenly shattered in front of her.

I blinked. One-Eye must have shaken her head and moved, but I couldn't follow the movement with my eyes. Then Spider Face's thread shot out at the back of the figure; however, it snapped off in the middle and disappeared into the air. She was just too fast. This wasn't a good opponent to get close to without fog or decoy. Now that Ms. Allo's major feint was over, there was no way for us to fight back.

Ah, Master, I believe we're doomed.

As I stood there, hopeless, I heard a loud roar.

"Goooouuuuuur!"

At the sound, One-Eye turned around and opened her eye wide. Master came toward us, though to our surprise, he was seriously injured. There was a gouge across his chest, some of the scales on his back had been broken, and blue blood was pouring out here and there. But the sight that met One-Eye's eye was not one of opportunity.

Master was holding two humanoids in his other mouth. They were piled one atop another, skewered on his fangs. The second head gazed up at the ceiling and moved its jaws. A nasty sound resonated throughout the room as the bodies were crushed, red blood dripping from between those teeth.

"A-aaaaugh!"

One-Eye kicked the ground, screaming. The next moment, she disappeared. When I looked around for the creature, I saw Ms. Allo was looking up at Master, so I followed her gaze and watched him swing down his raised front leg at tremendous speed.

A sharp sound resounded through the chamber, and when Master lifted his front leg, the one-eyed creature lay smashed underneath. Her large eyeball was cracked, and her thick leg was bent in the wrong direction. At this sight, I could finally breathe a sigh of relief.

I was a little flustered there, Master.

PART 5

GAINED 3,840 EXPERIENCE POINTS.
Title Skill "Walking Egg" Lv — activated: gained 3,840 Experience Points.
Ouroboros Lv 99 has become Lv 101.
Gained the Special Skill "Master's Demonic Gaze" Lv 1.
Gained 4,288 Experience Points.
Title Skill "Walking Egg" Lv — activated: gained 4,288 Experience Points.
Ouroboros Lv 101 has become Lv 103.

The usual Divine Voice announcement confirmed that the two Adams were dead.

Wow, this was the first time in a *long* time that I'd felt as if my life was in danger. I had to put recovery on the back burner and attack the two Adams together with Partner to hurry up and kill them. With both of them dead, the experience we gained was outrageous. It seemed like only a matter of time until I would achieve Ouroboros's stupidly high-level cap if I stayed on this island.

Hmm, what's this skill? Something like a level 100 present? Master's Demonic Gaze? Ah well, I'll have to check it out later. No time now.

I glanced at Partner, who was holding the Adams in her mouth, and she used Regenerate to restore my body, organs, and leg bones that had been destroyed by the Adams' Gravidon. Now I could move around freely again.

Perhaps I'd acted a bit rashly attacking the two Adams at the same time, figuring that it would be fine as long as Eve didn't heal them even if I suffered their kicks all over my body. However, thanks to that, although it took longer than I thought, I was able to kill them safely within a short period of time.

I loomed in close while they were hitting my body with Gravidon and used Roll to make them evade with a High Jump before quickly hitting them with a reverse Roll to smash their body and prevent them from moving. From there, the Adams were prepared to die and kept firing off Gravidons until their MP ran out. I was barely able to eke out a victory.

Humans...nay, dragons, can do anything. It'd never occurred to me that I could use my tail to make an instant 180-degree turn in desperation during Roll. I'd have to use that again.

If Allo and the others, who were holding the Eve in place, were in danger, I planned to break away from the Adams and let my companions escape. It took longer than I thought, so I was pretty impatient, but when I turned my attention to Allo, who was busy stopping Eve, I noticed that they were all safe, somehow.

When Eve saw Partner swallow the two Adams, she opened her mouth in amazement. After a short pause, she tensed her leg before bending it and staring at me with her one big eye.

"A...aaaaaugh!"

She charged at me in desperation. Atop her single leg, she ran about, swinging her body left and right at an unimaginable speed, kicking the ground and jumping at me. She was fast. She even tried to feint. However, she was way too easy to hit. Alas, there was no point in doing just a little damage to me in this place, so it was obvious that she was aiming for a spot that could be a decisive blow when she attacked.

I raised my front leg and guarded my head, and Eve slammed her heel into my forepaw. She must have really been aiming at my head. I shook it off and slammed Eve to the ground. I could feel her crumbling under my foot in that decisive blow.

Gained 3,584 Experience Points.
Title Skill "Walking Egg" Lv — activated: gained 3,584 Experience Points.
Ouroboros Lv 104 has become Lv 104.

I could still take out monsters with low HP with a single blow, even if they were rank A. I could even take out the Adams with my melee attacks, despite their physical proficiency, depending on where I hit. I really struggled with support types like Eve, and I never would've been able to catch up if she had ran away; it was a good thing she was obstinate and came for me instead.

Partner licked the crushed Eve off the ground and chewed on her a bit before spitting out a part of her skull.

("Hmm, not bad.")

I really don't want you eating those kinds of things. But I was shocked to realize that I'd lost a lot of my original disgust over seeing Partner eat humanoid figures. I'd need to watch out for that.

Since Allo had taken severe damage, I decided to ask Partner to cure her. Treant and Nightmare were unharmed, but Allo, who looked like she took a kick head-on, was gravely injured. There was a large hole in her body, and she was limp on the floor. Partner growled, and Allo was enveloped in black light; when the light cleared, everything was back to normal.

I felt bad, since I had intended to hurriedly take care of the Adams and then get right on Eve, but they were stronger than I anticipated. I might have underestimated the Adams too much after seeing how the sirens and basilisks had been able to handle them. In any case, I was glad everyone was safe.

I checked the group's levels. Allo went from level 14/85 to level 22/85, Nightmare from level 18/70 to level 20/70, and Treant from level 5/60 to level 10/60.

Allo's level had easily surpassed Nightmare's. Well... even if there was a level difference, Allo was the strongest in terms of rank, status, and skills. If I wasn't careful, she could end up with even better skills than me.

Treant also went up by five levels and was starting to catch up to Nightmare. Adam and Eve were real experience gold mines. This island was full of strange monsters. Well, Adam was abnormally strong, so it seemed like we got a lot from him.

Actually, should I try out that level 100 commemorative skill I just got? Let's check the skill details.

Special Skill "Master's Demonic Gaze." By using MP
and holding the target's gaze, the user can freeze the
movement of a target for several seconds. If a large
amount of MP is used or the target is on the same
wavelength, user can control the target's movement.

*Oh, whoa! Isn't this a pretty good skill? Let's try it out...
Hey, Treant, wait a moment. No?* Treant shook its trunk.
Apparently, it wasn't interested?

Allo quickly jumped in front of Treant and looked
at me with expectant eyes. *Well, I'm reluctant to use this
kind of skill on a girl, but...*

"I-I'll take it! I want to try it!"

Eh, yeah...no, but...maybe just a little. Allo's face flushed
as she fixed her gaze on mine. *Let's give it a go. Are you okay?*

I looked at Allo with magic in my eyes. *Master's
Demonic Gaze! Hmph!*

I didn't sense any particular change. Allo kept her eyes
wide open and kept her eyes on me. Now that I thought
about it, Allo had immunity to status ailments, so it might
not work. I didn't feel anything trigger at all, though.

"Graow." ("Hey, Partner.")

Yes? What's up?

When I looked at Partner, her red eyes emitted a glaring crimson light. I tried to close my eyes against the glare,

but my eyelids couldn't move, as if they were paralyzed. I was taken over too?! No way, this skill could only be used by Partner?? C'mon, let us both use it!

As I lamented, my front leg lifted up on its own and scratched Partner's neck. Partner let out a gentle roar and bent her neck.

"Oh, this is a good technique."

Had my body been hijacked?!

"Gaaoo!"

I broke out of Partner's magic eye restraint and slammed my front leg into the ground. Huh, this could seriously turn Partner into the main controller of our body. What a ridiculous skill. Partner snorted proudly. *Well, damn. Seriously, in the future, Partner won't have a problem with her head with a skill like this.*

When I turned around, Allo was staring at me with pale eyes. I felt kind of bad. *Why don't you have Partner cast it on you?*

"Never mind."

PART 6

I MOVED CAREFULLY DOWN the huge stairs. Allo walked alongside me, so I instructed her to stay low by motioning with my nose. I had no idea what was ahead. Without warning, Treant started slowly advancing behind us. I expected that as we went underground it would grow dark, but it seemed like the depths of the cavern were illuminated by a fire, possibly a candlestick. Theories of an underground Adam kingdom filled my head, becoming more and more intense as I thought about them, and I could sense an overwhelming presence rising up from the depths.

Until now, whatever lay ahead seemed to have been hiding its presence, but now I was struck almost physically by a strong wave of oppression. I felt almost intimidated. Should I back down? There was no doubt that whatever was in store for us was something greater than Adam. *No way, could it be the master of the Divine Voice?*

As long as I was dealing with that voice, there was no doubt in my mind that there was someone who wanted to guide me in some way. If such a thing existed, it would almost certainly be at the end of the world, and this place, which was said to be located at the end of the world, fit the bill.

Oh, hey, Partner, how are you doing?

("What, you came all this way and now you're finally asking me?")

No, no, it's just that your intuition is pretty accurate.

("This isn't something you can just look at and figure out, y'know.")

Her response was neither positive nor negative. Hmm. But even if we were to be attacked, I figured I could take Allo and the others and run away as long as I didn't get knocked out in a single blow. If there was a bad guy down here, he'd almost certainly attack me the moment I stepped inside.

As I chewed this over, a thought popped into my head.

‹It's been a while. You survived the Adams just fine. You aren't from the island, are you? Come closer.›

Hey, is that the Telepathy skill?!

It was just Telepathy, but it felt quite heavy. It was the first time I'd felt like this. Whatever it was, it was at least the same rank as Adam, so A or higher was a given. It didn't seem to be the Divine Voice, but I really couldn't say with certainty.

‹Hurry up, don't make me wait.›

There was irritation in his voice. He didn't seem terribly patient.

("What a cocky bastard. Let's eat 'em.")

Partner clacked her fangs.

It seems like it could be friendly, so let's try and play nice.

("It's looking down on you, y'know.")

Well, maybe, but... This being was actually acting quite calm even after I'd taken down that trio of opponents. If Allo and the others hadn't helped out, I probably wouldn't have been able to kill them, and I would've had to run away.

As I proceeded slowly, I saw a number of candlesticks lining the hall, and at the very back was a dragon that was one size bigger than me, with a body covered in a shiny, purple scales. It had thick fangs, large claws, and four wings, and its hide seemed to be quite thick.

Hey, what is this guy?

ELDIA

SPECIES: **Diabolos**

STATUS: **Normal**

LV: **130/130 (MAX)**

HP: **1697/1697**

MP: **1316/1316**

ATTACK: **1510**

DEFENSE: **835**

MAGIC: **1109**

AGILITY: **1139**

RANK: **A**

SPECIAL SKILLS:

   DRAGON SCALE: Lv MAX

   GRECIAN LANGUAGE: Lv 7

   FLY: Lv MAX

   DARK TYPE: Lv —

   WICKED DRAGON: Lv —

   AUTOMATIC HP RECOVERY: Lv 6

   AUTOMATIC MP RECOVERY: Lv 6

   STEALTH: Lv 6

   PSYCHIC SENSE: Lv 8

   KING'S DEMONIC GAZE: Lv 8

   DIVINE VOICE: Lv 1

RESISTANCE SKILLS:

   PHYSICAL RESISTANCE: Lv 8

   FALLING RESISTANCE: Lv 8

   HUNGER RESISTANCE: Lv 7

   POISON RESISTANCE: Lv 9

   MAGIC RESISTANCE: Lv 9

   FEAR RESISTANCE: Lv 5

   PARALYSIS RESISTANCE: Lv 6

   ILLUSION RESISTANCE: Lv 6

   INSTANT DEATH RESISTANCE: Lv 9

   CURSE RESISTANCE: Lv 8

   CONFUSION RESISTANCE: Lv 6

   BLINDING RESISTANCE: Lv 5

LONELINESS RESISTANCE: Lv MAX

SLEEP RESISTANCE: Lv 3

DARK RESISTANCE: Lv 7

FIRE RESISTANCE: Lv 6

WATER RESISTANCE: Lv 6

EARTH RESISTANCE: Lv 4

LIGHT RESISTANCE: Lv 6

LIGHTNING RESISTANCE: Lv 6

WIND RESISTANCE: Lv 7

FROST RESISTANCE: Lv 4

NORMAL SKILLS:

ROLL: Lv 6

SCORCHING BREATH: Lv 7

FREEZING BREATH: Lv 8

DRAGON TAIL: Lv 8

BELLOW: Lv 5

HUMAN TRANSFORMATION: Lv 7

REGENERATE: Lv 5

TELEPATHY: Lv 4

DRAGO FLARE: Lv 7

LIGHTNING BOLT: Lv 8

PHYSICAL BARRIER: Lv 7

MANA BARRIER: Lv 7

TITLE SKILLS:

CALAMITY: Lv MAX

DRAGON KING: Lv —

THICK SCALES: Lv —

FOLLOWER OF THE LAST DEMON

KING: Lv —

IMMORTAL: Lv —

FINAL EVOLUTION: Lv —

Wh-whoa! He's powerful! His attack is 1,510?!

That was about one and a half times as strong as me. At that rate, even I was sure to die if I took a round of attacks from this guy. I couldn't believe something like this was underground.

While I was busy being dumbfounded, Partner shot me an annoyed look.

("*What the hell is that thing?*")

This was crazy. It would be hard to escape now. Frankly, I would need to be in an enhanced state to simply survive this fight.

In this world, there were things far more important than HP and MP such as attack power, agility, and status ailments. This dragon had immensely high attack power and agility, and strong resistance. There was no room for trickery, and I didn't have any winning categories.

Well, this was kind of a common occurrence. Hmm? Ah, I'd seen that title before. Dragon King... Ah, yes, my skill was Dragon King's Son.

A guy whose resistance rises and whose levels increase easily. I wondered if it had anything to do with that. Did that make him my father in this world??

<Even if they threatened you, it doesn't mean that you can just take them and eat them. Those Adams were my servants, although they can be infinitely replaced. Or perhaps you just want to challenge me to a fight? That's fine too.>

The dragon with shining purple scales opened its mouth to show me its fangs.

Diabolos: Rank A Monster.
Its overwhelming destructive power is second to none.
Its tough claws can kill ten humans with a single swing.
The flame it shoots from its mouth can mow down hundreds in a single breath.
The evolution of the dragon that received the buff of the Demon King.

I knew it from his status, but if I was a recovery type, this guy was an attack type. Should I check the title skill? I was a little concerned about that.

Title Skill "Dragon King."
A title given to the strongest dragon in the world. Life
span and attack power status increase rate will be
corrected. The required experience value is reduced,
making it easier to acquire some basic resistance skills.
Also raises the resistance skill levels each time it evolves.
Greatly affects the evolutionary path.

Basically, it was the same as my Son of the Dragon
King... Well, it was a higher rank. I didn't have life span
or attack power correction, and my level increase of
resistance skill linked to leveling up didn't go up after 5.
However, by the time I got this title, I'd wondered if the
final evolution had already been met.

However... Demon lord, demon lord, huh... Hmm.
I'd seen other monsters' descriptions before...but I never
thought I'd see a former subordinate like this.

Allo, who had been following after me, now stood next
to me. After looking fearfully at the gigantic dragon, she
looked up at me with concern. Nightmare was behind
me, and Treant was standing all the way back, under the
stairs that led to the upper floor.

Everything should be fine. I had no animosity towards
Diabolos.

Diabolos glared at Allo. For a moment I felt a chilling, cold, oppressive sensation. I immediately heightened my vigilance, but it seemed that it was a needless worry, as the murderous intent quickly disappeared.

‹What is it—not a human but an undead?›

Allo was frightened by Diabolos' tone and quickly clung to my hind legs, trembling slightly. Even I was intimidated by Diabolos, so from Allo's point of view, he was probably many more times scarier for her.

‹What brings you to this island?› It seemed like he didn't know why we were here—I was surprised.

I wanted to confirm whether it was my father or not, but... was it really okay to ask that? *Is it awkward, or do I feel it too...* No, I felt a great sense of intimacy, but it wouldn't be right to call him my father right now. I was Ouroboros. *I haven't yet lived for a full year, but I'm a splendid adult dragon, okay?*

But if this dragon was staying on this island, it was strange that an egg would be left in the forest. However, this skill...

‹I've asked you a question. What are you so confused about?› Diabolos slammed his tail into the ground in disgust. The floor crumbled, and the whole area shook.

"Growl." ("What in the hell do you think you're doing?") Partner also shot me a look, her eyes narrowed.

I mean, he's my father?! And, since he's my father, he's

also your father, right? It's amazing that you're acting like you don't care. While I was arguing with Partner, Diabolos became more and more disgruntled. He probably wasn't keen on being ignored. I hurriedly turned from Partner to face Diabolos.

Oh, I'm sorry. As for why we came to the island, you see, I was too strong and didn't have a place to belong. Um, why did you come here, Diabolos?

<*Hmph, how do you know my race's name?*>

Was it bad that I knew?

Oh, that was right. Not everyone had access to Divine Voice and View Status. Diabolos was one of the rarest dragons. There are very few rank A monsters. How many Diabolos had even been born in this world?

I turned my face downward and scratched the back of my neck to play down the situation. I had no idea what the View Status skill meant about me, and I figured it was best to not mention it.

Diabolos gave me a skeptical look, but he said, <*Fine. I wondered why you were here.*>

It seemed that there was a lot he could teach me. I was itching to talk about it when he started talking about himself without holding back. He had [Loneliness resistance: Max Level] under resistance, so perhaps he was starving to talk too.

‹I am here because I heard a revelation from the will of the world.›

The will of the world? Was he referring to the Divine Voice's pseudo-gods? I was sure that Divine Voice should be under his skills.

‹I was originally a monster that served the Demon King. Since the Demon King was defeated by the hero, many monsters followed him and died. Some recklessly attacked human villages and were killed in revenge, others flew to the ends of the world and never returned. I was going to do the same.›

Eh, you've come up with a very heavy story. Um, is the hero that one we already know about? This dragon king, even if the three heroes attacked him, he should've been able to easily fight them off.

‹I don't know what you're thinking about, but that was about 500 years ago.›

Huh, so did he live 500 years?

‹However, when I decided to die, a divine decree descended upon me. I heard a voice in my head: "In the future, the Demon King will appear again in this world. You, the Dragon King, must survive until that time." I decided that, at that time, I would devote my allegiance to the next Demon King and bring an end to the human era. I knew right away. This voice is the will of the world that the Demon King predicted.›

Um, it seemed like the conversation was taking a disturbing turn.

<*"And until then, hide yourself and just keep waiting..."* It's been a long time. I hid myself on this island, occasionally walking outside, just watching the sun rise and fall. I doubted the owner of the voice many times. But I know. Now, that time is surely approaching. Before... I had just evolved and could not fight side by side with the Demon King. But not now. I will no longer lag behind the hero. The time has come for me to redeem myself and lead my new master, to create the world that the former Demon King desired, and use it as a hand for his soul.>

Diabolos gazed up at the roof above with an ecstatic expression. Those eyes must've been staring at the sky far beyond the ceiling. This was no good... My father was totally evil. He was either another final boss or a secret boss.

<You are a promising dragon. Come with me; I will make you my subordinate. Follow along with me to the next Demon King who will come someday.>

I was momentarily stunned. Diabolos lowered his head to meet my gaze and regarded me with dissatisfaction.

<What? Are you saying you don't like the idea of serving under me?>

Well, that wasn't it, but... I'd say it was more fundamental... What should I make of all this, what should

I do? Would the Demon King return? Was this the will of the world?

However, it seemed that I couldn't delay giving an answer. According to Diabolos, it was only natural for dragons to be attached to the Demon King. If I said something that favored the humans, he might regard me as an enemy and attack. There was one option to settle things down peacefully! I put my chin to the ground and lowered my posture.

Ha ha, thank you very much. If the time comes, I, Ouroboros, will do my best to accompany Diabolos!

("Hey, you sure about that, Partner?") Partner looked at me with a thoughtful gaze.

It's okay. These kinds of things rarely come so quickly. Isn't it okay if we just deceive him for now and let things blow over?

("That guy is probably the one who will kill the humans.")

That might be true, but...but it might be my father, you know? I didn't even see him doing anything, and he didn't seem to show any animosity toward me... I didn't know how to respond.

<Hmph, "Diabolos, Diabolos"... You don't even know how to be polite.> Diabolos shook his head in artificial disgust and let out a deep sigh. I guess he expected courtesy among dragons? <I have a name, Eldia, given to

me by the Demon King. I'll allow you the honor of calling me by that name. Diabolos is just a term that describes my form.>

He shot me a sideways glance as he proudly told me his name. This old man struck me as a tad stuck up. Normally, I would relax, but Diabolos—er, Eldia's—disturbing remarks unnerved me. I was grateful that he seemed to be welcoming me, but...I decided it'd be better not to stay on this island for too long.

PART 7

AFTER THAT, I started to ask Eldia about the ruins. I was in a bit of a daze after the sudden father-son reunion, but I had to get back to the main task at hand: exploring these ruins that were home to the incoherent inscriptions I believed were related to my previous life.

<All right, listen up.>

Eldia seemed a little proud, but eager to chat at the same time. *I guess this guy is willing to talk after all.* Eldia shot me an irritated look as I had that thought. I shook my head and looked away, desperately searching for something else to think about.

REINCARNATED AS A DRAGON HATCHLING

Man, what's up with these ruins and all the weird inscriptions, anyway? I'm so curious about them. Eldia seems super strong and cool too... Hmm hm hm hmmm...

<...Hmph.> Eldia gave an awkward sniff before continuing to talk. I had to be careful not to let my mind wander to unnecessary thoughts. <*This place had already fallen into ruin by the time I came to it. The Demon King was quite fond of it, though, and used to fly here often.*>

With this, he began telling me about the island and its ruins. Apparently, it had been a favored spot of the Demon King, one that he visited from time to time.

Eldia shifted his massive frame to reveal the wall behind him. On it was a large mural inscribed with a variety of Japanese characters, Latin letters, and other symbols. As usual, I couldn't glean any meaning from any of the writing, and as I looked closer, I realized there were some strange characters mixed in with the others, such as one that looked like a combination of the Japanese characters for "ra" and "ru."

Could this be a completely new language? No, there's no way. All the other characters are there...

The mural itself was just too abstract; I couldn't parse any meaning from it at all. There was art of some sort of giant eyeball-like object floating in the air, with six humans lined up beneath it. The images weren't very detailed either... The symbols looked deformed somehow, or messy, like someone had painted each of them in about ten strokes of their brush. The eyeball monster was also drawn in a round circle that looked like it was done in two swift strokes of paint.

Um... What am I looking at, Eldia?

‹According to the Demon King, this is a mural of the evil god, the Fallen, and the six Great Sages who opposed him. Long ago, longer than one can even imagine, the Fallen descended from the heavens to bring ruin to the land, sea, and sky. The six Great Sages were the most powerful beings from each of the different realms; that is, the realms of humans, majin, monsters, magical beasts, angels, and demons. After a long, fierce battle, the Sages were able to seal the Fallen away, and peace was restored to the land.›

Eldia's tale must've been one of the legends passed down about this world. As I looked closer, I realized that although the beings underneath the Fallen were indeed bipedal, one had the face of a wolf, a few had wings, and one looked like a skeleton from the neck up. This felt like something that was *way* beyond me.

So I guess this stuff isn't about my past life after all? I immediately shifted my focus back to Eldia's storytelling to keep my thoughts of other things hidden from his Telepathy.

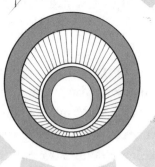

But also, majin? I've heard of demi-humans, but no one's ever said anything about majin to me before. I'm surprised that there are two separate realms for monsters and magical beasts too.

<*The majin are an ancient race. In the present day, the boundaries between the human, majin, monster, and magical beast realms have been lost. Only the realms of angels and demons remain separate. There is now little point in trying to distinguish between anything more specific than "human" and "monster." However, there is evidence to support the idea that humans and monsters once inhabited different realms. Namely...*>

Ahh, right. Evolution.

Eldia remained silent and glared, evidently annoyed at me for finishing his sentence. *S-sorry... I'll shut up and listen. Go on.*

I looked away from Eldia and gave myself a chance to think. I remembered having a lot of hang-ups about the concept of evolution in the beginning. This world was bound by a level-based system, and the existence of evolution completely overrode the level system. I was reminded of how strange and disconcerting it had felt, like my body parts were being pulled apart and forcibly put back together in a new configuration.

There were no ordinary animals in this world. Every living being was categorized as either human or monster. You'd think that humans with skills and stats would be considered monsters, but they didn't have ranks or evolutions, so they didn't count.

All things considered, the legend Eldia was talking about seemed like just that: a legend, something past humans had made up to make sense of the strangeness of this world.

I looked over at Partner and noticed her nodding off next to me. Eldia was glaring at her, so I quickly nudged the base of her neck with my paw. *Wake up, Partner! Professor Eldia's history class is in session!*

Partner gave me a doleful look, then moved her gaze over to Eldia.

("And where did the Demon King hear this from, exactly?")

H-hey, watch your tone! We don't want to put him in a bad mood.

Despite my worries, a smug grin broke out over Eldia's face, showing his gums.

‹There is a similar legend that is spread among humans. But my master, the Demon King, heard this directly from the divine will of this world.›

Oh! Like a Divine Voice?! I thought, surprised.

Eldia, mistaking my reaction as interest, sniffed gleefully. ⟨*There is more to it. We monsters cannot live in peace with humans because we are so different, in both our appearance and our way of thinking. Both sides are also powerful enough to be a threat to the other. However, because our four realms are intrinsically linked, neither of us can leave. Humans have tried to expel the monsters, and monsters have tried to eradicate the humans. Unfortunately, while we monsters possess superior power as individuals, it is not common for us to join forces. Over time, our numbers have slowly dwindled.*⟩

I knew this all too well. Looking and behaving differently from others could cause a massive divide. I was supposed to think the same way as the monsters, but this divide had caused a lot of hardship for me. Even if we looked the same on the outside, if we're different on the inside, we just couldn't get along.

⟨*But that is not all. The six Great Sages are long dead, but in order to keep the Fallen sealed away, their powers have been passed on to others. The one who possesses the power of the Great Sage of Monsters is able to control entire hordes of weaker monsters at will. Because of this, massive wars began to break out. What's more, the Demon King revealed to me that he himself possessed the power of the Great Sage of Monsters. From the moment he was born, the Demon King was destined to bring humanity to its end.>*

Partner gave me a skeptical look, but I knew I couldn't just disregard Eldia's tale. *I see... Maybe this relates to my new sacred skill?*

Sacred Skill "Human Realm Path." Allows user to gain power over the human realm. Although its original power has been lost, this skill will still greatly affect one's evolutionary path.

This skill was somehow transferred to me when I defeated the hero. The description didn't give me many clues as to what exactly the skill *did*, but along with Eldia's story, things were slowly starting to make sense.

("Er... Partner? What's up?")

Partner was looking up at me with an unusually worried expression. Eldia was alert and poised as well, his upper body raised as if in preparation to strike.

("What're you getting so stressed out about?")

The legend felt so abstract and hazy to me that I had a hard time gleaning any sort of higher meaning from it. But now I knew *something*, at least. Maybe the Divine Voice was the evil god of legend, the Fallen? Or maybe one of the Great Sages, or someone related to them?

Which would mean...both this legend and the war between the Demon King and the hero were nothing but a farce cooked up by the Divine Voice—and the world was once again getting caught up in it.

The current struggle for survival between monsters and humans felt like a stepping stone to all-out war. I couldn't shake the thought that the one behind the Divine Voice was intentionally pitting the Demon King and the hero with sacred skills against each other to ensure their mutual destruction.

The hero and the Demon King both possessed the Divine Voice as well. If there was only one entity behind the Divine Voice, that meant that they were offering advice to both the monsters *and* the humans. Laying it all out like this, the obvious conclusion was that the Divine Voice was deliberately trying to make beings with sacred skills fight each other.

Although now that I knew that there were six Great Sages, that did open up the possibility that my Divine Voice and the hero's Divine Voice came from different sources. The Great Sage of Humans and the Great Sage of Monsters could be waging a proxy war through the beings that now possessed their power... That possibility would make the most sense to me, anyway. But considering how confused the hero had seemed in his final moments, I had my doubts.

He probably got cut off from the Divine Voice, I mused. And after that, the Human Realm Path skill he had was transferred to me. It seemed to me like the Divine Voice arranged for two of its pawns to face off and made the victor its chosen one.

What was the Divine Voice up to, and what role was I expected to fill in its plans? I still didn't have the answers for those simple questions. Was I selected as a replacement for the Demon King from the very start? But I didn't have any sacred skills at first... If Eldia really is my father and has the Divine Voice, then did the Divine Voice simply stake its claim on monsters and their offspring that it thought would become more powerful?

I just didn't have enough information. There was no point in thinking about this now. If only the hero had been a little more willing to chat...we could've shared notes.

I suddenly snapped out of my reverie to find Partner looking up at me, her face centimeters away from mine. I jerked my head back in surprise.

Ack! Sorry... Got lost in thought for a minute there.

"Graaah?" ("Why do you care so much?")

Well, to be honest... I don't think I can just write this stuff off as irrelevant anymore.

I knew I couldn't think any more deeply about other things right then, though, or I'd risk Eldia getting angry at me. Besides, it'd be bad if he picked up on my thoughts with his Telepathy. *I'll come back to this topic later, once things settle down. I can decide what my next move is then. That way, when push comes to shove, I'll be ready to act.*

<What, are you lost in thought?> Eldia asked, stamping his foot impatiently. *<No need to have a discussion with your other head. If you have a question for me, ask it.>*

A question for you? Let's see... Oh, I do have one, actually.

<Yes?>

Er... Do you know if you have any sons off the island? As Eldia received the telepathic message, his eyes widened.

<Sons? All seven of them were slain five hundred years ago by the abhorrent hero, Mia.> He gnashed his fangs like he was ready to close them around that hero's throat. *Oof, looks like I stepped on a land mine... My bad.*

This "Mia" managed to defeat seven of the Dragon King's children? Wow... The name Mia sounded pretty feminine—was this hero a woman? Regardless, they must've been quite the character.

Anyway... If all his sons were killed, did that mean Eldia wasn't my father after all? If his story was true, he'd been holed up on this island ever since he heard the revelation. I was born in a forest all the way across the ocean, so it seemed unlikely that we were related. Maybe my Dragon King's Son title skill was just a coincidence?

<There was a Nomadic Dragon wandering the islands more recently with whom I had relations, but I do not know if she bore a child. Why do you ask?>

A Nomadic Dragon...?

<Indeed. That particular type of dragon does not stay in one place for long. They are fickle and free-spirited, prone to appearing one day and vanishing the next. She asked me to leave the island with her and I refused, and the very next day, she was gone without a trace. As I have decided to remain in hiding on this island until the next Demon King appears, we were simply incompatible. But such a weak dragon is beneath my concern.> Eldia seemed aggravated by the memory but also a little sad. The image of Eldia searching all across the island for this elusive nomad flashed through my mind, and I quickly looked away, not wanting to upset him further with my thoughts.

Then maybe Eldia really is *my father. I probably shouldn't tell him, though. When the Demon King appears, Eldia will be under his thumb—which will make him my enemy. I shouldn't get too involved with him.*

If it was true that he would be my enemy someday, then maybe the smart thing to do was to strike now, while his guard was down. I just didn't think I had it in me, though.

For all I knew that day might never come—he could very well just stay on this island forever.

I was suddenly struck with a strong desire to go home, which I let Eldia pick up on telepathically. Then I made my way back to Allo and the others and told them that we were leaving these underground ruins.

Allo looked up at me, confused, while Nightmare dashed for the stairs. Treant, who was sca—I mean, *wary* of Eldia, had kept its original position near the stairs and now slithered smoothly up them behind Nightmare.

<Hmm? What, you want to leave already?> Eldia asked. *<But I know many more things...and have heard nothing about you yet either.>* He had been hunched over at the back of the ruins, and he now stretched his neck out toward me.

Sorry to cut things short, I replied. *I'm exhausted from battling the three guardians of these ruins. I think I'll head back to the burrow and get some rest for now.*

<I see... Oh, that's right. I assume you do not have a name? You will one day join me in offering your allegiance to the next Demon King, and it would be improper to do so without one. Perhaps I can give you a name that suits you?>

I appreciate the thought, but I already have a name.

\<M-mmm...? If you have a name, then why have you not said it?\> Eldia asked in confusion, pulling back his outstretched neck.

I glanced back at him, gave a light bow, and then left the ruins.

CHAPTER

7

The Dragon King's Flames

PART 1

· ·

IT HAD BEEN TWO DAYS since I parted ways with Eldia. I was standing on the tip of a branch on the great tree near our burrow, looking out at the island spread out below. My eyes lingered on the deep, overgrown forest, then the massive waterfall, and then the edge of the world. I let out a deep sigh.

("Why the long face?") Partner asked, craning her neck around to look at me.

I've just got a lot on my mind. Things are probably going to get a little messy from here on out. I don't even know what I want to do about Eldia... And there's also the issue of the Demon King and the Divine Voice.

(*"Sitting here and thinking about it won't change any-thing. If something happens, you can decide what you want to do then."*)

No, yeah, you're right... But the reason I can't do any-thing about it is because I don't have enough information. I don't know how me defeating the hero who was supposed to take on the Demon King will affect things. If I had any idea of what it was like when past Demon Kings returned, I might've at least been able to figure out some sort of pattern...

Should I leave this island at the edge of the world and its dangerous dragon inhabitant behind and find some friends who were a little more well versed in the ways of the world instead?

I hadn't seen much movement from Eldia lately, although he sometimes glanced up from the base of the great tree to look at me. He didn't seem like he was doing it to scrutinize the movements of a strange visitor with a Sacred Skill, carrying out his duty as a faithful servant of the Demon King... He mostly just looked curious, and perhaps a little lonely. We *were* the first visitors he'd had in a while.

I felt bad, but I knew I just wasn't cunning enough to make friends with someone I knew was going to turn on me someday.

Speaking of things I'm worried about, there's also the issue of Allo and the others. I looked behind me to find Nightmare biting at a giant red and white two-tone wasp *(Death Needle: Rank C+)* that was caught in its web. Treant was hurling clumps of earth with its Clay Sphere skill to weaken the death needle, and Allo, perched on a branch nearby, looked on happily.

They've all become much stronger too, I thought. *But I'm sure we'll encounter enemies in the future that'll make monsters like Adam look like small fry.*

Suddenly, I got a telepathic message from Partner. *("Partner! Something's coming!")* I looked over to her and followed her line of sight.

Way out in the distance, I saw a figure flying through the sky. It was a massive bird monster with blueish-green feathers that made it look like a bronze statue that'd been left to oxidize. Unlike a bird, though, it was gliding along on four wings spread wide in a flashy display—and its face was undeniably human.

It had long, teal-colored hair that flowed behind it in the breeze. Its eyes were the only relief against the relentless teal; they were bright red and focused directly ahead. Fortunately, they were not pointed at me. In fact, it didn't seem so much like it didn't notice me as it wasn't interested in the first place.

Neptune: Rank A−.

A Siren who eventually came to be known as the Queen of the Sea after accumulating tens of thousands of human bones. Possesses overwhelming defensive capabilities and the ability to fly. Also boasts powerful ocean-bending skills. The entire sea is her domain. Revered as the "Guardian of the Sea" by the inhabitants of coastal countries and small islands.

Wh-whoa... Guess there are more rank A monsters around than just Adam and Eldia, huh? It seemed like the rank C+ monsters were considered weak around here, rank B were about average, and A was reserved for the big names on the island. In the forest where I was born, the highest rank I ever ran into was C, and those monsters were really strong.

This Neptune's rank put it roughly on par with the Adams. I was able to successfully take on two Adams at once, but Neptune's sea skills worried me a little. *Let's try to avoid getting involved with this one. If the sirens on this island evolve into* that, *then maybe culling their population a bit would be a good idea...*

("*That other one looks tasty too, but it's different. See? A little behind the first one.*")

Tasty? There's nothing tasty about that monster. It smells like iron. You can't fry that or stick it in a stew to make it edible.

I narrowed my eyes and looked farther out to where Partner was indicating. On the edge of the horizon, barely visible, I saw a small, shining white figure. How on earth did Partner see that one? As I squinted, its outline slowly became clearer: It was a dragon.

W-wait. Is that...a Nomadic Dragon? Could it be my mother?! N-no, no way, that's just not possible. It's probably just a random dragon who came to visit the island. That's all.

I had a feeling the dragon was looking at me, so I returned the stare with one of my own. As it got closer, it became apparent that there was someone riding on the back of the white dragon—*two* someones, in fact. Both were human: one wielding a sword, and the other, a staff. They both seemed to be women.

I was shocked. *A-are they here to try and take me down?*

I flew all the way here to reduce the possibility that the Lithovar tribe would get in trouble for the incident with Tolemann, and I'd deliberately shown myself to many villages along the way. I was guilty of a long list of crimes: wiping out the survey team the hero rubbed shoulders with, invading the country of Harunae, killing the hero meant to be their one weapon against the Demon King, approaching city perimeters, demanding sacrifices to the

Lithovar tribe, destroying Tolemann's private army, and even killing Tolemann himself.

I didn't think they'd be able to make it all the way out to an island this remote. But I guess it was a different story with a high-rank dragon under their command. Just one, though? Perhaps I had the sea to thank for that.

If they came all the way here believing they had a chance at defeating me, then that dragon's rank was probably somewhere between B+ and A. Along with its two riders, who I assumed were probably heroes, or maybe Mystic Knights, this was a very dangerous situation for me. If they'd sent heroes after me, then the humans must consider me something of a special case.

With Eldia's help, we could drive them away in no time, I thought. *I'm sure Eldia would agree with me too. But he'd probably want to kill them both, just to be safe.*

Should I transform into a human and show them that I have no hostility toward them? No, if they were planning to go on the offensive without any chitchat involved, then I'd be screwed. But even if I somehow managed to neutralize them so I could try to talk my way out of it, Eldia might get suspicious and launch his own attack.

The white dragon was gradually closing the distance between us. *First things first.* I activated my View Status skill and directed it at the dragon, who locked eyes with me and gave a loud snort.

HOLY DRAGON OF SALVATION

SPECIES: Seraphim

STATUS: Spirit

LV: 82/125 (Lock)

HP: 1101/1101

MP: 1279/1279

SPECIAL SKILLS:

DRAGON SCALE: Lv 6

GRECIAN LANGUAGE: Lv 9

FLY: Lv 8

LIGHT TYPE: Lv —

HOLY DRAGON: Lv —

AUTOMATIC HP RECOVERY: Lv 4

AUTOMATIC MP RECOVERY: Lv 5

RESISTANCE SKILLS:

PHYSICAL RESISTANCE: Lv 5

MAGIC RESISTANCE: Lv 8

PARALYSIS IMMUNITY: Lv 4

ILLUSION RESISTANCE: Lv 6

INSTANT DEATH RESISTANCE: Lv 8

CURSE RESISTANCE: Lv 8

CONFUSION RESISTANCE: Lv 6

DARK RESISTANCE: Lv 8

NORMAL SKILLS:

MEGA FANG: Lv 5

FLASHING CLAW: Lv 5

LIGHT SHIELD: Lv 7

HI-REST: Lv 7

HI-CARE: Lv 7

HOLY: Lv 7

YAWN: Lv 7

HUMAN TRANSFORMATION: Lv 7

TELEPATHY: Lv 5

CONCENTRATION: Lv 8

LIGHTNING RAIN: Lv 8

TITLE SKILLS:

VALIANT: Lv MAX

ANGEL: Lv —

PURIFYING LIGHT: Lv —

SYMBOL OF THE HOLY LAND: Lv —

DRAGON SPIRIT VASSAL: Lv —

FINAL EVOLUTION: Lv —

Another rank A?! It's a lower level than Eldia though, so it seems a bit tamer in comparison. I'd probably be able to take it on if we fought one-on-one. I'm a little concerned about the "Spirit" status, though...

Next, I turned my attention to the two humans atop the white dragon I now knew was a Seraphim. The first was a girl with white hair, devoid of any pigment, and kind jade-green eyes. Next to her was a woman clad in white armor sporting short, golden hair and looked to be in her mid-twenties. Her almond-shaped eyes followed me warily.

Of the two, the golden-haired swordswoman was the one who seemed the most openly hostile, but for some reason the white-haired girl's impassive gaze sent a chill up my spine.

I shifted my attention to the white-haired girl. She looked back at me and gave a small, satisfied nod.

> **LILYXILA LIALUM**
> SPECIES: **Earth-human**
> STATUS: **Normal**
> LV: **100/100 (MAX)**
> HP: **887/887**
> MP: **1154/1154**
> ATTACK: **673+76**
> DEFENSE: **476+98**

MAGIC: 1112+110

AGILITY: 679

EQUIPMENT:

WEAPON: Staff of the Holy Land: A−

ARMOR: Vestment of the Holy Land: A−

SACRED SKILLS:

HUNGRY GHOST PATH: Lv —

SPECIAL SKILLS:

DIVINE VOICE: Lv MAX

LIGHT TYPE: Lv —

GRECIAN LANGUAGE: Lv 7

MAGE: Lv MAX

PSYCHIC SENSE: Lv 7

STEALTH: Lv 7

RESISTANCE SKILLS:

PHYSICAL RESISTANCE: Lv 7

MAGIC RESISTANCE: Lv 7

DARK RESISTANCE: Lv 7

ILLUSION RESISTANCE: Lv 7

POISON RESISTANCE: Lv 7

CURSE RESISTANCE: Lv MAX

PETRIFY RESISTANCE: Lv 7

INSTANT DEATH RESISTANCE: Lv MAX

PARALYSIS RESISTANCE: Lv 7

NORMAL SKILLS:

VIEW STATUS: Lv MAX

HI-REST: Lv MAX

HI-CARE: Lv MAX

HOLY: Lv MAX

HOLY SPHERE: Lv MAX

HOLY SPEAR: Lv MAX

TELEPATHY: Lv 9

SPIRIT SERVANT: Lv MAX

FLOAT: Lv 7

HI-QUICK: Lv 7

HI-POWER LV 7

ILLUSION COUNTER: Lv 7

GRAVITY: Lv 6

GRAVIDON: Lv 6

GRAVIRION: Lv 6

CONFUSE: Lv 6

ILLUSION: Lv 6

FIRE SPHERE: Lv 6

CHARM: Lv 6

SLOW: Lv 6

DIMENSION: Lv 4

TITLE SKILLS:

CHOSEN ONE: Lv —

VALIANT: Lv 7

SAINT: Lv 8

WHITE MAGE: Lv MAX

BLACK MAGE: Lv 8

MASTER OF STAFF: Lv 8

ITTY-BITTY HERO: Lv MAX

PROTECTIVE SPIRIT: Lv MAX

CUNNING: Lv MAX

WRONGDOER: Lv MAX

LIAR: Lv MAX

DASTARDLY KING: Lv MAX

CALAMITY: Lv MAX

LAPLACE AUTHORITY INTERFERENCE: Lv 3

ONE TRUSTED BY THE HOLY DRAGON: Lv —

SUBDUER OF THE BEAST KING: Lv —

Tolemann told me that the people I should be wary of were heroes and saints, and this woman was the second person I'd encountered—the first one being the hero—who had a Sacred Skill. I knew that, but her status screen was just...bizarre. She had way more skills than the hero did. *Although he managed pretty well without them anyway.*

I'd been assuming that the dragon would be my biggest opponent, but it could very well just be serving as a mode of transportation for that saint. It felt like she took as many skills as she could get and spent her entire life grinding her skill levels.

She has Divine Voice too—and it's at max level. If I clash with her, I won't have any sort of informational advantage. This whole party's bad news. The other one too, the swordswoman...I doubt she's your average opponent either.

> **ALPHIS ATELITE**
> SPECIES: **Earth-human**
> STATUS: **Normal**
> LV: **58/75**
> HP: **352/352**
> MP: **217/217**

Phew. Looks like Alphis is just a normal human. Well, still one of the strongest humans I've ever seen, but compared to Lilyxila, she looks like a cakewalk.

So a rank A, a human who'd probably be rank A, and another human who'd probably be rank B. And Lilyxila knew View Status? Maybe I should've been a little more careful. She probably saw my Status when we locked eyes before.

While I was distracted by the white dragon and its two riders, Allo came up beside me, followed by Nightmare and Treant. Allo must have guessed from my expression that something was wrong; she followed my line of sight and then looked back at me, nervous. I wanted to tell her it was going to be okay, but I didn't have any way to back up that statement.

Should we run? No, that dragon's agility was way higher than mine. I'd still have to inflict some serious damage on it if we wanted any chance at getting away. From the look of Lilyxila, I didn't think things will immediately turn into a battle anyway, but maybe that was just hopeful thinking. I still didn't know if they were here to talk to me or to take me down. But whether we ended up negotiating or I had to do enough damage to try and escape, we needed to make contact with each other first.

I resigned myself to sitting patiently and waiting for their arrival. Eventually, the white dragon reached the great tree and landed on a branch a good distance away. Then it turned its face toward the heavens and roared.

Lilyxila raised her staff. "Thank you, Holy Dragon. You may rest."

The white dragon began to glow. Its outline started fading, almost like it was dissolving straight into the air.

The phosphorescent light that remained swirled around Lilyxila and then seemed to enter her body.

I guess that explains the Spirit status, I thought. *It seems like Lilyxila is somehow able to summon a monster spirit at will.*

Lilyxila and Alphis landed on their branch and stood tall. I tensed, preparing myself to react to whatever they had planned.

"Master...Illusia, I presume?" the saint asked. Despite her stiff words, she smiled softly. "I was surprised when I learned of your name, but it fits you well. Much better than that monstrosity from the desert. We have been hearing rumors about you for quite some time now. I always hoped I would meet you one day."

PART 2

. . . .

SAINT LILYXILA BEGAN to move closer, stepping lightly from branch to branch, until she stood next to me. As you'd expect from someone with such an extraordinary status screen, she leaped and darted about with ease.

I crouched without thinking and assumed a wary stance.

"Grrrh..." Partner gave a low, restrained growl.

Allo and Nightmare, alerted by Partner's growl, stepped in front of me and glared defiantly at Lilyxila. Treant stood tall and straight behind me, trying to blend in with the background.

Jeez... One of these three is not like the others, huh?

Alphis, the woman in armor who seemed to be Lilyxila's attendant, hurriedly stepped in front of Lilyxila and blocked her path.

"Saint Lilyxila! I ask that you do not approach them so carelessly!"

Lilyxila responded by puffing her cheeks out in a pout. "It's all right, Alphis. No need to be so protective. They don't seem to be looking for a fight." She craned her neck up to look at me, and her eyes widened. Beneath her jade green eyes, I sensed a faint glimmer of red light.

"I would say that there is less than a one-percent chance of a battle from here on out."

"But even so..." Alphis said. "Your gift of prophecy is not always correct."

Gift of prophecy? I didn't see that in her list of skills...

But wait, she used a percentage. Back when I fought that Little Rock Dragon that showed up in my village, I remembered the Divine Voice gave me information in terms of probability too.

I had come to not rely as much on the Divine Voice since evolving into the Plague Dragon. To be fair, I would've had no idea how bad Myria's village had gotten without it. However, I had a sneaking suspicion that it was the Divine Voice who made those slimes attack the village in the first place. I'd stopped trying to make pointless conversation with it since then, and I'd also avoided asking about any probabilities related to that period in time.

Take the hero, for example. I didn't know what the Divine Voice had told him to do near the end, but whatever it was, it made him go into a rampage. Fortunately, in this case, it didn't seem like Lilyxila was in any danger of allowing the Divine Voice to decide things for her, but...

"Besides, Alphis," Lilyxila responded, "it's rude to be so openly leery after we've come all this way. We've traveled here—with full knowledge of our respective ties and differences—to make a request. We must accept the risk involved or our journey is meaningless. It would be a shame if our chances were ruined because of your rudeness. My life is worth far less than that of the world itself, yes?"

She paused for a moment, then added, "Although...it *is* somewhat difficult for me to imagine them being the type to sit quietly around a negotiating table."

Alphis, upon hearing Lilyxila, turned back to me with a blank expression and bowed her head, eyes still full of hostility. Allo met her gaze with a scowl of her own.

"...Hmph. Is that an Undead? How vile."

"Alphis!" Lilyxila chided her again.

So this is a saint, huh? Based on how they've acted so far at least, they don't seem to want to be our enemies. Those Title Skills make me uneasy, but I can't really speak for humans as far as Title Skills go... Maybe there's some reason or explanation for them, but still.

Lilyxila, with Alphis at her side, crossed over to our branch and moved to stand directly in front of me. Allo and Nightmare both tensed.

"Your Oracle level is still quite low," Lilyxila said. "I'm... not sure where I should begin with all of this."

Oracle level...? She must be talking about Divine Voice. I remembered seeing her Divine Voice skill was maxed out, while mine was only level 5.

"I suppose they may not be necessary, but let's start with introductions. My name is Lilyxila Lialum. I was born into this world with the Title Skill of Saint, destined to be the symbol of the Holy Land of Lialum and one day lead the world to peace. It's a pleasure to meet you. This is Alphis, the finest swordswoman in Lialum and a member of the Order of the Holy Knights."

Alphis bowed her head with a sullen look. I mirrored it with a bow of my own.

N-nice to meet you. I don't have any Title Skills important enough to attach to my name, but...

At this, Lilyxila covered her hand with her mouth and giggled. "I'm relieved to find that you're exactly as I expected you to be. I don't know what we would've done if we came all this way only to be attacked."

Partner stared at Lilyxila suspiciously. Lilyxila glanced at her but quickly turned her gaze back to me.

"I've had the displeasure of meeting that hero you fought," she said. "I've also visited Harunae to find out what happened and spoke to those who were there. Because of this, and because I believe you are willing to aid humans, I have a request for you. That is why I've come to this island."

That hero I fought... She must be talking about the blond-haired jerk from Harunae. I could tell that he didn't amount to much in her eyes either. So she found my track record promising and came to ask for a favor? Maybe they really weren't here to pick a fight.

"Master Illusia, I would like you to subdue the Demon King of this era, who has taken over the body of the princess of Ardesia and infiltrated the Ardesian royal family."

Th-the Demon King? In the Ardesian royal family?!

I had kind of assumed that her request would've had something to do with the war between monsters and humans, but I had no clue that the kingdom of Ardesia had been taken over by the Demon King. Ballrabbit and Nina were supposed to be in Ardesia right now. Had all the top brass of the kingdom been overrun and replaced with monsters?

Despite myself, I let out a low, worried groan.

Lilyxila watched me with a steady gaze. "I see you have someone important to you in Ardesia."

D-did she just read my mind?!

I figured it was only natural—she did have the Telepathy skill, after all. Even if I wasn't intending for her to hear, I thought about it powerfully enough that she probably picked up on my thoughts anyway. Besides, Lilyxila's Telepathy skill was at level 9. No wonder she picked up on them. It was hard for me to control my thoughts when I got emotional, but I needed to be careful around that Telepathy skill.

Lilyxila continued. "There has been a string of deaths due to illness in the Ardesian royal family as of late. As such, control of the kingdom was transferred to the rather young princess; however, she has been acting quite strangely. She frequently invites skilled swordsmen and mages to visit her castle, but unfortunately...it seems that most of them have gone missing."

Wait, you don't mean...you think she's killing them to gain more experience points?

"That is what I fear. She very well could have cursed the royal family to death and then took her place on the throne in the ensuing commotion. However, I have no proof. And if I take any action against her, it could be used as an excuse for war between Lialum and Ardesia, which would only reduce human forces. I would like you to confirm with your own eyes that the Demon King has taken over the Princess's body and then assassinate the Demon King."

I hesitated, not sure whether I should believe her or not.

It was certainly true that relations between Lialum and Ardesia would suffer if Lilyxila involved herself in the matters of the Ardesian royal family. Entrusting this task to an outsider monster like me was probably her best option. I still had my suspicions, but there was no need for Lilyxila to go to such great lengths to trick me. If they just wanted to destroy me, it would be much quicker and more convenient to attack me now; even out here, I doubted I could win a fight against both of them.

"Do you not trust me?" Lilyxila asked. "Perhaps I can allay your concerns by explaining things in a little more detail. I see that you know little about your position and the Holy God. I would be happy to tell you more about them, if you like. I'd also like to lay all my cards on the table; there's no point in hiding one up my sleeve from you. I wouldn't want there to be any misunderstanding between us because of it."

The card up her sleeve? Was she talking about her Spirit skill?

That skill was definitely weighing on my mind. If she had the ability to control monsters as she pleased, there was no need for her to rely on me. Judging by her Title Skills, it seemed like she had some other monsters under her control as well.

"And naturally...I have a reward to offer you in return for your help. I know we haven't been acquainted long, but from what I know of you, and the things I've picked up through Telepathy, I think you will like it."

A reward...?

"First, let me reveal my trump card. My Spirit Servant skill, which I rely on so heavily, is one that can be acquired with the Title Skill 'Saint: Lv 5.' Please analyze that skill."

It seemed that, like the Hero Title Skill, the Saint Title Skill also had its own skill attached to it that could be learned once the skill was leveled up enough. As requested, I asked my Divine Voice for a description of her

Spirit Servant skill, and immediately a familiar message window appeared in my mind.

> **Normal Skill "Spirit Servant." Allows user to bind the souls of monsters with whom a contract has been made and use them with the "Spirit" status condition.**

I continued, turning my attention to the description of the Spirit status condition.

> **Abnormal Status "Spirit." Affected user takes on a spiritual form. Unable to gain experience points.**

So...it made them into a spirit? Did that mean the Holy Dragon they rode here, Seraphim, was a spirit under Lilyxila's command? It'd be pretty handy to be able to summon a rank A monster whenever you wanted. A skill like that without any restrictions would be terrifying in the wrong hands.

"Seraphim's soul was sealed away in the statue of the Holy Dragon in Lialum," she explained. "According to the statue's description, it was left there by the previous generation to be used as a Spirit Servant for the next saint when they appeared."

So Lilyxila took the Holy Dragon's soul out of its statue...and now she could summon Seraphim whenever she wanted, which meant her strength was basically equivalent to two rank A's. That was insane!

But wait, there's still another thing I'm curious about with Lilyxila's Title Skills. Along with "One Trusted by the Holy Dragon," she also has "Subduer of the Beast King." Does that mean...

"Yes, you seem to have the general idea. Seraphim is not the only Spirit Servant I can summon. When I maxed out my Spirit Servant level, I gained the ability to summon two spirit beasts simultaneously. I also possess the soul of the Beast King, Beelzebub, a vicious monster that I vanquished with help from the Holy Knights. However, that soul is quite difficult to handle, so I prefer not to use it unless absolutely necessary."

Lilyxila has the power of three rank A beings at her disposal...? Well, if what she was saying was true, that monster was one she defeated with the help of Seraphim and the Holy Knights. If she wasn't careful, it could even get strong enough to overpower her.

A mental image of three Eldias standing together in a row appeared in my mind. *Yikes... I definitely don't want to get on her bad side. I thought they were here to negotiate with me as equals, but with such a huge power gap, it doesn't feel like I can say no.*

But if Ardesia really was in such dire straits, I was willing to put my life on the line to help them. Nina and Ballrabbit were in Ardesia. I couldn't just leave them to a fate like that.

Not to mention, from Adoff's tales about Ardesia, I had the impression that it was a rather large and influential country. It was pretty easy to imagine that the Demon King occupying the land and gaining power there could incite a conflict that would involve the entire world one day.

The stronger Lilyxila was, the less we needed to worry. Of course, that was assuming that Lilyxila was trustworthy. With her Divine Voice, though, and those questionable Title Skills—all of which were max level—there was no way I could just trust her unconditionally.

I also had to think about Allo and the others. Should I leave them here or take them with me? It'd be dangerous, so I'd prefer to go alone, but I doubted Allo and Nightmare would be okay with that.

Lilyxila did deserve some credit for disclosing her powers to me up front, though. If I had taken it as a threat, it would've made negotiations a lot more difficult for her. But that second spirit was just too valuable of a trump card. Unless she genuinely intended to cooperate with me, it would've been far more useful to keep that card tucked up her sleeve.

...I'm curious, Saint Lilyxila. Why not use one of your Spirit Servants to attack the Demon King?

As I sent my thought to her, her gaze lowered, and she slowly shook her head. "The fact that I was the one who defeated Beelzebub is well known. If I use one of them to attack the Demon King, he will know immediately that it was my doing. It wouldn't be impossible to release one of them and acquire the soul of a more appropriate monster, but the Demon King is likely a high-rank B... and no doubt he has defensive measures in place. A weak attack would only serve to put him on his guard."

A high-rank B, huh...? I mean, I hope that's true, but I'm pretty sure he's a rank A or higher. Was this the point that Lilyxila had been trying to get across? She'd said she wanted to lay her cards on the table first to prevent any misunderstandings, and I could see why now. She had a lot of cards, but right now, she couldn't play a single one.

"Now, that's enough of my story, I think. Next..."

Wait. Before we move on... I'd like to hear what you think about the Divine Voice, Lilyxila. Forgive me if I sound rude, but that's the part I'm most concerned about.

Lilyxila hesitated for a moment, which surprised me; she hadn't shown a trace of hesitation before now. After a short pause to think, she exhaled.

"In Lialum, we are taught that four of the six Great Sages who once sealed the evil god away divided themselves into two groups: one to advise the humans and one to advise the monsters," she said. "The beings who inherited the power of each of these Great Sages were the hero, the Beast King, the Demon King...and myself, the saint. According to the teachings of the Holy Land, our god is thought to be speaking through the will of the Great Sage, who has taken me as their vessel."

That lined up with what Eldia told me in the ruins. But that stuff was just an old myth—it couldn't be true, right? Lilyxila said that she had been in contact with the hero and the Beast King. In that case, there was no way that I was the only one who'd felt uneasy about the presence of the Divine Voice. The way Lilyxila talked about it—from a distance, as if the Divine Voice were inhabiting someone else—made me suspect she felt that way too.

"However," she continued, "that is false. My position does not allow me to outwardly deny the content of our scriptures, but no matter what the legend says, the Holy God is one individual. Not even I have unraveled all of his mysteries. All I know is that the Holy God has entrusted us with a certain degree of control over the future."

W-wait, what? I'm lost all of a sudden. What're you talking about?

Lilyxila seemed somewhat taken aback. "Ahh, I see. You haven't heard anything from the Holy God, have you, Master Illusia? I was concerned that you intentionally sought out the Human Realm Path to take as your own, but it seems it was a coincidence after all... Or rather, your destiny."

She went on, "In the innermost room of my country's crypt, we have unveiled a secret of great significance, and it pertains to the Holy God. One of the rewards I intend to give you once the matter of the false princess of Ardesia is settled is an invitation to visit that crypt because I believe you have the right to know that secret. I daresay you will find the answers to many of your questions there."

Interesting... It had to be a secret about the Divine Voice. I had no intention of getting fixated on finding out the truth of that matter, though.

"My second reward for you will be a personal guarantee of safety in my name. If you are able to defeat the Demon King without any issues, you will also be pardoned for attacking the castle, and you will be known as a great savior to the world. I will protect that truth from being twisted and warped by those around me. I can tell by what you've told me thus far that your size and formidable power have exposed you to many who harbor misconceptions about your kind."

My shoulders jumped in surprise. Lilyxila's eyes followed the movement.

PART 3

. . . .

LILYXILA'S PROPOSAL WAS, in a sense, what I'd been aiming to do since the moment I was born into this world as a monster. With the saint to back me up, I could clear up the misunderstanding with the village where Myria lived and finally reunite with her or maybe even travel around to look for the orangurangs and my black lizard friend. I should also be able to reunite with Nina and Ballrabbit in Ardesia, and it might even be possible to end the prejudice against the Lithovar tribe and visit them as their Dragon God.

I didn't know how influential the saint's support would be, and I was sure it wouldn't all be smooth sailing. I didn't even know how long defeating the Demon King would take, but there was hope, at the very least.

"Grrrh..." I growled softly. I missed my friends. In my current state, I couldn't even check to see if they were alive and well.

"...Finally, as your third reward, I may be able to make you human with my magic. However, I cannot yet guarantee that it will work."

M-make me human?

"Yes. There is an anecdote told in the Holy Land about a saint who was able to transform an evil monster into a sweet, good-natured boy. If I raise my Saint skill level, I may one day learn of the magic needed to perform such a miracle."

Did I...want to go back to being a human? In the past, the answer to that would've been an immediate yes. But now, strangely enough, I wasn't sure. For one thing, what would happen to Partner if I became human? I had no idea.

When I stayed silent, Lilyxila began to speak again. "I know I've said a lot...but in short, I will give you credit where it is due, and I will do everything in my power to spread the word about your achievements. Not to mention, I'm sure allowing the Demon King to regain his unlimited power would not be good for you either, would it?"

I thought for a moment and then glanced at Partner. She was watching Lilyxila with narrowed eyes but turned when she noticed me looking at her.

What do you think about all this, Partner? I imagine we'll run into the Demon King someday, so I feel like it would be better to get rid of him while we have a powerful saint on our side, but...

("It's your body. Do what you want with it. But I'd rather not get unnecessarily chummy with humans. I don't trust this girl much either.")

Yeah, that's the thing. I'm way behind Lilyxila, both in information and in strength. If I'm not careful, they'll definitely take advantage of me.

I turned to the saint. *Let me ask you one thing, Lilyxila. Where did you get that "Calamity" Title Skill? That will help me decide whether I'm willing to follow you or not.*

"Oh, I thought you knew... My Calamity skill allows me to take in new Sacred Skills when the need arises. It's not difficult to acquire, so long as you know where to look."

I see. So that Title Skill is related to Sacred Skills? I did remember that Title Skill changing a lot when I defeated the hero, so that made sense.

"Without that specific Title Skill, you would be unable to acquire new Sacred Skills. According to the Holy God, this is a mechanism that was created in a long distant era, to ensure that the power of the ruler of men would always be in the hands of someone who tampers with monsters and vice versa."

But if that was correct, then it seemed like the Holy God—the Divine Voice—was working to poke holes in the system while still existing within it. I'd always thought of the Holy God as more of an external entity, like statuses or skills...but instead, they seemed to still be bound by the laws of this world.

Maybe this Holy God wasn't related to the myth at all? Maybe it was a monster in its original world who reincarnated here long before I did and became immortal?

Lilyxila continued, "I could've acquired the Sacred Skill of the Beast King if I wanted to, but I opted to keep Beelzebub as my Spirit Servant because there were no other suitable candidates. If you fail to defeat the Demon King, and we can no longer afford to consider the survival of the Holy Land or relations between Lialum and Ardesia, then I will do what I must. And if I determine that I am no match for him, I will summon Beelzebub as my last resort."

W-will that be okay...? You don't have complete control over him, right? And even as a spirit, Beelzebub still has his Sacred Skills, doesn't he? I think the worst-case scenario would be for Beelzebub to snatch the Demon King's Sacred Skills and then for you to lose control of him completely...

"Which is why he is my last resort. Not even the Holy God knows what is going to happen. Perhaps Beelzebub will break the shackles his soul is trapped in by force and allow him to resurrect himself. It's like tossing a coin again that has already landed on tails. But it's better than nothing."

I glanced back at Allo, Nightmare, and Treant.

So...what do you guys think? Personally, I think I'm going to try and get to the castle in Ardesia.

Allo had been staring at me like she was still annoyed that Alphis called her an undead, but when our eyes met, she nodded. Nightmare looked at Partner and, once it confirmed that Partner wasn't opposed, tilted its head slightly to indicate that it was willing to participate.

Treant backed away as I asked, looked at Allo and Nightmare, and then stepped forward like it was trying to stretch its trunk.

All right, all right, no need to strain yourself. If you're afraid to stay on this island, I can try to find a safe forest for you or something... I could maybe ask Lilyxila to take you there, if you want.

My eyes landed on my next addressee: Gyva, who had appeared next to Treant at some point.

"Kuuu! Kuuu!" It gave an adorable wiggle, leapt into the air, and did a perfect somersault.

Allo, if you would.

"...Gale!"

"Kuuuuuuu?!"

A gust of wind blew out from Allo's fingertips. It peeled the bark off the branch we were on and broke a bunch of thin branches around us. Gyva, caught in the strong wind, was thrown into the air and fell down. *Sorry, Gyva, but you're not coming with me. How long have you been here, anyway?*

"May I assume that you have accepted my request?" Lilyxila asked. I nodded.

"Wonderful. I'm happy to hear you approve of—wait. Something is coming." A look of panic suddenly crossed Lilyxila's normally well-composed face.

Seconds later, my Psychic Sense skill detected something. I followed the signs it gave off with my eyes, turning my head to look below the great tree, searching for the source.

At the base of the tree, I saw the glint of shining purple-blue scales as light bounced off the hide of a familiar giant dragon. Glaring at Lilyxila and me in turn, with eyes that burned with fury, was Eldia, the Dragon King. My father.

C-crap! Did he sense humans and leave the ruins to investigate?! No, the underground ruins were way too far away for him to have sensed anything. It's hard to believe he could pinpoint the presence of two humans—ones he didn't know were here—in this gigantic tree full of monsters...

Wait, was he spying on me again?!

"Grroooooooohhh!"

Eldia's roar of fury reverberated through the wood of the great tree.

PART 4

ELDIA SWOOPED UPWARD, flying almost vertically at me. He bared his teeth, showing off his reddish-black gums and massive fangs.

<*Why?! Why are you laughing and chatting away with humans and their ilk?!*>

I looked down at Eldia and checked his stats.

> **ELDIA**
> SPECIES: **Diabolos**
> STATUS: **Enraged (Major)**
> LV: **130/130 (MAX)**
> HP: **1697/1697**
> MP: **1316/1316**

Oh, God! He's totally pissed! I can't seem to get through to him so we can talk either...not that there seems to be much room for discussion.

"What...? Those stats..."

Lilyxila, who also seemed to be checking Eldia's status screen, frowned. With an attack power of over 1,500, Eldia didn't seem like the type of enemy even the max-leveled saint would like to take on very often.

"An acquaintance of yours?" she asked, narrowing her eyes at me—I avoided looking at them. Even so, I could feel Lilyxila and the swordswoman Alphis' piercing gazes on me.

I didn't want to fight Eldia, to be honest, but he would definitely attempt to join forces with the Demon King once he learned he'd been born. There was no way we could just get along with each other anymore.

I raised my upper body off the ground and flapped my wings, letting the magic-charged wind travel down my arms and shoot out from my claws. The gust of wind from my Whirlwind Slash severed a thick branch of the great tree right in front of Eldia. He swerved to the side to avoid it and then hovered in the air, glaring at me.

I-I'll hit you with the next one! If you're planning to retreat, now's your chance!

It was me, my three companions, the saint and her attendant, and the saint's dragon, versus him. We outnumbered him seven to one. Plus, Lilyxila, Seraphim, and I were the equivalent of rank A's. Even maxed out at level 130, he was still at a huge disadvantage!

"Did you miss him on purpose?" Partner asked, disgusted.

I-It was a warning. Sure, there's a psychological reason why it's hard for me to fight him, but more than anything, I just don't want him to hurt my friends. I'm pretty sure neither of us want to fight each other here. If things work out the way I want them to, he might back off for now.

<I see. So that is your answer, you two-faced, backstabbing dragon? So be it!> Eldia roared, leaping vertically toward me once more. It was no use. There was no way to de-escalate things when he was this angry. Besides, Eldia didn't seem like the type to let things go, regardless of the practical benefits.

"Saint Lilyxila! Summon the Holy Dragon!"

Lilyxila thrust her staff into the air and cried out, "Spirit Servant! Come to me, Holy Dragon of Salvation, Seraphim!" In an instant, the Seraphim's massive figure appeared once more.

The divine white dragon looked serenely down at Eldia, then leapt from the branch of the great tree toward him, spreading its wings wide to slow its descent. Numerous lights appeared behind its wings and rained down on Eldia, chipping away at the branches of the great tree. *That must be its Lightning Rain skill,* I thought. From our position above him, it was the perfect skill for the job. It'd be difficult to avoid completely, and, as a rank A monster, Seraphim should be able to do a decent amount of damage.

"Grooooooaaaa!" Eldia roared, and a sheer film of magic enveloped his body. A Mana Barrier. Eldia was already resistant to magic, but now it was even less effective. He broke through the barrage of light with a single ram. Balls of light landed on his cheek and back and burst, cutting through his scales and gouging out his flesh.

But that didn't stop him. The high-level dragon reached Seraphim's side with ease and raised his massive, purple-blue arm.

"Kraaaaaaah!" Seraphim cried out. A wall of light appeared between the two of them. It had to be the Light Shield skill. Rather than raising the user's resistance or stats, it seemed to create a barrier that prevented the user from being attacked.

I thought Eldia would swing his arm down immediately, but he took advantage of the moment it took Seraphim to use Light Shield and swung his arm even wider. Then, his arm came down, sending a blow with the highest attack power value I've ever seen straight at Seraphim.

The Light Shield shattered like a pane of glass, sending shards flying that embedded themselves in Seraphim's abdomen. At the same time, Eldia slashed at it with his monstrously large claws.

"Kryaaaah!"

Seraphim's shriek of pain echoed in the air. It flung back, slamming against the trunk of the great tree. Its abdomen was ripped to shreds, but there was no blood coming from the gaping wounds. The flesh that was ripped from its body began to glow with white light, then vanished. It really was a spirit after all. It'd still seemed to take a decent amount of physical damage, though...

<You pitiful dragon, forced to serve the whims of your human masters! A nothing like you should stay out of matters that do not concern you!>

It happened so fast that there was no time to react.

N-no way. But Seraphim's a rank A like me?!

"Holy Dragon?!"

Alphis's face paled. "I... I never thought that such a monster still walked this earth..."

Lilyxila was shocked too, and I could see why. She had come to me to increase her fighting power against the

Demon King. She clearly wasn't expecting to be attacked by a monster even stronger than the one she was seeking.

It seemed like I had underestimated Eldia as well. He was tough, fast, and heavy; straightforward traits, but difficult to beat all the same. His stats were much more valuable than a bunch of superficial skills. The blow that Eldia struck Seraphim with wasn't a skill or anything; he didn't have any claw or striking skills. Considering the fact that the Demon King was apparently masquerading as royalty while he improved his skill levels, I was suddenly pretty convinced that Eldia was much stronger than him.

When I met Lilyxila, I shuddered at the thought of her commanding the power of three rank A monsters, but Eldia was not far behind—and aside from magic, Lilyxila's stats fell far short of Eldia's.

Eldia flew upward until he was level with me, then whirled around to build momentum and lashed out with his tail. He hit the branch in front of me, gouging it wide open and sending up a spray of wood chips. The sharp recoil from the Dragon Tail attack sent him reeling back before he landed on another branch. I couldn't react with an attack of my own without taking a hit.

‹Consider that payback for your preemptive attack,› he said calmly. He regarded both Partner and me with

glittering, crimson eyes. I made my first attack miss on purpose—Eldia must have done the same thing with his.

I was frozen in place, staring into Eldia's eyes. Suddenly, I was reminded of a saying about a frog staring into the eyes of a snake; that was exactly how I felt in that moment. I didn't think the gap between our stats and resistance skills would be quite this glaringly obvious.

I received a thought from Partner. *("Hey! Get moving!")*
H-huh? What're you gonna do?

While I was confused, Partner's eyes—still directed at Eldia—glowed suspiciously crimson, and she used our Special Skill, Master's Demonic Gaze. Eldia squinted uncomfortably at the sudden red light.

Y-you did it!

For those wondering, Master's Demonic Gaze was a skill that froze enemies in their tracks if they gazed into your eyes, but I had no idea how effective it'd be on Eldia. If it wasn't effective, it might just provoke him. I could only hope that it would stop Eldia long enough to create an opening for us to act.

"Groooohhh!"

I launched off the branch of the great tree with my hind legs, then swung my front paw down toward Eldia. His eyes caught the movement, and he raised his own paw.

No! He's going to counterattack! The Demonic Gaze didn't have any effect!

Eldia had his own Special Skill called King's Demonic Gaze, I remembered. That might give him resistance to other Demonic Gaze skills.

I expected Eldia to fight back, but instead he flew backward onto another branch, keeping his front legs raised. At that moment, three spears of light pierced through the spot where Eldia had just been, cutting through the branch with clean, cylindrical holes.

I traced the spears' trajectories and found Lilyxila standing at the source.

<You're a clever little one, aren't you!>

That had to be her Holy Spear skill. It was pretty powerful. It would do some damage if it hit Eldia, even with all his Resistance Skills.

"Hi-Quick! Hi-Power!" Lilyxila shouted, this time pointing her staff at me. Two different lights flickered around my body in turn. *Those're both stat-adjusting skills. Are they gonna be enough to give me a chance against Eldia?*

"Forgive me, but I'll have to leave the front lines to you! Do what you can to impede his movement!"

It felt reassuring to have someone of such a high level watching my back; few had the stats to fight side by side with me since I evolved into Ouroboros. Sure, Allo had gotten much stronger, but she still wasn't strong enough to be able to hold her own in a battle between two rank A's.

Out of the corner of my eye, I saw Seraphim raise its head and howl.

"Kraaaaaaaaa!"

Seraphim had been taken down by Eldia's blow, but it recovered quickly, thanks to its Hi-Rest skill. However, there was still a large scar on its white abdomen where Eldia's claws had dug into its flesh. I could never think of Seraphim as some small fry, but the fact that it didn't have Regenerate to restore its body to its original state was a little embarrassing.

Unfortunately, Eldia *did* have Regenerate. This meant that even if we could successfully break his wings, he could easily grow them back by just expending MP. I usually considered regenerating broken limbs an expensive undertaking, but Eldia had plenty of MP to spare.

Seraphim met my gaze, and I soon received a thought: *‹I suggest you not be too dismissive, Evil Dragon, for I am the guardian deity of the Holy Land.›*

It then looked at Eldia and let out a huff.

S-Seraphim knows Telepathy too?! And apparently it also had a lot of pride... I *really* had to be mindful of my thoughts.

Seraphim lowered its neck and tensed, putting all its strength in its hind legs. *‹Unlike before, when I was caught by surprise, I now have the saint's magic supporting me. I shall not display such ineptitude again.›*

With that, Seraphim kicked off its branch and spread its wings, heading directly for Eldia. *Th-that sounded awful foreboding to me, but maybe it'll be okay…?*

I flew after Seraphim, trying—unsuccessfully—to suppress my doubt.

Eldia swung a massive paw at Seraphim. Seraphim bit down hard on his paw, then quickly grabbed it with both legs. Eldia slammed his captured paw into the branch they stood on, and Seraphim's body twisted in pain. *Ouch, that hurts just to look at! There's no way Seraphim's getting out of this in one piece!*

Seraphim, determined not to let go, continued staring at Eldia with bloodshot eyes. I dove down from above them and used Whirlwind Slash to try and divert Eldia's attention. Eldia raised his front leg high, causing the blade of wind to carve itself into Seraphim's back instead.

"*Kraaah?!*"

Seraphim shrieked, released its jaws from where they were biting Eldia, and fell to the ground, completely limp.

‹Fool. You attacked without thinking. A novice mista—›

Eldia's telepathic message was cut short.

Fortunately, I never attacked without thinking, and I had a pretty decent amount of experience in battle. I knew that if I picked the perfect time to shoot at Eldia, he'd immediately raise his arm up and use Seraphim to block me, which would block his view. So I managed to swoop in and slip into a blind spot. Unfortunately for Seraphim, that meant being intentionally used as a meat shield.

I reduced the power of my attack just in case. I didn't want Eldia to notice, so I couldn't lower it by much, but I did what I could. However, I knew if I was moving in a straight line, he'd notice me even if I was temporarily out of sight. That's why I used my Roll skill.

"Groooooooohhh!"

‹What?!›

I dropped down from above Eldia's head with Roll. The momentum of flight, gravity, centrifugal force, and my body weight all combined to deliver a crushing blow to Eldia's back as I fell. The great tree shook violently as my huge body slammed down onto the branch he was standing on. Since my Roll was strengthened by Hi-Power, I expected him to take a great deal of damage, but as he fell, Eldia flapped his wings and regained his stance.

I stopped using Roll in midair and bit down on Eldia's wing as he tried to fly out of my reach. I was wrenched through the air by my jaw.

<Eat the open sky!>

The next moment, I was punched in the jaw by a powerful uppercut. My upper and lower fangs collided, sending the impact reverberating through my brain.

O-ouch...that sure was a 1,500-attack power uppercut! I was quickly reminded of the fact that this was not an opponent I could approach so easily.

I had a lot of HP, so I was somehow able to endure it, but there was no way I could deal with hits like that over and over again. I needed to back off and recover. If this was how I felt, even with all my HP, Seraphim would've died twice over already if it wasn't lucky.

My mind was hazy, almost paralyzed. I saw Eldia swinging his paw for another mighty blow.

Dodge! I've gotta dodge! I thought, but I couldn't get myself to move. The impact of the last blow to my brain was too great.

At my side, Partner's glaring eyes glowed bright red. A moment later, my body moved automatically to avoid Eldia's claws. It seemed Partner had moved my body with Master's Demonic Gaze to keep me safe, then gave me back control right after.

Th-thanks, Partner. I thought I was a goner for a second there.

Partner bit down hard on Eldia's wing. Eldia struggled to pull her off him, which made it impossible for us to continue flying, so Eldia and I fell, tangled together.

Hey, Partner, this isn't good! If he attacks you first, you'll die! Let go and get outta the way!

("*I can't bite all the way through, and I can't pull my fangs out either...*")

S-seriously? How tough is this guy's body?!

Our bodies, still entangled, slammed into one of the branches of the great tree. The impact broke us apart and we leaped away from each other.

I used Regenerate to repair the broken fangs and shattered bones from Eldia's uppercut, then Partner used Hi-Rest to finish the job. Eldia also seemed to be repairing the damage we'd done with his own Regenerate.

<*You're more skilled than I thought... I was careless. I didn't realize conserving my MP by not using Physical Barrier would have such a negative consequence.*> Eldia stared at me with bloodshot eyes. His body was cloaked in a magical light. As he said, he must've decided to use Physical Barrier now. *This guy's about to get even tougher to beat?*

As Eldia lurched to his feet, a thin cube of black light unfolded around his body, large enough to envelop him completely.

<...Hmm?>

I thought it might be one of Eldia's skills, but none of them seemed to fit the bill. As I watched, the black light got darker and more opaque, and at the same time, the cube began to shrink as though it was being compressed.

"Grrraaaaah!" Eldia's howl echoed through the foliage. Eldia and the branches inside the cube, barely visible behind the black light, were becoming more and more squished. Eldia cowered, his wings pressed tightly against his body.

What is this...?

"This is the most powerful type of gravity-based magic: Gravirion," Lilyxila said from the branch above us. "It takes...a bit of skill to handle one this large, but..." She was kneeling in place, panting from exertion; her attendant, Alphis, was gripping her shoulders to support her.

Gravirion, huh? Gravity and Gravidon were both pretty incredible skills, but this one was easily several degrees more brutal than the other two.

Spatial compression due to supergravity in an enclosed space. It seemed the reason Lilyxila told me to restrict Eldia's movement was so she could use this when she had an opening. Eldia, despite all his stats and resistances, had been crushed to about three-quarters of his original size.

PART 5

· ·

ITURNED MY EYES BACK to Eldia, crushed inside the tiny black cube of light. Then I bowed my head.

I had a lot on my mind. *That dragon was more than likely my father in this world. He served the Demon King. He had been stuck waiting on this island for his resurrection for hundreds of years. Couldn't he have looked for another way to live his life?*

Partner came over to me and pulled my head to hers.

("You're overthinking again. Aren't you tired?")

...Maybe. But stopping is easier said than done.

I turned my attention once again to the compressed cube of what had once been Eldia, and suddenly, I felt strange.

"Um...forgive me for interrupting such a solemn moment, but you haven't acquired any experience points yet, have you?" Lilyxila asked in a quivering voice, her staff still pointed at Eldia. Bright red veins stood out on the pale skin at her temples. It was clear that she was exerting a great deal of effort.

Hm...? Oh, you're right. I haven't gotten any experience points yet.

"I'm sorry, but I can no longer...maintain the Gravirion spell. It's not...really something meant to be sustained for a long period of time, so..."

Huh?

The black cube of light faded, then disappeared. Eldia's compressed body began to swell, scales cracking and blood spilling from every joint. Fresh blood flowed from the empty holes where his eyes had been.

But as I watched, Eldia's injuries began to close up, and his distorted body started to regenerate.

‹A powerful spell. But unfortunately, not powerful enough to finish me off.›

Eldia's newly emerged eyeballs lit up. *No matter how I look at it, this recovery is going way too fast. Wait... That's right, he was already using Regenerate when he had Gravirion cast on him.*

However, his body was a mess: His wings were broken and shriveled, and although he could move his legs, his joints cracked like they were being destroyed with every movement. He still wasn't fully recovered. If I hit him now, he wouldn't be able to fight back. I kicked off the branch and swooped down at Eldia.

<The distance is not ideal, but this is beyond my control. It seems I have underestimated the humans providing backup a little.>

Eldia glared past me, directly at Lilyxila. Then, with a thud, he stomped on the branch of the great tree with his hind foot and roared.

"Groooooohhh!"

Even in midair, I felt a powerful pulse reverberate throughout my body. A blinding light obscured my vision, and I was blasted back. I tried to catch myself but failed; my entire body went numb. Instead, my back struck a branch with a loud thud.

Somehow, I managed to reach my arm out and grab onto the branch below me. I looked back at the spot where I'd been attacked and realized that that branch was on fire.

Is that Eldia's Lightning Strike skill? I didn't expect it to be so fast! I might've been able to spot it before he used it, but there's no way to deal with it once it's already been cast. What a nasty skill!

A sphere of scorching fire appeared in front of Eldia's face, which he immediately sucked into his mouth.

I had a strong sense of déjà vu; this was the Drago Flare skill I'd seen used by one of Tolemann's subordinates, a man who could turn into a dragon. I remembered it being incredibly powerful when he used it. Eldia was trying to use it on me, to kill me. *C-come on, man, that's not cool!*

Eldia bent his neck and shook his head, then opened his mouth, aiming straight my way. A crimson laser sprayed out at me in a horizontal line.

I leaped into the air, barely avoiding it. The beam passed right under me. The scales on my hind paws seared with pain from the heat of the terrifying blast.

The beam hit the trunk of the great tree, carving a deep groove into the side that continued to burn and spread.

Damn, that skill is no joke. It seemed really powerful when Tolemann's underling used it too, but this one had even more range and scope. It was probably more powerful to boot—not that I wanted to find out.

I'm in trouble. If he keeps shooting out skills with such a ridiculous range, I won't be able to dodge 'em forever. That skill's gotta drain a lot of MP, though...

I looked back over to Eldia. His wings and scales were still broken, which made me think he had stopped using Regenerate because he was trying to preserve his MP. *Almost there! Just a little more!*

"Kraaaaah!"

Seraphim, who seemed to have recovered again, flew up from the lower branches and landed on one at about the same height as me. It lowered its head and glared at Eldia, preparing to strike.

I'll match your timing to make sure our next attack does some real damage. I glanced over to Seraphim, who gave a small nod. *Looks like Seraphim got my message.*

Just as I was about to close the distance between us and Eldia, his mouth glowed red again, and out came more fiery rays. Eldia moved his head haphazardly, spitting the fire out at random. Some of his attacks hit the great tree, only serving to intensify the blaze.

I spread my wings, leaped off the branch, and soared into the air. It would be a lot easier to dodge his attacks with the ability to move in three dimensions.

The blaze of Eldia's Drago Flare followed me. I desperately tried to evade, but the high-density flames were closing in right behind me. As soon as the onslaught finished, Eldia conjured up another mass of flames, engulfed it, and readied himself to attack again.

I thought Eldia was more of a melee type who capitalized on his high stats, but I was wrong. Maybe he didn't prefer long-distance skills, but he definitely liked to use ranged attacks.

‹I'm not done yet!›

Eldia stomped his foot. I knew that didn't mean anything good, so I rolled to the side to throw off his trajectory. A blinding flash of light hit the spot where I'd just been, and the branch in front of me fell to the ground, charred black.

C-crap! I can't even afford to try and get close! Between his Lightning Strikes and Drago Flares, it's a miracle I'm not fatally injured yet!

"Master Illusia! Our opponent's body isn't completely regenerated! He can't fly with those crushed wings! Let's get out of here while we have the chance!" I looked to where the voice was coming from and saw Lilyxila and Alphis on top of Seraphim.

She was right; Eldia was just too strong. A max-level rank A was no joke. If he kept firing off Drago Flares, it was only a matter of time until our luck ran out.

I launched up, endeavoring to retrieve Allo and the others. The Drago Flares paused once more. When they did, Lilyxila pointed her staff at Eldia.

"Holy Spear!"

Five spears of light appeared and shot down toward Eldia. He jumped out of the way, causing the spears to hit the branch he'd been standing on instead. The branch snapped off and fell to the ground.

I kicked off from the thick branch of the great tree and jumped to an even higher one. The branch I was just standing on was engulfed in a powerful ray that sparked flames. It broke off and fell, charred and burning, to the ground below. If I'd been any slower, I would've been grilled to a crisp.

As I looked behind me, I noticed the mass of heat that had just burned off the branch was following me. Below me, branches of the great tree were burning and breaking off one by one.

Partner sent me a thought. *("I'll watch our backs! You just focus on watching where we're going!")*

R-right, got it. I'll leave it to you, then, Partner.

Eldia was just too strong. He held the most powerful dragon Title Skill of the modern era—he was clearly no ordinary foe. In fact, I wouldn't be surprised if he was the most powerful dragon in the world. If we wanted to defeat him, we should've caught him off guard with a surprise attack before he engaged us. Lilyxila might've had the guts to do something like that, but I unfortunately did not.

He was bleeding through the cracks in his busted scales, and his wings were broken. He couldn't move properly in that condition, let alone fly, and he hadn't had any time to use Regenerate. He probably thought if he stopped his onslaught to focus on recovering, he'd risk another attack from me or Lilyxila. There was no doubt he was getting backed into a corner, but his eyes remained fixed firmly on me and Lilyxila, in the air.

Once again, the sound of destruction caused by Drago Flare stopped. *Did he run out of MP? Or is he going to Regenerate now that we're keeping our distance?*

("*The last volley is over! He's just recharging!*")

Oh. Right...

I didn't want to assume this was a recurring pattern, but it *was* an opportunity for me to grab Allo and the others. I picked up speed and flew to the branch where they were waiting.

Allo clambered onto my lowered head while Nightmare shot some spider silk onto my back and hopped on. I grabbed Treant with my front paws, then launched off the branch of the great tree. Lilyxila and Alphis, atop Seraphim, started moving in my direction.

Lilyxila called out to me. "Let's just get out of here! That dragon is wounded; I doubt it will give chase. Those random attacks are likely just a deterrent to keep us away, and it has lost a lot of MP. I do not think it will try anything rash." I nodded in agreement.

But...this is an opportune time to defeat Eldia. He didn't use Drago Flare in the beginning; I don't know if that was because I was there or out of consideration for the great tree, but no doubt his own pride and recklessness played a part too.

Because of that, we managed to begin with a close-range battle, and, with Lilyxila's help, we launched a successful attack. She followed up with her super powerful Gravirion attack. Then he used Drago Flare, attacking at random to keep us away while he was immobilized, and that wore his MP down a lot. But next time, he'd probably start using Drago Flare from the very beginning. Not to mention, it would be much harder to hit him with Lilyxila's Gravirion now that he knew about it.

However, I had Allo and the others to worry about. Eldia wasn't an opponent they could best with the attacks they had currently; he would destroy them. I doubted whether Allo's earth magic, Nightmare's webs, or Treant's gravity magic could even make a dent against him.

It'd be next to impossible to hit Eldia while he was flying around, and even if they did, it wouldn't mean much in the face of his huge size, sturdiness, and overwhelming power. From the very beginning, it was clear that Eldia was not an enemy they had in their sights, but it wouldn't surprise me if they got caught in the middle of a fight like that.

And, although I knew I couldn't say it out loud...on an emotional level, I didn't want to fight Eldia. But I knew that if he knew about the Demon King's resurrection, he would try to meet up with him immediately, killing any humans he saw along the way. I couldn't just leave a monster like him to his own devices.

That being said, if I could defeat the Demon King before he gained enough power to reveal himself, Eldia might be able to continue living out his retirement years in hiding on this island. Eldia's Divine Voice might clue him in sooner or later, but it didn't seem like the Demon King had made any attempt to contact him so far. *There's still time before he finds out,* I thought, perhaps naively.

Eldia had been waiting for the Demon King to rise for five hundred years, though. It felt a little cruel to keep him in the dark.

As I flew away, I looked behind me from time to time. The eerie island on the edge of the world—which I had tentatively named Adam Island—with its huge trees and rolling black clouds, was getting farther and farther away. Was Eldia still crouched at the base of that tree?

"Wh-what was the meaning of all that, you dreadful Ouroboros?!" bellowed Alphis, who had just stood next to Lilyxila with her mouth agape during the fight, pretending to guard her. "You and that monster knew each other, didn't you? Do you really mean to place your trust in this beast, Saint Lilyxila?!"

Seraphim, clearly also put off by Alphis's behavior, gave its passenger an annoyed look.

"Enough, Alphis. You're being rude." Lilyxila's gentle expression had disappeared; she now stared blankly at Alphis. It wasn't until Alphis lowered the hand she had gripped around the hilt of the sword strapped to her waist and stepped back that Lilyxila nodded, and her original expression returned.

"F-forgive me, Saint Lilyxila," Alphis said.

"Goodness, no need to apologize to *me*, Alphis. You certainly are a strange one sometimes, aren't you?"

Lilyxila's somewhat venomous tone made Alphis's shoulders shake. The knight turned and bowed deeply to me instead. *O-oh...no, it's fine. I'm used to it.*

"Allow me to rephrase my question. I am curious to know what your relationship is with that Dragon King. Would you be willing to discuss what you know of him?"

W-well, he's not just your average, neighborhood dragon. I didn't see any reason to rub shoulders with him, so I avoided fighting with him. He hates humans, but he's been alone on that island for hundreds of years. Because of that, I doubt he'd go out of his way to come after us, even if he thinks of us as his enemies.

Lilyxila pondered this for a while, staring at me with a finger in her mouth. I didn't lie, but...did she get the impression that I was talking about myself?

I decided to think about something else, so she wouldn't catch on with her Telepathy.

So, in my mind, I envisioned rolling up a whole bunch of ballrabbits side by side, then concentrated on stacking them, one by one, into a ballrabbit tower. There were hundreds, maybe thousands of ballrabbits of various sizes scattered around in the vast white space, and I continued building my ballrabbit tower until it seemed like it reached the end of the sky. Thousands of "Pfeff!"s echoed through my mind.

"...I see. I knew of this island from folklore, but I had no idea there were such powerful monsters inhabiting it. I suppose my perspective is still rather limited." Lilyxila frowned skeptically for a moment...then her expression softened, and she laughed.

I-It worked?! Great! I'll use that as my new anti-Telepathy skill from now on!

REINCARNATED AS A
DRAGON
HATCHLING

1

A Certain Dragon King's Past

PART 1

MY HOME was deep within an ancient temple, half buried in the earth, on the westernmost island of the world. I woke there, contemplated life itself, frolicked with Adam and the others, and then went to sleep. My days were filled with little else. "Remain hidden deep underground until the next Demon King awakens." This was the mission given to me by the Will of the World, the god in which the previous Demon King, King Noah, believed.

I was to assist the next Demon King in his quest to rid the world of mankind. That mission also served as atonement for my sins toward King Noah and my compatriots, who entrusted their hopes to me before meeting their demise. Back then, I was still too weak to be involved in King Noah's battle. If I'd had the power then that I had now, things would have ended differently. I was weak, foolish, and most of all, a coward.

"Hyoo?"

As I sighed over the painful memories of my past, I heard a high-pitched coo from nearby. It was a Nomadic Dragon; an island-hopping dragon that had come to visit this island in the West just the other day. Her body was a pale blueish white, with a long, slender neck. Her eyes were large and blinking, and her massive wings shone when the light hit them.

Nomadic Dragons were those who made a habit of traveling around the world to find and mate with more powerful dragons, then flew to even more distant lands to leave their eggs. But there were few Nomadic Dragons with the courage to come all the way to the edge of the world. I had been living in hiding on this island for nearly five hundred years, but until now I had never seen one visit this island before.

The Nomadic Dragon came closer and rubbed her cheek against my shoulder.

"Hyoo!"

‹You have never before seen a dragon as beautiful as I, have you?› the Nomadic Dragon asked.

I sniffed back. *‹You are nothing compared to Hanera.›*

The Nomadic Dragon glared at me, frustrated. Her eyes were filled with reproach. *Hmph. Do I seem like the type to go out of my way to ensure a female dragon is in good spirits?* After a period of silence, the Nomadic Dragon cooed once more.

"Hyoo..."

‹Well, well, well. It seems the Nomadic Dragon wishes to hear what I have to say after all. Hmph, very well. Listen carefully, then. I wish to speak of my former mate, Hanera; my best friend, Todorius; and the Demon King Noah, whom I still respect and admire to this day.›

‹My tale begins around five hundred years ago, when I was still a rank B Dark Dragon. This was when I met Demon King Noah for the first time. I was weak back then, and in danger of being defeated by the private army of a human noble...›

PART 2

. . . .

I WAS SURROUNDED by more than twenty men dressed in armor with iron helms and red plumes. They were the private army of Viscount Domaz, the man who owned the forest where I dwelled.

"Come on, men! This time, we'll bring that Dark Dragon's head back to Viscount Domaz on a silver platter!" the private army's leader, Quixote, shouted from the rear of the pack. He was a tall man with a cleft chin and small, beady eyes. It was not easy for me to remember the faces of humans, but I was tired of seeing this one. This man had already challenged me to a fight five times, and each time he had lost. I had assumed he would not come again after I bit one of his arms off, but he simply showed up with an artificial limb this time. Perhaps incensed by his hatred for me, instead of backing down, he was better equipped than ever and had come with a plan.

At Quixote's instruction, countless swords struck me in unison. I kicked off the ground and jumped into the air, but several of their blows still collided with my legs, cutting my scales.

"It's in the air! You know what to do!" Quixote shouted excitedly, his big mouth wide open.

"Fire Arrow!" "Fire Arrow!"

The swordsmen near my feet began to shoot magical fire arrows upward, sending a line of bright red flames at me. I dropped down to try to dodge them, but a flaming arrow pierced my wing and set it ablaze.

"Grrrooohhh..."

Were they intentionally aiming at my wings from the beginning?! There were not many humans who could handle the magic of Fire Arrow. It was long-range and quite powerful. They probably all crowded around me to coax me into the air so they could shoot me down as I flew.

The first time I battled Quixote's group, I emerged the clear winner. But each time we fought, his tactics became more sophisticated and specialized, and now Quixote had finally set my wings on fire.

As I fell awkwardly from the sky, the swordsmen all swung their blades at me. Countless shockwaves cut through the wind toward me. *Don't you dare underestimate me, fools...!*

I raised my tail as I fell and swung it viciously at the soldiers. Their swords slashed, carving thick lines across my body. But I endured. My tail struck a wide swathe of his men, knocking them off their feet. I knew I had broken some backs and some necks and had rendered some soldiers completely immobile. Even those who hadn't been directly hit tumbled to the ground from the force of the impact.

"Q-Quixote, sir! W-we just lost three men!"

"A necessary sacrifice! The time is now, men! Give 'im all you've got!"

Hmph. How many more men can he afford to lose? The space behind me had been cleared out by my tail swing—there was no way they could attack my blind spot now.

I'll burn them all away at once. I took a big step back, gathered magic power in the pit of my stomach, opened my mouth wide, and inhaled.

"Now! Release the powder!!" Quixote shouted. The men around him began slashing at the binding of several burlap sacks to open them, then threw them in my direction. A yellow powder flew through the air past me. *What is this?*

I was still in the process of inhaling to release Scorching Breath, so I breathed in some of the yellow powder. Within moments, my throat erupted in searing pain, and my entire body went rigid.

"Ghhg, oghh, grraaagh!"

They... They did it. They found a way to counter my Scorching Breath!

"Tch! I told you all to hold your breath! What're you all getting all choked up about?!"

"I-It's no use, sir! It's a mixture of powdered lightning shrooms and flame moth scales; it's a poison designed for use against medium-sized dragons. The men at the front are getting paralyzed!"

A few of the soldiers who had fallen back looked at each other and stepped forward once more.

"Care!"

"Care!"

Care was a spell that removed status effects. They must've prepared it to counteract the effects of the poison. This was not good. Not only could I not move my body, but I also couldn't breathe properly, and my throat was in agonizing pain.

"Yes! You've finally done it, sir!"

"Now we'll all be recognized for our feats!"

The soldiers all slashed at me with glee. Countless blades sliced through my scales, gouging out my flesh. I'd never thought these lowly soldiers would one day defeat me. I had hoped that when I died, it would be at the claws of another dragon, in a one-on-one fight, but it seemed as though that dream would not come true...

My death is imminent...eternal sleep awaits. My ravaged body would become food to the humans, my existence just another paragraph in their heroic sagas. It was shameful, but there was nothing I could do.

Be proud, Quixote, for you have won. Your persistence and strategies have defeated me. I did not like you, and I did not wish to see you here, but I praise you for your victory over me.

"Rest."

Suddenly, lifeforce returned to my body. *What...? What is happening? Who in the world...?*

"S-sir?! Why did you heal him?!"

Q-Quixote was the one who cast it on me? Why?

"Why? The bastard still owes me for my left arm... I won't let you die so easily, Dark Dragon scum!"

My closed wounds were opened once more by Quixote's sword. Again, he cast Rest, and again his sword slashed into my flesh.

"Give me back my left arm! I was the best swordsman in the land until it was taken from me! You ruined me!"

Did these men have no respect at all toward those who have fought for their lives against them...?! Perhaps this was the difference between the hearts of humans and dragons. It was a shame to lose my life to such wretched beings.

At that moment, a voice echoed in my head. *‹Losing to a bunch of humans...how pathetic. You truly intend to make him one of us, King Noah?›*

‹He is a rank B– dragon. There is no reason to pass him up.›

Quixote's soldiers looked around in confusion. Then their gazes turned skyward, and their faces paled.

"S-sir! Call a retreat! There are...there are two adult dragons coming!"

"Wh-what?! Damn it! After all I've endured to get this far! I'll just finish off the Dark Dragon, and then—"

A dragon descended from above and landed squarely on top of Quixote, no doubt killing him instantly. The other soldiers screamed in terror and scattered.

<Well met, Dark Dragon. You're in luck. The Demon King, King Noah, says he's going to save you. You should be grateful.>

The dragon who'd trampled Quixote had a blueish-black body and a third eye on its forehead. Two massive, wicked-looking horns grew from either side of its head.

<I am Todorius, a B+ Nidhogg. It's a pleasure to meet you, little rank B-.>

Another dragon descended from above. Like me, it had a jet-black body, but it did not look to be of the same species as me.

<And I am Noah, a Plague Dragon. I am only rank B now, but one day I will rule over the entire world as the Demon King.>

<The Demon King?>

As I knew it, the Demon King was a king of monsters who appeared once every few hundred years to command monsters in an effort to wipe out all of mankind. It was said that long ago, there was a time when he succeeded in killing the hero who was meant to be the

savior of mankind, and thus established a paradise for
monsters.

But such tales were not to be believed. Besides, why
should I follow a dragon who was only as powerful as me?
From what they'd both said, his subordinate, Todorius,
had a higher rank than Noah himself, who was supposed
to be the Demon King. I was surprised Todorius followed
him willingly.

*‹Todorius, was it? A dragon is not meant to grovel to a
dragon who is beneath him. Have you no pride?›*

*‹...King Noah, don't you think this guy would be more
use to us as experience points?›* Todorius asked Noah,
ignoring me completely.

‹I don't mind dragons with a bit of pride,› Noah replied.

‹As my king commands, then...›

With that, Todorius turned his head toward the heavens and let out a roar. Light enveloped my body, and the
wounds marring my flesh healed. Hi-Rest. It seemed he
had some decent skills.

‹What are you playing at? I am—›

‹You obey dragons who are above you, yes?› As he spoke,
Todorius pounced on me. His B+ rank was no fluke. He
was fast; too fast for me to react.

‹Then bring it on!›

He raised his arm and unleashed a Whirlwind Slash.

I couldn't evade it. I blocked the attack with my wings, which shredded them, but allowed me to avoid a direct hit.

<Not so prideful now, are you?>

Todorius headbutted me. A heavy thud reverberated through my wings, making me see stars. I fell to my knees.

<Taste my poison claws!>

His claws ripped through my still-guarding wings. After those hits, I understood. I would surely die under this dragon's onslaught if it continued. I tried to fall back, but I couldn't get free of him.

<Get the picture now?!> He struck me with blow after blow. He easily overwhelmed me, and I fell headfirst to the ground.

<Enough, Todorius. Any more and you'll kill him.>

<If he won't join us, then he's no use to us anyway, right?>

While Todorius was distracted by Noah, I seized my chance and lunged to bite him.

"Graaaaah!"

Todorius blocked with his arm, protecting his throat.

<B-bastard! You can still move after all that?!>

But that was as far as I got. The poison had taken its toll. My consciousness began to slip away, and I collapsed on the spot.

<I never thought I'd be bested so easily in one-on-one combat...>

There were no excuses to be had. I had even been restored to full health before the battle. I was defeated. I was nothing more than the king of a tiny forest. I had convinced myself that the only reason those soldiers had defeated me was because they had used their numbers and cowardly tricks against me. But now, this Todorius had defeated me head-on. *How shameful. If only I'd been fast enough to respond to his attack, I would've won...!*

Todorius's claws pierced my neck.

<We've got no time to waste. Choose. Swear allegiance to King Noah or die here.>

<...I shall submit. For now.>

<That's a good attitude. You're an unexpectedly honest one, Dark Dragon.> Todorius looked down at me and gave a hearty laugh.

<However, one day, when I am more powerful than you...I will eat you alive, Todorius. You should prepare yourself for that. I do not approve of your self-proclaimed Demon King either...but he is too puny to be my opponent, so I will let him go for now.>

With that, I lowered my head to the ground. I had reached my limit. At my current strength, even keeping my head raised was painful.

<...Well, that's how it is, King Noah. Shouldn't we get rid of him after all?>

<Now, now, Todorius. He makes for interesting company, don't you think?> Noah responded, sounding amused. I heard a noise. Todorius seemed to be moving his face closer to mine.

<Listen up, Dark Dragon. King Noah is on a mission to lead us monsters against the humans. He's still growing, but eventually he'll evolve into a dragon who'll outclass us all!>

A sharp pain jarred my skull. He must've kicked my head with his foot. *Do as...you like now, Todorius...but one day, I'll...!*

PART 3

AFTER THAT, I followed Noah and Todorius out of Viscount Domaz's forest. We made for the great forest at the corner of the continent, which the humans had not yet civilized, and settled there for a while.

<Hey, Dark Dragon! I've hunted us a tasty bird to eat!>

Demon King Noah wandered by with a huge bird in his mouth. The sight of him made me furious. Why should I have to defer to such a stupid, carefree dragon?

<You want some?>

Ignore him. Just ignore him. I crouched in place, hiding my presence.

The other day, when I challenged Todorius to a duel for the twelfth time and was instantly defeated, Todorius said, *‹Just so you know, King Noah is even stronger than me. He even defeated me once.›* I could tell he meant it, but looking at Noah's stupid face now, I had a hard time believing it.

"Groooooohhh!" Noah roared.

You fool, what the hell do you think you're doing, letting the entire forest know your whereabouts? Did he really believe I got lost? I was only hiding like this because I don't want to get needlessly chummy with him! Offering for another adult dragon to take your food...how shameful. Was he an idiot? How could Todorius follow the command of someone like him?

‹King Noaaaah! You called?› Todorius responded, flying toward the sound of his roar. *Oh, right. They're* both *idiots.*

‹Todorius! I was hoping to share my meal with that Dark Dragon to deepen our friendship, but I can't find him anywhere! Find him for me, would you?›

‹Good idea! Leave it to me; that useless dragon must be hiding from us again! Give it up, Dark Dragon! You can't hide from Nidhogg's Eye of Truth!›

As soon as he said it, Todorius soared up, then swooped down directly toward me. The third eye on his forehead was glowing. *Can that detect other skills? Crap, not good!* I immediately took off at a run, but Todorius landed squarely on my back. He pinned me to the ground effortlessly and clasped his jaws around the base of my neck.

<Dark Dragon secured!>

What the hell?! He's even faster than he was during our duel! Could he give me a break for once?!

<I'll do no such thing. This is simply a reflection of my loyalty to King Noah.>

"Grooooohh!"

With a howl of fury, I pulled my neck out of Todorius's jaws and swiped at him point-blank with my claws. Todorius blocked my attack with his long tail.

<This makes thirteen wins, Dark Dragon.>

Then his tail collided with the side of my face. My brain rattled from the impact. I fell to my knees, writhing with pain. *D... Damn it...it's no use. I still can't beat him.*

<Dark Dragooon! Come and dine with us!>

Noah landed in front of me, the giant bird still clutched securely between his teeth.

<Hm? What happened to him?>

I decided to pretend to be out cold.

<He seems to be knocked out, but my Eye of Truth tells me he's faking it.>

Damn you, Todorius...!

<Up and at 'em, Dark Dragon! Come on, don't make me tickle you!>

Numerous sharp, red-hot pains erupted all over my body.

"Gwaaaaaagh!"

<Wah ha ha ha ha ha! Seems like your belly's pretty ticklish, eh? How cute!>

<King Noah, your claws are too sharp for jokes like that! You're not a baby dragon anymore, you know!>

<O-oh, right! C'mon, get it together, Dark Dragon! You're fiiiine!>

<Don't try to rub him with your claws; you'll only make it worse! Here, I'll use Hi-Rest, so please just stay back!>

D-damn them both... One day I'll tear out their throats with my fangs...!

Later, when I was feeling better, I ate every last bite of roasted bird Noah had offered in abject humiliation. I was in such a bad mood that I couldn't even taste it. To make matters worse, Noah kept calling out to me as I ate, saying, *<It's good, right?! It's gotta be delicious!>*

Now that I thought about it, this was the first time in my life that I'd shared a meal with another monster.

When one eats, they opened themselves up to attack. I had always thought that eating with others made me too vulnerable.

The next day, Noah brought me prey again. The day after that, I managed to hunt something down first, so we split the catch between us. It was unpleasant for me at first, but as the days went by, it became the norm for us, and I lost my desire to resist.

But let me make one thing perfectly clear: I still haven't agreed to be one of Noah's underlings!

PART 4

"M*wooooooo!*"
    "*Grrraaaaaah!*"

I was standing alongside the idiot Todorius, watching Noah's battle. He was fighting a massive golden-haired bull, a particular species of Graffant called King Graffant according to Noah. King Graffant was rank B; Noah was a B– Plague Dragon, which meant his opponent was slightly stronger than him.

Even so, King Graffant was clearly outmatched. Noah kept some distance between them and used Whirlwind

Slash to inflict some damage. Then, when King Graffant charged at him, he counterattacked with a tail strike. Next, he retreated and released another Whirlwind Slash. The moment King Graffant gave him an opening, he unleashed a series of blows on it, striking alternately with his tail and claws. Finally, he lifted King Graffant off the ground and hurled it against a large tree. Its massive frame shattered the tree, then fell to the ground, lifeless.

Wh-whoa... This is the first time I've ever seen Noah really fight. He's no joke. It's not that he's fast, or that his attacks are particularly powerful, but it's just that he always finds the most advantageous position and uses all the right moves on his enemy before it has a chance to react. With skills like this, he really could go head-to-head with Todorius.

<So? What do you think? This is why I say King Noah is even stronger than I am.> Todorius said proudly. He must've noticed I was watching Noah's moves. I turned my head away from him, furious.

<Fighting like that...it's cheating.>

Todorius blinked in surprise.

<Oh? I'm shocked you noticed. But what he's doing isn't cheating, per se. He's simply using a skill granted to him as the Demon King.>

I knew it. He was way too good at anticipating his enemy's actions. The fact that he won every engagement was unnatural too. Was that the power of the Demon King at work?

‹As you know, King Noah's eyes can see the strength, status, and skills of living creatures. He reads his enemies' thoughts with Telepathy and predicts their actions by comparing them against their skills and his own experiences in combat. On top of that, in critical situations that will determine the outcome of the battle, he gives himself some insurance with Laplace.›

‹...Laplace? What's that?›

‹Ahh, yes. That is a power bestowed to King Noah by the Will of the World. With this ability, he is able to analyze the information provided to him to read and gauge the probability of simple events. That is why King Noah never loses: He can already see the scene that will follow before he even thinks about what the enemy will do next.›

What the hell? What kind of foul play skill was that? If I intended to tear his throat out one day, how was I going to get past something as unbeatable as that...? He seemed even harder to take down than Todorius!

‹Hmph,› snorted Todorius. *‹Let me be clear: You are no match for King Noah. You may challenge me to a hundred battles, but even still, you will never be able to*

land a single blow on him when he's taking things seriously. Your moves are too predictable.>

Grrr...! I hated to admit it, but he was right. As I was, I'd never be able to beat Noah. I had underestimated him because he was a lower rank than Todorius, but I was simply no match for him. I thought all that stuff about him being the Demon King was just talk, but...there was something in his movements that felt strange.

<Woo-hooooo! I did it! We're eating King Graffant steak tonight, folks!> Noah said, wagging his tail happily.

And he's back to being a simpleton. What the hell is his deal?

<More importantly, your level, King Noah!> Todorius said. *<Have you maxed your level yet?!>*

<Just leave it to me! I'll make this dinner perfect!>

<First tell me about your levels! I don't care about that big golden cow!>

<You don't care, Todorius?! How can you say that?! It's a golden cow! It's gonna taste amazing!>

...It seemed like even Todorius had trouble reining in Noah's stupidity.

<Anyway, I guess with this I can be a rank A dragon now? Let's see... I've got "Gorgon Dragon," a cursed dragon with evil eyes...multi-headed giant dragon "Hecaton Dragon"... Ooh, this "Pandora" one seems the coolest to me!>

<What are their details? You are blessed with the ability to choose which evolution you desire. Let's wait three days to decide, my lord. We must also consider when to time your evolution. You will be at a huge disadvantage while you are at a low level.>

At that moment, black, magical light began to pour from Noah's body. His black exterior transformed; branches sprouted from his entire body like plants, and his limbs grew thicker.

"*Urooooooooogh!*" Noah bellowed. I stood alongside Todorius, watching Noah closely.

Noah now had six eyes: two on the left, two on the right, and two more centered under his forehead. A broad, pointed exterior like coral protected his innards. In his chest, a massive crystal gleamed with a blackish glow.

<Mm, feels nice. So this is a Pandora?>

<King Noaaaaah!> Todorius shrieked. *<How glorious! I'm overwhelmed by your majesty, my king! However! Before we continue, I... I must say one thing!>*

I didn't like Todorius, but I did feel a little bad for the guy. Anyway, did this mean Noah had evolved? He wasn't just a dragon but a dragon capable of seamless combat, thanks to his foresight abilities. And now he was ranked even higher than Todorius.

I looked at Noah. Countless horns branched out in intricate patterns from his shiny black body, protecting him from harm. As I looked at the shining crystal in his chest, I could feel its monster battle instincts overflowing. There was no doubt about it: This guy was *strong*. Just looking at him, I was painfully aware that I was no match for him. He may actually have been born to be the Demon King after all. He had the sort of aura that just drew you in.

I had been staring at him, enraptured, but suddenly came back to myself and shook my head. *No, no, no! Inside that body is still the mind of an idiot! Don't be fooled, me!*

However, at that moment, a feeling sprouted inside me: the feeling that I'd quite like to stick around and see just what would happen to this dragon who called himself the Demon King.

PART 5

ALL AROUND US lay the scattered remains of huge, bright red butterflies. These butterflies had massive wings and three eyes.

<*A flock of Ogre Butterflies?*> Noah muttered. The countless magical black hands that Noah had summoned to make quick work of the swarm of butterfly monsters disappeared. It happened so fast that it felt wrong to call it a battle or a hunt. The Ogre Butterflies didn't even have a chance to notice it had begun before it was over.

<*Your skills are too overwhelming, King Noah.*> I was so disappointed. I couldn't even consider defeating Noah at this point. Pandora was on a different dimension. He was simply too powerful.

There were several other reasons why I had also begun to refer to Noah as "King Noah."

"Waaaah! Aaaah! Aaagh!"

The strange voice came from the hulking, humanoid mass of black scales that King Noah had created, known as a demi-man. His skill "Human-Monster Mirror" gave him the ability to transform humans into monsters and vice versa. It only worked on those with low magical power, but it was perfect for making a small army of minions. If he used it on a human, he could turn them into a demi-man: an ugly humanoid with scales and low intelligence. The demi-man would go on and on to Noah about how disrespectful I was to him, which annoyed me so much that I had to change my attitude toward him.

Although, admittedly, that was only one factor in why I now called him King Noah. I had been drawn to his strength for some time.

In total, we had about thirty demi-men under our control now. They had almost no intelligence; they would eat even their former human brethren with impunity. They were a pitiful species. I wasn't particularly fond of this type of skill, but King Noah said it was the Will of the World that he had them under his command.

King Noah's current species, Pandora, was incredibly strong. Along with his Human-Monster Mirror skill that straddled the boundaries between humans and monsters and his Dark Hand skill that conjured multiple powerful arms, his stats were also extraordinary. He was not as fast, but in return, his magic power, physical strength, and defense were well beyond the level of mine and Todorius's.

It was nigh on impossible to break through King Noah's defense with melee skills. If attacked with one, he would inflict his opponent with Pandora's Special Skill "Tainted Blood," which caused his opponent's body to rot away and turned them into Undead. If he was struck down, he would release "Light of Ruin" and a powerful death curse would be sprinkled all across the target area. Noah had said—entirely nonchalantly, as if it didn't concern him at all—that its range was wide enough to exterminate the population of an entire country.

<...King Noah, did you choose to evolve into Pandora in order to prevent yourself being defeated by the hero?> I asked. The hero was apparently a human hero who appeared in order to oppose the Demon King. King Noah said that the hero's mission was to join forces with an assistant, the saint, to defeat him. As the Demon King, Noah's mission was to unite with the Beast King—who was currently acting independently—and the monsters.

However, not only was it impossible to defeat Noah as Pandora, but if he was somehow felled, he would cause a great deal of death and destruction to the humans. For this reason, not even the hero, champion of the humans, could defeat him.

<I heard this from a human traveler before I met you, Dark Dragon, but...the name of this new hero is said to be Mia. Rumor has it they are much stronger than the hero of the previous age. But it is said that this Mia also has the disadvantage of being too kind.>

<Then...you didn't actually choose your evolution at random?>

<Oh, Laplace has been telling me all about my evolutionary tree for a long time. What evolutions will be possible once I reach my level cap, which evolution I should choose...

all of that. I kept it quiet, though, because Todorius's reaction was so funny.>

King Noah made his Dark Hand float into the air and then pointed at Todorius with a single finger.

<K-King Noah?!>

I had mixed feelings about this.

<But Pandora's powers...they're unlike you, my king. I mean, toying with those you've defeated, exploiting your enemies' weaknesses, it all seems—>

At that moment, Todorius swung his claws at me.

<Watch your tongue! You dare to disrespect the Great Demon King Noah?!>

Noah's Dark Hand floated over to block Todorius's swipe.

<That's of no concern to me. It's not what I intended either. But Laplace, who has been manifested through the Will of the World, has told me that there will be no victory for the world of monsters without Pandora. That is how powerful a hero Mia is said to be.>

King Noah had spoken about this Laplace before. He was able to actively use Laplace's probability calculations. However, using it consumed MP, and its calculations were based only on information that was available to the user. Therefore, when King Noah used it in battle, it was only as a type of insurance for anticipating his enemy's next, single action. Using it for anything more than that would be risky.

That being said, Laplace required only a small amount of MP to use, and it could give accurate answers to a wide range of questions without regard to the amount of information the user had. It gave King Noah helpful predictions and gave him direction from the Will of the World on what he was to do next. He said it had guided him three times so far, including deciding his evolutionary path, and that if he had not complied the other two times, he would undoubtedly be dead by now.

Hmm... Am I the only one who can't help but think that the Will of the World smells a little fishy?

I had recently started to feel like King Noah was changing a little on the inside. It felt like he was losing his former cheery, playful demeanor. If this was due to the fact that he was forced to live his life as Pandora, which wasn't by his choice...could we really consider that a trend in the right direction?

No, enough. That shouldn't be any of my concern. I didn't like the stupid dragon he used to be anyway. It was precisely because Noah was the way he was now that I was willing to serve him. *Of course it is. That's how it should be.*

<Oh, also, you see, er...calling you Dark Dragon all the time feels a little clunky. Can I give you a name?>

I looked back over at Noah with a start.

<No? You don't want one? Okay, that's fine. I just thought it felt awkward, that's all,.> Noah said sheepishly, scratching at his chin with his Dark Hand. For some reason, I felt my eyes begin to burn. I didn't know why, but I suddenly found myself crying.

<Would you...give me the honor of granting me a name?> I asked.

<O-okay, okay! There's no need to cry about it!>

I couldn't say why I was crying. Words swirled around frantically in my brain; I tried to speak, but it came out in bits and pieces.

<I... I have heard from Todorius that you were the one to give him his name, my king. I fear that I am not yet considered worthy enough to be one of your servants...>

<D-don't be stupid! To be honest, I thought you might not want it... You see, I thought you still didn't want to follow me, and... Ack! It's hard to find the right words...!>

Just like that, I was convinced. Noah had not changed. And at the same time, I realized that I had unknowingly come to adore the somewhat scatterbrained Noah of the past.

<Believe it or not, I had your name picked out a long time ago. How do you feel about the name...Eldia?>

From that day forward, I was no longer just a Dark Dragon trailing along behind him but a dragon named Eldia, who served my one true king, King Noah.

PART 6

. . . .

WE'RE LEAVING THIS FOREST *and heading for the island to the West at the edge of the world.*>

About a year had passed since the day that I had begun to adore King Noah when he said this to me.

I vaguely recalled a lesson that King Noah had taught me once. Beyond the edge of the world lay a vast expanse of nothingness that extended for eternity. And near the boundary between that nothingness and the sea, one could find powerful, high-rank monsters that had lived for a very long time.

It was also said that in the northernmost ravine, the westernmost island of giant trees, the southernmost volcanic island, and the easternmost foreign lands, lay legends passed down for millennia by the humans. And that a huge black dragon was spotted flying around the island to the west nearly ten years ago.

<Ahh, I see. We're going after the dragon. If it still lives, it's likely a rank B or higher,> Todorius said.

King Noah nodded. *<Yes, that's right. You remembered.>*

Todorius looked at me proudly as he received Noah's praise. *Damn it, I should've said it first. Now it looks like I forgot.*

<But that's not the only reason, is it?> I asked, and Noah nodded deeply. *<You've seen the army of the Harunae Empire heading our way, haven't you?>*

The Harunae Empire was the largest human nation in the world. It was said that the hero was always born in this empire because they had the blessings of the Holy God.

Harunae's army was quite large. They apparently didn't believe that there was a Demon King walking the land, but when they learned of three adult dragons living together in a remote forest, they came to take preventative countermeasures. Although the hero, Mia, was not among them, a total of around two thousand soldiers had attacked the great forest where we lived. We fought them mainly with King Noah's Human-Demon Mirror skill, turning the enemy soldiers with low magic power into demi-men to wreak havoc. Then we informed them of King Noah's Light of Ruin skill that would activate when he died, to invite unrest among the soldiers. We somehow managed to defeat them in the end, but it was a dangerous battle. Any of us could have been killed.

And although we survived, we still suffered many losses. Noah lost all of the demi-men he had created. Because they couldn't fly, they couldn't escape when they were cornered, and the human soldiers greatly outnumbered them.

I had come to realize that we were at an overwhelming disadvantage against the humans. At our current levels, if they were willing to sacrifice everything and sent out human soldiers in droves, they could very easily drive us back. Making sure they knew about King Noah's Light of Ruin skill could act as a very useful deterrent moving forward...but on the other hand, because we told them about it, the hero Mia might have learned that Noah was the Demon King and that his true identity was a Pandora.

<*The humans won't be able to send their armies after us if we're at the edge of the world. It'd be impossible to send that many humans across the ocean at once. For now, at least, we must avoid engaging with the humans' main forces, rally strong comrades to our cause, raise our levels, and strengthen our forces.*>

It was said that every bit of land at the edge of the world was host to a plethora of strong monsters, which was why we'd never been there before. However, if that was our one chance at survival, then we had to take it. If we stayed here, we'd be annihilated.

<Do you think we're ready to take on that huge human army and the hero?> I asked.

Noah shook his head. *<Not yet. In addition to Mia and the human army, there's also the issue of Saint Lumira. She herself is not much of a concern, but if the legends regarding saints are to be believed, she should be able to use her skills to subdue powerful monsters. Since we haven't received any information from the human side for a long time, we don't know what kinds of monsters she has under her command or even if she truly has the power to command monsters in the first place.>*

I'd underestimated the humans. I should've been defeating them one by one before I ever discovered that Noah was the Demon King. The fact that our battle with the Harunae army had alerted them to his existence was not good either. We should've been stronger earlier. We were a move too late.

<There is still hope,> said Noah. *<If I'm able to find and kill the Beast King, and take his power, I can evolve into the legendary dragon of calamity and wipe out all the humans.>*

‹Why not try to work with the Beast King?›

‹Because there are too many variables. According to legend, the Beast King is a bit of a loose cannon. He lives a life of violence and rage and does not bow to the Demon King; in fact, he thinks of himself as king. Naturally, I cannot bow to such a being.›

We really couldn't cooperate with the Beast King? It felt a little unfair, seeing as the two human saviors got to work together.

‹However, if I acquire the power of the Beast King, I should be able to evolve into the legendary Calamity Dragon, Azhi Dahaka! Then those human armies will no longer be an issue!›

The legendary Calamity Dragon, huh? So in other words, for us to stand a chance, Noah had to evolve one more time.

‹I don't know where the Beast King is, but the fact that he hasn't appeared yet leads me to believe he's probably somewhere at the edge of the world. After I've increased my strength enough, I'll go to defeat him, then I'll evolve into Azhi Dahaka and start a great war against humanity!›

And so, we left the great forest behind and headed for the giant tree island in the west; not only to hide from the humans but also to pursue the black dragon that had been spotted there.

PART 7

‹*So this is the edge of the world?*›

It was a terrifying place, even for me. King Noah had described it as an island of giant trees, and that was certainly accurate; there were trees on this island so huge that even dragons like us could stand on them. They were more like mountains than trees.

To the west of the island, the sea was cut off by a waterfall so massive that it seemed to spill down into an endless void beneath.

‹*It's certainly true that only a few of the strongest humans could possibly reach this place. But don't you think we could have avoided contact with the imperial army and kept your identity hidden for longer if we'd come here earlier?*› Todorius asked Noah.

‹*Are you trying to accuse King Noah of poor leadership, Todorius?*› I asked, glaring at him with murderous intent.

Todorius just snorted, clearly annoyed. ‹*Eldia, you're just following him blindly. King Noah, you are fighting a war against the humans in which a single move can be decisive. If you do not act with reason, you will eventually be driven into a corner. If you have any doubts, you should speak up so that you can make the best use of them in the*› future, right? Why can't you understand that? Even you, with your brain half-eaten by avyssos, should be able to consider that.>

I was irritated. There might be some truth in what Todorius said, but even so, why did he have to put it like that? <What? Why are you saying all this? What's the point? You're just complaining about something that's already over.>

<If you have no intention of supporting King Noah and just want to run around without thinking, that's fine. I don't expect much from you, and I'm sure King Noah doesn't either.>

<I see. You've been taunting me. Very well, then. Dragons have no need for clever chitchat. From now on, let's speak with our fangs and claws, shall we?>

<I believe you were the one to poke at me first, Eldia. But all right. You are aware that I have won each of the eighty battles we've had against each other, correct?>

As much as I hated to admit it, I was still no match for Todorius. He was faster than me, and he also had a recovery skill, status skills, and a magic absorption skill. On top of his physical prowess, he had a more expansive set of skills, and his mind was quicker than mine.

<The eighty-first round is mine to win, though! Todorius! I will devour you and give your remains to a den of lion cubs and ants!>

<Bring it on, then, Eldia! I'll beat you again, and make sure you never open your cocky mouth again either! I'll carve the difference in our rank into your bones! It's a good thing you have Regenerate, because I'm going to tear off all your limbs and shake you until you cry and beg for forgiveness!>

Todorius spread his wings, his third eye glowing red. That was his sign that he was ready for battle.

<Come on, let's get this over with!>

I leaped into the air and flew low to the ground, approaching Todorius.

<That's enough, you two!> As King Noah shouted, a glowing, black spherical orb of magic deployed around us, trapping both me and Todorius inside. This was King Noah's Gravity skill.

<K-King Noah! Wait—>

The entire area was hit by a crushing wave of pressure. The terrain inside the circle sank deeper into the earth, and I was forced to crawl on my belly with my head on the ground.

<Honestly,> said Noah. *<I relax for one second, and this is what happens. I'd like to remind you both that we came to this place out of necessity and to keep an eye on what the humans are up to. I didn't* really *want to come here.>*

<But that's—> I began to ask, but Noah shook his head.

<There's a line in a human book that reads, 'When one ventures to the edge of the world, they will be absorbed by the strange indigenous peoples there with whom they can hardly communicate.' I only know what I've read about in books, but I doubt that I'll be able to convince them to serve under me.>

<Then why not just eat them alive, my king?>

<If I could, I would... Eldia, look behind you for a moment.>

At the sound of my name, I turned around immediately. Three unarmed humans were running straight at me from the center of the island.

<What? I thought you said they were a strange species, but those're just humans.>

<...Look closer,> Todorius said, his voice trembling. I stretched my neck out further and realized that the humans running toward us had no heads; instead, their faces were embedded within their abdomens. I rubbed my eyes with my paws. I wanted to believe that what I saw was a hallucination.

What the hell were those things?

<I'll tell you right now, each one of them is much, much stronger than Todorius. I'm getting out of here as soon as I can. I'll meet you two at the top of that great tree.> With that, King Noah spread his wings and took to the sky.

<King Noah?!>

<Noah?!>

Todorius and I couldn't believe it. Our commander had just deserted us in the face of the enemy!

<Aha ha ha ha ha! Watch out, they have Gravidon! Now then, I'm leaving you two stupid dragons who like to fight over nothing behind and getting the hell out of here!> Noah's huge body quickly soared up and away. I stood there for a moment, watching him, then Todorius suddenly remembered I was there and headbutted me.

<Hey! What do you think you're doing?!>

<Look out, El-diot! Gravidon! Three of 'em, coming this way!>

<What?!>

I turned back to look and saw the three headless humans lined up, with black spheres of light floating in front of their faces. Gravidon had excellent power and speed, and it was one of the most powerful among the many offensive magic skills. Even so, the three of them in a row looked more comical than threatening. What a ridiculous island! It was certainly much better than getting attacked by a thousand humans...but it was still terrible. No wonder King Noah didn't come here any sooner. Until he'd learned to use Pandora's powers, he probably didn't think he could survive here.

‹King Noaaaaah! Wait for meeeee!› Todorius was already making a beeline for Noah.

‹King Noaaaahhh! You used us as decoys, didn't youuu...!›

I followed suit. An orb of black light came swirling past me, right above my head. *Ah, that was a close call.*

‹Wah ha ha ha ha ha!› Noah laughed, some distance ahead. Unfortunately for him, though, Pandora was very slow for a dragon species. Todorius and I passed our heartless majesty in no time and went far ahead.

‹Wah ha ha ha! Okay, my bad. Eldia, Todorius, get back here. H-hey, wait! I'm sorry, all right?! I'm sorryyyyyy!›

‹Hey, Todorius. How about the winner of the eighty-first round is whoever can make it to the top of that giant tree first?›

‹Okay, sure. But you do know that I'm faster than you and my flying skill level is higher than yours, right?›

We sped up, vying with each other for the lead.

Behind us, King Noah screamed, hit by two Gravidon orbs.

"Uwoooooogh!"

Todorius sighed and slowed down. *‹...Guess it's about time we go help him, huh?›*

‹...Yeah. I guess.›

Now that I'd thought about it with a cool head, I knew that what King Noah did was just a joke. I already knew he wasn't the type to actually abandon his subordinates and run away laughing. Maybe he was just trying to lighten the mood between me and Todorius.

Suddenly, I saw something in the distance and tried to look closer. It seemed to be a dragon, crouching on a large cliff on the other side of the island, far off in the distance. Most of the cliff was thickly covered grass, but the area around the dragon was completely barren. Perhaps the ominous miasma rising off the dragon's skin was deadly to plants—or to *everything*.

The dragon looked sinister, with a dense, wicked veil of magic coating its entire body. Something was constantly dripping from its skin, as if the surface itself was dissolving. It looked like it was made out of mud. Two pink lights gleamed beneath the fog of darkness; I realized after a second that they were eyes. Our gazes met, and suddenly my stomach felt like it tied up into knots. Was this some kind of skill attack? *Nah, no way. Not at this distance.*

Is that the dragon you're looking for, King Noah? It doesn't seem like the kind of dragon that'd be interested in joining up with you.

PART 8

AS WE LANDED on the upper branches of the giant tree, we were relieved to find that those strange, headless indigenous creatures weren't chasing after us. We definitely hadn't expected three monsters as strong as Noah to show up side by side. Noah breathed a deep sigh of relief when we landed and shook out his large frame.

<No, Eldia. We've been through enough for today already. You can't go off on your own.>

Hmph... I understood his point, but being forbidden to go off on my own like this made me feel like a hatchling being scolded by his mother. It was embarrassing to be treated like a baby, even if Todorius and I undoubtedly were like spring chickens to the rest of the inhabitants on this island.

<Hmm...? Oh, so that rule only applies to me? Todorius is fine?>

<Todorius is an excellent flier, so he can easily flee from danger. You're not allowed, Eldia.>

Hnnngh...! Out of the corner of my eye, I saw Todorius give me a small, mocking look.

<But what in the world were those things anyway, King Noah? I've never seen such a strange monster before. Neither has Todorius.>

<It seems they're known as Adams. They have high magical power, but they apparently excel in close combat. If they were able to surround me and hit me with a barrage of blows, even someone like me, whose strength is my greatest advantage, could be in danger.>

Impressive... They could unleash such powerful Gravidons and excelled in close combat as well? It seemed I was still stuck in a realm of monsters that were beyond my reach. But in order to be as useful as possible in the coming battle between the hero Mia and King Noah, they were monsters that I had to overcome in the near future. Would I ever be ready? I couldn't even imagine it from where I was now.

<O-oh, right! King Noah! When I was flying away, I saw an ominous-looking dragon crouched on a cliff on the other side of the island! If that's the dragon we're after, then I must say, I'm against adding it to our forces!>

<Ahh, you saw it too?>

King Noah had apparently spotted it as well. I glanced at Todorius, who shook his head. He must not have seen it.

<Guess you were too focused on running away,> I taunted.

<Excuse me...?> Todorius's eyes filled with anger, but Noah cleared his throat to interrupt our bickering.

<Why are you against it joining us, Eldia?> he asked.

<Because, well... Did you feel anything strange when you saw it? I've never seen a more sinister-looking dragon before. It felt like something unfortunate would happen to us if we let it join us. And it was just dripping with ominous magic. I feel like it'd be difficult to work together with it.>

<Hmm...a sinister-looking dragon?> said Noah. *<Sounds good to me. We are the Demon King and his subordinates, after all—beings who exist in the shadows of this world. We aim to exterminate the humans who rule this world and build a paradise of chaos infested with monsters. Sinister? Ominous? I am the Demon King Noah, and I do not fear such things. Do you disagree with anything I've said thus far, Eldia?>*

<...No, my king. If you insist it join us, then of course I will obey.>

King Noah was more determined than he'd ever been before. I thought it would be impossible to make that dragon bow to him, but if anyone could do it, it was him. I thought back to the eerie features of the dragon from earlier. Beyond ominous, it had also felt...vast, somehow. Immeasurable. If we had it on our side, I had no doubt it would be a valuable asset.

Todorius and I followed behind Noah as he made his way to the miasma-covered dragon crouching along the cliff at the edge of the island. The dragon turned its sinister red eyes toward the three of us. Noah took a few steps toward it, then stopped. Still, the dragon did not move.

<Hmm...>

<Don't get too close, King Noah,> Todorius said, stepping in front of him. *<The dragon's miasma seems to induce abnormal status effects.>*

<That goes for you too, Todorius. You've already been cursed and poisoned.>

The two of them retreated and used Care to heal their status effects. King Noah was a rank A dragon, and Todorius was equal to or better than me—and resistant to status effects as well. And still, the two of them were proceeding with extreme caution. It didn't feel like the right moment for me to make an entrance.

<What kind of dragon is it, King Noah?> I asked instead, and Noah's head turned to face me.

<A Nameless Ugly Dragon... It's said that there's never been a proper sighting of this dragon by humans because the poisonous gas it emits from its entire body makes it impossible for it to coexist with any living creature. Even I have to keep well away. It's also a rank A, like me. Its level is lower than mine, but even so, it could likely hunt me down if I gave it an opening.>

Was King Noah really going to let this dragon join us?

I noticed Todorius was also looking at the Nameless Ugly Dragon with discomfort.

Noah took a step forward, then rubbed at his eyes with his paw. They must've been stinging from the miasma.

‹Lord of this island, Magic Mist Dragon. I am Noah, the one born to become the Demon King. I am gathering forces in preparation for the coming battle with the humans that will decide the future of our world. I humbly ask that you join my cause and serve me as my subordinate.›

"Magic Mist Dragon" felt like a bit of a mouthful, but I figured our new acquaintance wouldn't take too kindly to being called a miasma dragon.

The miasma dragon looked up slightly, then gave a small shake of its head and returned to its original position.

‹Leave me. I belong to nothing and no one.› The dragon gave a small groan as it gave its telepathic reply; something it seemed inexperienced in. Its eyes, glowing red underneath the miasma, closed. The meaning was clear: This dragon was finished with our conversation.

‹But that's not how this works! We can't just leave you be if you refuse to join us. You're too powerful!›

The miasma dragon could have easily taken Todorius's words as a threat, but it did not react at all. Although Todorius usually acted quite calmly, he was as hotheaded as me—that was why we always clashed.

<A high-rank dragon who doesn't want to follow the Demon King is a threat to us! If you won't obey, then you'll be our food!>

Todorius leaped into the sky and began to attack the miasma dragon. I followed suit, kicking off the ground and aiming for the dragon's flank, but I kept my distance. I was going to cover Todorius, but while he specialized in resisting status effects, I knew I'd only be a burden if I got too close to the miasma.

The miasma dragon was a higher rank than both of us, so I didn't think there was any shame in the two of us working together.

<Fools...>

The miasma surrounding it thickened. It began to gather together and take shape, forming itself into a second, and then a third, gigantic tail. The tails struck the ground at a high speed and rebounded at random. Todorius was hit hard by one of them and was flung back.

<Todorius! Damn it...>

I flapped my wings and sucked air into my lungs. *Get ready to taste my Scorching Breath!*

<Dual Dark Sphere.>

Two shining black magic orbs shot from the miasma dragon. *Yikes, that was fast...and it shot two at once?!*

I exhaled the breath I had stored within me and shot out flames in a diagonal direction above me, the recoil sending me flying backward. I couldn't avoid the second orb; it hit my left thigh and exploded on impact. Blood spurted out from the wound, and I hissed in pain.

"Gwooooooogh!"

I fell headlong to the earth. *It's no use. We're no match for this dragon. It hurts, the miasma, it's sinking into my wound. Is my leg going to rot away?*

King Noah stepped forward to protect me and Todorius. He was quite close to the miasma dragon now and seemed to be struggling to breathe.

<...Magic Mist Dragon, I apologize for my underlings' rudeness, but if you intend to go any further, I shall have no choice but to put my all into stopping you.>

The miasma dragon lowered its tail dismissively and dissipated its additional miasma tails.

<Leave this island,> it intoned. *<The next time you come into my view, Noah, I will destroy you. I despise all living things. That is why I have come here, where there are few others around to bother me.>*

King Noah grabbed me in his jaws and dragged my body away. It was no use; the miasma dragon was unapproachable. On top of that, it said that if we stayed on the island any longer, it would treat us as enemies. We needed to leave and find another place to be, out of sight of the humans.

Have we dragged King Noah down with us? As I thought this, the miasma dragon turned its tail toward us and crouched on the ground again. Suddenly, I saw something strange from my line of sight. *Is that...a flower? What's a flower doing in the miasma dragon's domain?*

PART 9

HAVING FAILED to recruit the miasma dragon to our cause, we were perched on the branches of the great tree, reflecting on our failure.

‹*Forgive me, King Noah! In my haste, I made such an unforgivable blunder! I am entirely to blame!*› Todorius apologized, bowing deeply.

‹*...What's done is done. Even if we had approached it normally, things would have ended the same way. I wasn't expecting it to turn us away immediately, though.*› Noah shook his head in disappointment.

Todorius stared at me with wide eyes. ‹*Eldia! You need to apologize to King Noah too!*›

‹Why? I thought you said you were entirely to blame for all this, Todorius,› I said, playing innocent.

‹Bastard! There's such a thing as proper etiquette, you know! You attacked the dragon without the king's permission too! Don't you think it's disrespectful to not apologize to him?›

Noah held Todorius back from attempting to eat me. *‹Stop it, you two! Enough! There's no point in fighting!›*

That night, I slipped out from the branches of the great tree.

I couldn't stop thinking about the flower I'd noticed growing right in front of the miasma dragon. I wanted to be sure, but it was too dangerous to stop and check at the time. I had no idea what would happen if I incurred that dragon's wrath. So this time, I decided to go on my own. If things went awry, at least King Noah and Todorius would be able to escape.

I didn't know why I cared so much about that dragon. I doubted there was a chance I'd be able to convince it to join our cause. But I couldn't help it; for some reason, it made me uneasy.

‹...I thought I told you to leave me be.› The dragon in question was sitting along the cliff's edge.

‹I wanted to ask you one question.›

‹Too bad. I will not answer.›

The miasma dragon raised both its distorted wings. The poisonous gas in the air thickened and spread out further.

‹You say you despise all living things...so why is it that you're always staring at the flower in front of you?›

‹What?!› the dragon demanded, flustered. It seemed I wasn't mistaken after all. Neither Todorius nor Noah had noticed the flower growing behind the dragon, but I did, because I'd been shot down while I was trying to flank it.

Pieces of information began to connect in my mind, one after the other, as I observed the miasma dragon's reaction.

‹I think I get it now. That flower is the only one that can withstand your noxious fumes. That's why you're sitting on the edge of the island. If you move, you'll only add to the dead landscape.›

‹You...you dare provoke me...› The miasma dragon stared at me and lifted its paw. Its long claws took on a luminous glow in the darkness of the noxious air.

Ahh, now I know why I'm so curious. This miasma dragon was a lot like the dragon I used to be, when I hunted silently on my own. My pride wouldn't allow me to befriend another dragon, and this dragon was unable to do so because of the skills it possessed.

‹Come with us. Only dragons with strong scales like ours can stand by your side. Join us and use that power of yours for King Noah's sake.›

‹Go away, I said! Don't presume to know what it is I want! Your assumptions have offended me!› The miasma dragon raised both its wings completely, further increasing the range and density of the miasma. *‹If your wish is to die, then I will gladly grant it! Take your Demon King and run away as fast and far as you can!›*

I almost retreated, but I willed myself to stay.

‹Yes, I know. Saying all this from a distance doesn't seem very persuasive, does it?›

I kicked off from the ground and leapt at the miasma dragon. Its black shadow flinched, then trembled violently.

‹Y-you idiot! Do you truly have a death wish?!› Nine pseudo-tails made of solidified miasma sprouted from the dragon's body, giving it ten total tails that danced like tentacles in the air. *‹Get away! Leave this place or else! I'll kill you! I mean it!›*

‹How many times are you going to warn me?›

The closer I got, the hotter my scales became, burning in the miasma. Soon the heat turned into excruciating pain. My scales began to inflame and peel off in tatters. I countered with Regenerate.

<How about that? I don't have the same properties as that flower of yours, but I can still stand beside you! And when I evolve, my body will get even stronger! Your miasma will be nothing to me!>

"Kiiii, kyaaaaaaaahh!"

The miasma dragon roared and swung its long tail. But it missed me, as if it wasn't aiming for my body in the first place.

<You have a beautiful voice, you know. It doesn't match your appearance.>

<W-waah! Ahhh, ah! I! I am...!> The miasma dragon flinched and moved away from me.

One more push, I thought. *One more, and it will be willing to join us. But I don't think one more push is enough.* I already felt like my attraction for this miasma dragon was about much more than just increasing the number of powerful dragons under King Noah's command. I also just believed that this dragon would be better off coming with us instead of staying here to gaze at flowers for the rest of its life.

Let's see...right. One of the things that strengthened my loyalty to King Noah was when he gave me my name. Once he did that, I became very aware that he saw me as one of his companions. This dragon believed that there was no way it could have a companion. It suddenly occurred to me that the best way to break down this belief would be to give it a name.

<Magic Mist Dragon doesn't suit you as a name. I, Eldia, wish to grant you a name. From this day forth, you will be our fellow compatriot, Hanera. Hanera, come with me!>

With that, I reached out my arm and touched the shoulder of the miasma dragon I had named Hanera. My hand burned and began to dissolve. *Welp. Knew that was a bad idea.* As I reflected on this, Hanera's red eyes darted around in a panic, and her pseudo-tails wagged haphazardly through the air.

<D-d-don't! Don't t-touch me!>

Two blows from her tail struck my abdomen in quick succession. I was blasted back by the fatal blow and rolled a few dozen meters along the ground before stopping when my head hit a large rock. I desperately used Regenerate, but I couldn't keep up with the blood flowing rapidly from my body, and my consciousness began to fade.

So this is how I die...forcing my way through a miasma and getting smacked by two consecutive blows from a dragon much stronger than me. If only my level had been a little higher, I might've been able to hold out...

"K-kuoo, kuoooo?!"

Hanera rushed toward me, stricken.

"Gwuuuuuuuh?!"

Hanera's miasma was seeping into my entire body. *Well, it was a great idea, but it sure didn't work out the way I'd hoped.* I was going to die. My body slammed to the ground, and I writhed in pain.

Hanera paced back and forth at a distance for a little while, as if she were performing some sort of strange dance. Then she suddenly kicked off the ground with her hind feet, spread her wings, and flew away. She seemed somewhat agitated. After she left, all that remained of her was the one flower that didn't meet its end at the hands of her miasma.

At that point, I lost consciousness once more.

The next time I awoke, I was lying on the ground near the cliff where I had collapsed, with no idea how much time had passed. I looked up to find Todorius staring down at me.

<Care, Rest, Care... Oh, good! You're finally waking up. Thought you'd take matters into your own hands, eh, El-diot?>

<Is this Hell? It's just like the legends say: I see a three-eyed, pompous, brainless-looking dragon...>

<You want me to send you there for real, you scumbag?>

I stretched my neck and looked around. I saw Hanera looking at me from a good distance away, her face etched with worry.

<So, what kind of magic trick did you pull out of your hat to turn that terrifying Magic Mist Dragon into an innocent little lady dragon?> King Noah was there too, looking at me happily. Apparently, Hanera had searched all over the island for the two dragons and brought them to me. If I'd had to wait any longer, I might've truly died.

<I was shocked. She circled the whole island, crying out, "The black dragon! The black dragon, he's..." and then flew up to where we were sleeping. And not to mention...> Todorius's shoulders shook as if he was trying to hide his laughter.

"Kwoooooh?!" Hanera's body jolted upright from where she'd been watching from afar, then she flew over to us in a flash and unleashed a tail cleave that knocked Todorius into the sky.

<I-I-I-I, I, I told you not to tell him that! I told you not to! You promised!>

Todorius, who'd been thrown into the air like it was nothing, fell to the ground on his back with a thud, then bounced heavily and rolled with a continuous thumping sound.

Todorius...you already know how much stronger Hanera is than us. You'd really risk your life for a single joke...?

PART 10

. . . .

AFTER MAKING THE Nameless Ugly Dragon Hanera our companion, we continued to level ourselves up by battling against the monsters that inhabited the great tree island at the western edge of the world. Things had been progressing as usual, but...for some reason, I'd been a little out of sorts lately.

<E-El! Y-you, you looked g-g-great today!>

Hanera had started to fondly refer to me as El.

In the end, even after Hanera joined our group, I never really found a chance to be in close contact with her. She always looked sort of lonely, and even though I didn't mind, she seemed to be concerned about the fact that she had almost killed me once. However, that incident notwithstanding, she seemed very happy, and started to walk behind me at a distance.

That being said, because Hanera was much stronger than I was, I started to feel like I was being made fun of. Todorius, Hanera, and I fought against two Adams today, and Hanera had essentially had the upper hand from start to finish. Hanera unfurled her wings to spread her miasma while Todorius healed me. Then, Todorius and I tried to attract one of the Adams to split them up, but we couldn't handle it on our own. In the end, Hanera used Dual Dark Sphere to cover us while she overwhelmed the other one with her melee attacks, which was the decisive factor in our victory against them.

At night, Hanera left us and went to sleep on her usual cliff. She couldn't sleep on the great tree with us because the tree branches would rot out from underneath her during the night. Besides, if she'd slept alongside the rest of us, we could've all been dead by morning. Her miasma was that powerful.

<...I just feel a little out of sorts.> I was complaining to King Noah and Todorius.

<You're telling me. Hanera calls Eldia 'El' and calls Noah 'King Noah,' but she just calls me Todorius. It feels like she likes me even less than the El-diot...>

You're still making fun of me after all this time? I thought, but when I looked at his face, I realized he was serious. I was more annoyed than kidding, so I contemplated getting our eighty-fourth battle started here, but in the end, I opted to hold back.

<I've got some good news for you, El,> King Noah said. *Please don't let that nickname catch on,* I pleaded with my eyes.

<Your time as a Dark Dragon is numbered. You'll be evolving soon.>

<I-I'm going to evolve?!>

Wow, I was going to be a rank A dragon? I'd thought my next evolution was still long off, but since becoming King Noah's subordinate, I'd been growing stronger at an unusually fast rate. It was partly because I had more opportunities to fight strong enemies, but I'd heard that it was also due to King Noah's Special Skills as the Demon King. However, I didn't realize that it'd made me evolve this fast...

<If you get to rank A, you might gain the skills you need to withstand Hanera's miasma. Then maybe the two of you can actually get together.>

<K-King Noah, please! D-don't tease me like that! I have no intentions of doing something like that!>

<Really, El? That's a shame. Hanera's totally on board. If I told her that your evolution is near, she might die of sheer joy.>

<W-would you please stop calling me El?!>

Todorius snickered. *<C'mon, El. What's the big deal?>*

<Bastard! You're dead!>

I leaped at him, but Todorius was already ready for me.

<You've been looking down on me far too much lately!> I roared. *<I'll knock some sense into you so you won't be able to disobey me again for a while!>*

<While Hanera's not around, you mean? The other day you rushed into our battle and got yourself half killed!

Aren't you a little wiser now, Todorius, or is your brain still tiny because of the pressure of your third eyeball?!>

<You've fallen real low if you need a female dragon around to protect you, Eldiaaaaa!>

Todorius and I began to grapple with each other.

<Hey, guys, knock it... Actually, I'll let you two have at it today.> King Noah said, evidently deciding it was too much trouble to stop us. He curled up against the tree's trunk and fell asleep.

True to Noah's prediction, I evolved the very next day.

The monster we fought that time was called Neptune, a monstrous bird with blueish-green feathers that looked like oxidized copper. It danced in the sea near the island of giant trees. Its rank was A–, higher than mine and Todorius's. However, while Todorius and I kept it distracted, Hanera struck it with a barrage of miasma-coated tails. These caused deep cracks to appear all over its body, and it fell into the sea, dead.

At that moment, I realized that my body was changing. My level increased, and it was time for me to evolve.

<Nice work, Eldia!> Noah called out to me. He possessed the eyes of a god, which allowed him to see our conditions at a glance. Without saying a word, he knew that I'd reached my evolution.

I told Todorius and Hanera that I was about to evolve,

moved to the cliff where I had first met Hanera, and then started the process of evolution. I felt myself expand from the inside like an explosion. The heat felt like it was destroying and remaking my entire body. My body swelled like it was being pushed apart, and at the same time, my scales mutated into something stiff and hard.

"*Grrroooooooaaaaaaaah!*"

As if driven by impulse, I let out a roar.

‹*Congrats, Eldia...you've become the rank A dragon, Diabolos. Whoa, these stats... You have the potential to surpass even my Pandora in pure melee capabilities.*›

Not just Hanera but Todorius too looked at me with fascination. *Am I really that impressive now?* Todorius certainly looked smaller than he did before.

‹*E-El...!*› Beneath the miasma, Hanera's skin looked slightly pink. Todorius turned away from me as though he'd suddenly realized he'd been staring, then crowded around King Noah.

‹*King Noah! King Noah! When do I get to evolve next?!*›

‹*Err...good question. I wonder...*› Noah mumbled, gently turning away from Todorius. I had no idea how long it'd take for him to get there, but for now, I'd finally taken a huge lead over Todorius. *Heh heh. I won't be the eternal loser anymore, Todorius.*

PART 11

APPROXIMATELY HALF A YEAR had passed since I evolved into Diabolos, and a lot happened in that time.

First, Todorius did not end up evolving; he was still a rank B+ Nidhogg. King Noah had been aware of the fact that he was near his evolutionary limit for quite some time; however, he kept quiet about it, hoping that there would be a way to release it. As the Demon King, he was supposed to have been given much knowledge about evolutions, stats, and levels by the Will of the World, but that didn't mean he knew *everything*.

In the ninety-nine matches between Todorius and me, I'd now won eight and lost ninety-one. I had a lot of ground to cover before we'd be even, but I'd won the last five, so things were looking up. I sometimes thought about losing on purpose, but I knew Todorius wouldn't want me to do that. And for the past three months, we hadn't faced off against each other even once.

For the past three months or so, Todorius had been wracked with worries, and was, at times, on the verge of defecting. I'd even had to prepare myself for the possibility that a time may come where I'd have to kill him.

However, Todorius often disguised himself as a human and visited various places to obtain information on behalf of Noah, who couldn't gather intel himself. This gave him a role outside of combat to focus on instead. In addition, he contacted monsters across the world and formed cooperative relationships with them, sometimes bringing dragons with high flying ability to the far west to meet with King Noah. In turn, Noah would make them full-fledged subordinates and send them to live on the island.

Our army of monsters, with King Noah at its head, was growing steadily. The number of rank C, B, and A dragons on the giant tree island had increased to thirty, eight, and three, respectively.

One day, while I was out hunting Adams to increase my levels, I spotted Todorius flying in from the east. It didn't seem like he'd spotted me yet. I contemplated whether I should just pretend I hadn't seen him and move on but instead decided to say hi and went ahead to ambush him.

There's no reason to avoid him. Todorius is Todorius, and his role in all of this is important. Besides, if I avoid him, we probably won't see each other again for a while.

<Todorius! Long time no see. Seen any movement among the humans lately?>

Todorius stopped, closed his eyes once, and then huffed like I was making fun of him.

‹You know I don't report to you, Eldia. If there's something you need to know, King Noah will tell you.›

Then he started moving again like nothing had happened, hurrying along to King Noah. He didn't meet my eyes.

‹Hey, you! That's no way to behave!›

‹Why? Because I'm the weakest of the three Demon Dragons?›

The three Demon Dragons were me, Todorius, and Hanera; we were the three leaders of the Demon King's army. However, Todorius was the only rank B between the three of us.

‹I didn't say that! But...› As I bared my fangs, Todorius quickened his pace.

‹I'm not getting into a petty fight with you, Eldia,› he said. *‹Besides, I'm no match for you. You shouldn't bully those who are weaker than you. I was pretending not to notice you before. Please just take the hint.›*

My eyes followed Todorius's back as he departed. We used to poke fun at each other all the time. When did those pokes become more than just harmless banter? Nowadays, I couldn't even do things like launch a surprise attack on him. If I did, I might accidentally kill him.

"Roooooooar!" *<Master Eldia! Master Eldia!>*

With a cry, Capra, a flying dragon, descended from overhead. Capra was a white flying dragon who was reasonably fast, and as such was often assigned to serve as a messenger on the island. Capra also left the island on occasion for various missions.

<What is it?>

<It's your wife, sir! Her eggs! They've hatched!>

<Wh...whaaaaat?!>

Yes, this was the second major change that had happened in the past six months. Hanera was now my mate. When I first met her, I would've thought it impossible for us to be together. Hanera's wings were warped, and her body surface was constantly melting due to her noxious fumes. She may not have been what one would consider beautiful, with her strange, glowing red eyes that were quite eerie and the miasma that made it difficult to even get close to her.

But Hanera was also gentle, pure, and strong-willed. And strangely enough, we had certain similarities that I'd picked up on from the day we first met. Now I could say with certainty that there was no other dragon as beautiful as Hanera. The miasma that had kept me away for so long was no longer a problem, thanks to my strong stats as a Diabolos, and I'd developed a resistance to it through daily contact with Hanera.

"Grruuuoooooooogh!" *‹Haneraaaaa! Your eggs hatched?!›*

"Kuuuo! Kuroooo!" *‹El! Look, look! Come meet your children!›*

Hanera spotted me and shook her body to relieve it of its dryness. The miasma would spread if she moved around too much, so she tended to restrain her movements. Lately, I'd noticed that Hanera's telepathic messages were getting less and less awkward. She must've gotten used to using Telepathy to communicate.

Scattered on the ground were the remains of seven eggshells, covered with siren feathers. Among them were seven Baby Dragons who were playing with the feathers. They were all the offspring of Hanera and I, our children.

‹But look! They already have black skin...›

It was rare for Baby Dragons to be born with skin any color other than yellow, but six of ours were black and one was white. I'd considered the possibility that our children would be born with unique constitutions that allowed them to withstand Hanera's miasma, but I didn't tell her that because I was afraid it might upset her.

‹Heh heh. They're our kids, all right. I'm sure they'll be very strong one day. We should show them to King Noah and ask him to name them and predict their futures.›

I knew if anyone could tell us about our oddly colored baby dragons, it would be King Noah.

\<Shh, shh. You're all going to be big, strong war drag-ons someday, just like me and your mommy... You know, Hanera, there are probably no more than five of us rank A dragons in the world. I doubt there's another bloodline as blessed as ours.\>

"Gaaaa?"

"Graaah!"

"Ngaaaah?"

When I brought my face closer, the Baby Dragons all gathered at the tip of my snout.

\<...Well I, for one, would not want to take my children into battle with me against the humans.\>

A small, hazy thought leaked out of Hanera that I couldn't pick up on properly.

\<Hanera? Did you say something?\>

\<N-no, nothing...\>

\<You sure? Heh heh, I'd like to get these kids up to at least a rank B. With our blood and King Noah's blessing, I'm sure they'll eventually make it to rank A. Then instead of just three of us, we'll have ten Demon Dragons on our side.\>

Hanera remained silent.

We found out from King Noah that our children were indeed rare species. The black dragons were Dark Baby Dragons, and the white one was an Albino Baby Dragon. Both species were expected to have stable, high-rank evolutions. And, as I'd expected, all of them had strong resistances against status effects, likely due to their adaptation to Hanera's miasma.

While I was overjoyed at the good news, Hanera seemed strangely anxious.

PART 12

ONE DAY, King Noah held a meeting in the underground ruins at the root of the great tree. A total of fifty dragons were gathered in a large room. By that point, all of my and Hanera's children had already completed their second evolution and grown into rank C dragons. After consulting with King Noah, we planned to create a dragon unit under my direct control when they'd all grown to about rank B.

Todorius was the same as ever. Our battles hadn't resumed since the ninety-ninth one, and we had stopped talking to each other altogether.

‹According to Todorius's information, the humans have discovered the current Beast King in the great ravine in the northernmost part of the world. They probably intend to send their hero, Mia, after him soon. Of course, we cannot

allow the hero to take the power of the Beast King. We will journey into the great ravine ahead of them, and I will defeat the Beast King and seize his power. This will allow me to evolve into the Calamity Dragon.>

King Noah continued, *<Here's the catch. In order to defeat the Beast King, I, as the Demon King, must be the one to go there. However, there is little hope that I can win alone with my current skills. Therefore, I will take my three Demon Dragons, Todorius, Eldia, and Hanera, with me. Any more than that, and we risk alerting the humans to our presence, which would not help our chances in battle.>*

That meant the ones leaving were the top four commanders of the Demon King's army. It seemed like a drastic measure, but our opponent this time was very different from the ones we'd faced up until now. We were going up against the Beast King; one of the four entities that would decide the fate of this world. Time was running out. There was no other way.

However...there was a huge gap between Todorius's stats and mine. I wondered what Noah's intentions were in taking Todorius along with us to defeat the Beast King. It was true that he was good with support and recovery skills, and he was quite smart. He also had powerful magic skills that could be used against higher-ranked enemies, although he'd rarely had a chance to use them.

It would not be a loss to take him along, but I wondered if it would've been better to leave him behind and let him manage the Demon King's army in King Noah's absence. *Or maybe I just think that because I want to avoid him?*

Why do I want that? Although we were on bad speaking terms with each other, it was never to the point where we hated each other's guts. I supposed we just no longer knew how to talk to each other.

We left the giant tree island in the west and headed for the great ravine in the north, where the Beast King had allegedly been sighted. It was truly a voyage from one corner of the world to the other. With our wings, it would not take long if it were a straight line, but we had to avoid human habitats. If word about King Noah reached the hero's ears, everything would be ruined.

Todorius and I did not speak a single word to each other on our journey. We matched our speed with Noah, who was slower, sometimes getting lost, sometimes avoiding human settlements, sometimes meeting with cooperative monsters, and so on, for about a week. Then, at last, we reached the great ravine in the north.

The northern edge of the world was just as impressive as the western edge. It was an island-like mass of huge rocks with cliffs that stretched down forever. If someone without wings stepped off the edge, there was no chance they'd be able to survive.

<I never knew a cliff like this existed. I think I'd like to visit the eastern and southern edges of the world some-day too.>

<Yes, I agree. The edges of the world are so wondrous and beautiful.>

As Hanera and I casually exchanged conversation, King Noah's face went deathly pale. I looked back at him, concerned.

<King Noah? What is it?>

<...Eldia, I was wrong. I had said that the hero of this generation was out of the ordinary compared to the heroes of lore, but it seems it's not only the hero who's unusual. No, the Beast King is a monstrosity. Even more so than the hero.>

<What...? Such feeble words are unlike you, my king.>

<We're doing this in the wrong order. We should've killed the hero and the saint and then come here. You three...we need to leave. Now.>

<King Noah? What're you talking about?> Todorius asked, also doubtful. *What in the world does Noah see?* Hanera remained silent, but she looked at Noah in confusion.

At that moment, one of the rocks in the ravine exploded.

"Grrrraagagagagagagagaaaaaaaa!"

What appeared at the top of the pile of rubble was a huge dragon. Larger dragons tended to walk on all fours, with their forelimbs as front paws, but this one was bipedal. Its legs and arms were unusually long, but it supported its huge body effortlessly, giving it a very strange appearance. Its four eyes flashed, and its mouth opened wide in a smile. Then another mouth opened even wider on its abdomen. From the second mouth extended two unusually long, slimy tongues.

<What the hell? His stats, they're...>

That was the first time I saw Noah truly afraid. When I saw his face, I understood. We really shouldn't have come here.

<A rank A+...he's the strongest monster I've ever seen. But that rank is just a little higher than mine. Why is there such a huge gap between our stats...? Is it due to his Bad Skill "Constant Madness" constantly granting him the Berserk status...?>

<King Noah, is that...>

<Yes. That is the Beast King, the Frumious Maniac: Bandersnatch. If we're going to fight that...that thing, we may as well fight Mia the Hero right here and now.>

Whoa... Is he truly that dangerous?

<But your Majesty! We cannot know the outcome of our battle until we fight!> Todorius interjected.

‹Laplace says we have a twenty percent probability.›

‹You mean...we only have a one in five chance of besting him? But if we run away now, things will be even more difficult for—›

‹No,› Noah said. *‹That is the probability that we all escape unscathed.›*

I finally understood just how dire our situation truly was.

"Grrrraagagagagaaaaaaaa!"

Bandersnatch leapt off the top of the rock pile and disappeared. No, it was coming toward us at a terrifying speed. Faster than I could even imagine.

I must buy time for King Noah to escape. With this in mind, I moved forward. Hanera stepped forward at the same moment.

‹El... I'm sorry, but this will probably hurt.›

The miasma swirling around Hanera became dense, then spread out in the shape of huge tentacles. Status effects that managed to penetrate through even my thick hide began to attack my body. *Maximum output...* Even the seawater beneath us began to stagnate, and the carcasses of monsters who had died in the sea began to float to the surface.

The Bandersnatch would have a hard time getting through this. Even for me, with my well-trained resistance, staying close to Hanera at this moment was draining my physical strength significantly.

If I hesitate here and show the Bandersnatch that I'm weakened, he'll go after me, and I can strike a blow on him with all my might...! If I injure his wings, he won't be able to follow us!

<Eldia, Hanera, run! If you try to fight him, you'll die for nothing!> King Noah's voice echoed through our minds.

<Icky icky icky ickyickyick...kiiiiii!>

Before my mind even registered his movement, Bandersnatch moved in behind Hanera.

<Huh?!>

Bandersnatch's second mouth, lined with a great number of fangs, chomped down on Hanera. His mouth opened and closed with frightening speed, and in no time at all, the miasma-filled tentacles disintegrated between his teeth. His fangs pierced Hanera's shoulder, spraying her blood everywhere. Green bodily fluids dripped from Bandersnatch's four eyes.

<Yuck, yuckyuckyuckyuckyuckyuckyuck, yuck...yuuuck, bleeeeeeegh!>

Bandersnatch's thoughts echoed over and over in my head, giving me a headache.

<Yuuuuuuuuuuuuccccccccccccckkkkkkkkk!>

<Haneraaaa!> I leapt at Bandersnatch, who spun in midair and whipped me with its three tails. The force of the impact left me stunned. My consciousness wavered.

"Groooaaaaah!"

I slammed into the surface of the water with a roar. It felt like a different dimension.

Bandersnatch pierced Hanera's right leg and abdomen with the claws of both hands, then spread his arms wide, literally tearing her apart. Her lower and upper body split in two; Bandersnatch held both pieces of her high above him, and fresh blood poured down onto him like a waterfall.

‹UwaaaAAAAAAaaahahahahahahaaAAA!›

Bandersnatch's deranged thoughts flew through my mind.

‹H...Hanera...?›

The miasma Hanera constantly produced had stopped. For the first time, I saw her without any miasma dripping from her skin. Her body was a serene blue, like the sky on a summer day. She was beautiful. Her mouth, stained with blood from her vomit, opened and closed again and again.

"Kgggh..." *‹El...our children, take good c—›*

Hanera's telepathic message cut off there.

‹Hanera! Haneraaaaaa!›

‹Eldia, retreat! This was a mistake on my part! We should've never gotten involved with him yet!›

Bandersnatch! Your head is mine! I will do to you the same as you did to Hanera—no! That is not enough! I will tear your body into eight pieces and make them my play-things until you finally succumb to death!

<Physical Barrier!>

My body was enveloped in magical light. I now had a strong resistance to physical attacks. *As far as I can tell, Bandersnatch just rampages using his own ferocious power! This magic will give me a lot of resistance to counter those attacks!*

<Useless, useless uselessuselessuselessuselesslesslesslesslesslessahahahahaha!>

Bandersnatch's tail struck me sideways with a powerful swing. It was a ridiculously large motion, but I couldn't react to it. The bones in my wings broke, my scales shattered. Once again, I dropped head-first into the water, spraying a huge splash of water into the air.

My wing was broken. Until I healed it, I could no longer fly properly, and it seemed unlikely Bandersnatch would give me that chance. Four hungry eyes stared down at me. Bandersnatch dropped in a straight line from directly above me. *It's over.* The mouth on his belly opened wide.

<Thaaaaaankssss for the meeeeeaaaaaaalll!>

<Damn it, Eldia! King Noah told us all to run!>

Todorius flew in from the side and rammed me with his wings, knocking me out of the way. Bandersnatch's jaws latched on Todorius's body instead, slowly gnawing through him as if toying with him. Every time his jaws closed, Todorius's body lurched, and blood sprayed from his mouth.

‹T-Todorius...why? I thought...I thought you hated me?›

‹El-diot! You want to discuss this now?! If you, the only rank A member of the Demon King's army left other than the Demon King himself, disappears, there's no way we'll be able to recuperate from this loss. Regenerate your wings and get out of here!›

‹B-but...I didn't run before, and now you, you...›

‹Go! Or are you going to make me sacrifice my life in vain?!›

‹Todorius... I'm so sorry, Todorius, my dear friend...›

I used Regenerate to heal the bones in my wings, then broke free of the surface of the ocean and flew up. Todorius's eyes fluttered back to life for a moment, and he sent me another thought.

‹...Eldia, I'm sorry for taking everything out on you. I've done more to contribute than you this time, Eldia. I helped King Noah escape... Shall we say I won our hundredth battle?›

‹...Of course. You win, Todorius. I always knew I was no match for you.›

I turned my back to Todorius and told him of his victory as I flew away. I felt as if I had returned to the time when I was still a Dark Dragon.

I heard a wretched gurgling sound behind me. I turned my head and saw the bloodied body of Todorius, his head torn off, falling into the sea. Bandersnatch's four eyes turned to me.

<Tch! So impatient... I have the Single Dragon Scale skill, which allows me to preserve my life force for a short while after being mortally wounded... Which means he's about to taste my strongest skill: Mana Glass!>

A magic circle unfolded in front of Todorius, then rays of intense blue light shot out from it and covered Bandersnatch completely.

"Nghaaa?!"

Mana Glass... This was an attack spell that converted all of the user's magic power into energy waves and shot them out. If the user had a lot of magic power, it was a mighty spell. However, it had a huge disadvantage. Large monsters like us were supported by the magic power in our bodies, so if we released all of it, we'd no longer be able to move properly. The other disadvantage was that it took a long time to activate, so it couldn't hit an alert opponent. Using it in a situation like this, where Todorius was almost certainly about to die and Bandersnatch already believed him to be dead, was absolutely perfect.

"Wraaaaaagaaaagagagagagaaaaaaa!"

When the bright light subsided, Bandersnatch was cowering behind both wings, which he was using to shield against Mana Glass.

Even Bandersnatch had to be on the defensive against Todorius's dying blow. But that was all. There was a slight wound on the surface of his body, but it wasn't serious, and it healed as I watched. *He really is a beast.*

"*Wraagagagagaga! WragaaaaAAAAaaaAA!*"

Bandersnatch, perhaps aggravated by the damage inflicted by the lower-rank magic, swung both arms in a vicious motion and thoroughly destroyed Todorius's lifeless remains. My vision went red, but I knew if I acted on my emotions, Todorius's death would've been for naught. I left the great ravine at the northern edge of the world as Bandersnatch toyed with Todorius's corpse behind me.

PART 13

LOSING BOTH Hanera and Todorius at the same time dealt a huge blow to the Demon King's army. We had lost half of the four top dragons. Todorius was also a dragon who had formed cooperative relationships with monsters in other regions. In that aspect too, our loss was immeasurable.

If the information obtained by Todorius was correct, the battle between the hero, Mia, and the Beast King, Bandersnatch, would soon begin. It would be good if Mia escaped, but the worst possible outcome would be Bandersnatch killing Mia and taking her hero powers. Although the hero and the Beast King's powers would be undermined by the human forces, Bandersnatch, at that point akin to an uncontrollable god of destruction, would continue to live in solitude in the far north. What Bandersnatch would do with all this new power was not difficult to guess.

It was no exaggeration to say that the forces at this time were divided into three: The Demon King's army led by King Noah, the humans led by the hero Mia and Saint Lumira, and the lone force of the Beast King Bandersnatch. Bandersnatch had his own dangers to watch out for.

King Noah's strategy upon his return to the giant tree island at the western edge of the world was, "To proceed with preparations, observe quietly, and hope the situation becomes a stalemate." While the end to the conflict between Mia and Bandersnatch dragged on with no end in sight, the Demon King's army had to become stronger than the Beast King.

I was not left without a chance; I had seven children with Hanera. If they all grew up to be rank A, Mia would be no match for them. If that happened, King Noah would emerge victorious.

I'll get my children to rank A as soon as possible. If the humans haven't noticed us by then, and Bandersnatch is defeated, we monsters will win the war of our era. But how much time do we have left...?

I am now the only surviving member of the four leaders of the Demon King's army, excluding Noah himself. I must support him. Todorius, Hanera, watch me. I'll avenge you by killing Bandersnatch, and I'll fulfill the dream we've held all this time.

For those reasons, I was devoted to leveling my children up. Fortunately, there were many high-level monsters to fight on this island. Their numbers had been decreasing since we took control of the island, but if I left the island for a while and flew around in the sky, I could find many strange rank B monsters like giant birds and giant fish. I took to the skies with my children and hunted endlessly for monsters to fight. We needed a force strong enough to defeat the hero as soon as possible.

Several months had passed since those leveling days. The hero Mia had been defeated by Bandersnatch twice but survived both times. I didn't know what the most recent developments were, but the stalemate between them continued. I hoped things stayed like that for as long as possible. That being said, I thought Mia was rather impressive for having the strength to go right back up against Bandersnatch after being defeated, without a moment's pause.

<Papa, I'm tired.>

<You talk to father like that?!>

<Nims doesn't understand the fact that we're the hope of the Demon King's army.>

<I don't care what we eat, as long as it tastes good!>

<Wah ha ha ha ha! We don't need you, stupid! As long as King Noah's got me and father, the Demon King's army will be victorious!>

<...I'm out of magic power. Can I go home now?>

My children were flying in the sky near me, chattering as they pleased. They'd grown...physically, through leveling and evolution, but I didn't think they were quite caught up mentally and emotionally yet. They were already rank B dragons, but their words and actions were still those of Baby Dragons.

"Krrrr!" *<Father, are you all right? You look tired.>*

The white dragon that was flying alongside me looked into my face. He was born as a white Baby Dragon, unique among my seven children. He was now a B+

"Moon-Viewing Dragon" and was the strongest of my children, manipulating powerful gravity magic. His name was Tsukuyomi.

<Hmm? Instead of worrying about me, you should focus on getting stronger as soon as possible.>

"*Kyuruuu...*" Tsukuyomi chirped anxiously. I pretended not to notice his expression and looked forward.

There were only two ways for us to win. Either I raised all of my seven children to rank A and used them to destroy Mia the Hero and the human army, or we used King Noah's Pandora collateral damage and human-monster transformation skills to take them out. Personally, I didn't want to use the latter measure. It wasn't a pleasant victory, or a stable one. For humans and monsters alike, the days of hell continued, and there was no telling when they would end.

<Papa, um, I saw a human riding on top of a dragon. They were coming this way.>

A three-eyed dragon with blue-black skin flew up next to me and sent me a telepathic message. It was my daughter Lilos; she was a Nidhogg, the same species as Todorius. However, her skill levels were lower than his, and she had far fewer skills, so she was still far behind him in abilities. *I suppose that's the downside of short-term power leveling...*

\<A human? Are you sure it wasn't an Adam?\>

\<Lilos, are you trying to scare father with one of your awful jokes again?\>

\<Nuh-uh! King Noah yelled at me for doing that before, so I'm not doing it again!\>

Lilos's third eye gave her the power of Far Vision. This report was no joke.

\<What did they look like, Lilos?\>

\<She had, uh, bright blonde hair with some yellowish-green bits, I think? And she was wearing a cape, but not carrying much. And for weapons...none, I don't think?\>

As she described the rider, my vision distorted. There was no doubt in my mind; the woman she saw was the hero, Mia. Mia had the Dimension skill, which allowed her to store tools in another dimension and take them out as she pleased, so she had no need to bring any visible weapons along with her.

B-but why was she here?! Was she a fool?! Bandersnatch was her priority! Did she realize she couldn't beat him and decided to prioritize defeating King Noah instead?!

This was an emergency. My seven children were not yet a force to be reckoned with against Mia the Hero. And I didn't know how much support I'll be able to provide either.

\<...Lilos, was she alone?\>

<Mm, yes? It's just one human. But she's riding on a traitor dragon who's supporting the humans. What're you gonna do, Papa?>

Even alone, we were in trouble. I stopped moving and stayed suspended in place in the air, and Lilos followed suit. My other children also began to gather around.

I took a few seconds to think. What was the best thing to do? No matter what, I had to tell King Noah about Mia the Hero's attack as soon as possible. Noah was slow; even if he ran away, the other dragon would be able to catch up if they gave chase.

<Mia the Hero is attacking. I will buy us some time... All of you, report to King Noah at once.>

My seven children buzzed with nervous energy.

<Mia the Hero?!>

<H-how did she find us?!>

<I-I-I-It can't be!>

<I-I'm sure it'll be fine. Besides, how many dragons d'you think are on this island? And there aren't any of those Harunae soldiers that Father and the others were so worried about, right? W-we've got this!>

<D-don't be stupid! We were told that Mia the Hero survived several battles with Bandersnatch, the one who killed Mother and Todorius!>

They were confused and panicking. It seemed like a fight would break out at any moment.

<H-hey, guys, enough! Don't stir up a fuss now! Hurry, go to King Noah's!> Tsukuyomi, my son, floated in front of me. <And that goes for you too, Father. You're not calm either. There's no reason to send all seven of us to report in and leave you as the decoy when you're faster than all of us.>

My other six children had stopped moving, their bodies trembling with fear.

As someone dedicated to King Noah, my first thought was that the best solution would be to leave my seven children as decoys and report back to him, then return. However, if I did that, the lives of my seven children would be in danger. They were the last remnants of Hanera that I had left. I refused to use them as decoys for my own survival.

<You... You are all the hope of the Demon King's army...> I said.

<If we spread out and fight, we should have a chance to escape. After we've bought you some time, we'll split off and run away. It's all right... Mia the Hero has to rely on her dragon for her mobility. There's no way it's as fast as she is. We'll all be able to escape.>

Tsukuyomi was right. That was what we should do. And yet...!

<Father...leave this one to us!>

<Don't worry! Tsukuyomi always loves to exaggerate! Maybe he's being extra cautious, but he's also making everyone nervous! We'll all be back together before you know it! I promise!>

My seven children did their best to encourage me. It was originally my duty to command and encourage them. How pitiful of me, to make them do the same for me.

<My children...forgive me.>

I flapped my wings and made my way back to the giant tree island.

PART 14

A S SOON AS I RETURNED to the giant tree island, I started howling telepathically at anyone who could hear me.

<Mia the Hero is attacking! Inform King Noah at once!>

The dragons on the island were terrified and started to tremble as soon as they heard the news. Some even fled the island immediately. However, if all the dragons jumped into battle with Mia and lost their lives, it would take a very long time to regroup. It was necessary for some of the dragons to run away. That is, as long as King Noah survived.

Soon after, King Noah appeared in front of me, with a rank B dragon trailing him on either side.

<Eldia! Wh-what happened?! Tell me everything you know!>

<King Noah! Mia the Hero is on her way here! We don't know how certain they are that the Demon King is hiding here! My children are buying us time, but I don't know how long that will last! Let's get out of here!>

<...It seems the time has come.> Noah lowered his head in disappointment. He then turned his attention to the rank B dragons that accompanied him.

<Eldia will take over as my guard. You two, tell the whole island what Eldia has just said and then flee in opposite directions. If too many of you leave together, you risk being tracked by the hero. We will meet up with you eventually.

The two rank B dragons glanced at each other, bowed their heads deeply at King Noah, spread their wings, and took off in different directions. After he watched them depart, King Noah also spread his wings.

<Eldia, follow me.>

<Which way are we headed?>

<Toward the Harunae Empire, the home of the hero. Once there, I plan to head to the imperial capital, Breigal,

and the city of Mafis, which is right in the middle of the empire! This is the time for revelations from the Will of the World...!>

Even I was shocked as I heard this. The Harunae Empire was in the middle of hostile territory. It was probably the worst place for us to go to escape Mia the Hero.

<Now that she's onto me, wherever we escape to, it's only a matter of time before she finds me again. Mia is not Bandersnatch; she doesn't just do things out of love for violence. In order to protect the humans and get rid of me, she will chase after us to the ends of the earth.>

<But why there, of all places?>

<Have you forgotten? I have my skill, Light of Ruin, that will activate after my death. This way, it is possible to not only destroy the hero Mia but also to turn her entire homeland into a wasteland. She can't make that choice... If we attack her at the same time, we should be able to defeat her.>

It was the last resort that I never wanted King Noah to take. However, this course of action may have been one decided from the moment King Noah evolved into Pandora at the behest of the Will of the World.

<...Very well, your Majesty. Let's head to Harunae.>

He and I headed in the direction of the Harunae Empire, largely avoiding the route that Mia the Hero would have taken. Our destination was the empire's center point, between the imperial city of Breigal and the city of Mafis. Here, if King Noah was killed, his death curse would cover the entirety of the Harunae Empire, and every living being there would be destroyed. Mia's home would be utterly desolated.

I followed King Noah to our destination; sometimes we strayed off the beaten path, and sometimes we took routes that seemed like a waste of time. I had my doubts here and there, but when I asked him about it, he said, *<This is the route Laplace predicted. It is the safest way.>* If that was the case, I decided not to press him further.

After flying for three whole days, Noah and I finally entered the Harunae Empire. Far below us, we could see the terrified faces of the humans.

<King Noah, beyond those mountains is the center of the Harunae Empire.>

Noah remained silent.

<I have been constantly on the lookout from the rear, but there has been no pursuit by Mia the Hero so far.>

<Then that is the Will of the World and Laplace's decision. I must obey their commands and destroy the humans.>

When King Noah flew ahead past the mountain, he stopped in his tracks, hovering in the air.

<My God... Is this truly the place where the Will of the World wants me to be?>

He was acting strange. I sped up, trying to catch up to him.

<King Noah...?>

In the center of the plain beyond the mountains stood a female swordsman. Her blonde hair, slightly tinged with yellow-green, was tied in a single braid. She had large doll-like eyes, a high nose, and a small mouth—the embodiment of ideal beauty. She looked up at Noah expressionlessly. I had heard stories about her, but this was the first time I had seen her in person. This was Mia the Hero, the human born to be Noah's foil in order to destroy him.

"So this is where you fled to after all. It was difficult to follow you because of your strange route, but it was easy to guess your ultimate destination from all the sightings. I knew that if I waited here, you would show up, Demon King. Noah, as you are called."

Mia raised her arm into the sky.

"...Dimension!"

Her body was suddenly clad in shining white armor, and she held a huge, reddish-black sword in her upraised hand. The strangely shaped blade pointed directly at Noah. Blood was splattered all along it. In my mind's eye, I saw my seven children.

<You... How many of my seven children are dead at your hands?>

"I see, you are the parent of those seven dragons. They all met their fate at the end of this sword. They all fought quite valiantly. I was going to ignore them and hurry away, but...they came back to bite me again and again."

Mia answered my telepathic message easily. For a moment, I couldn't understand what she meant, but my brain finally caught up after a delay and was suddenly struck with a feverish heat. The world felt like it was shaking. As though it were pushed out of me by the black rage bubbling up in the pit of my stomach, I let out a roar.

"Gurooooh, groooooaaaaaah!"

Tears welled up in my eyes and spilled over. My brain was on fire. *I told them all to escape after distracting the enemy... Why, why, why are all of my children dead?! Hanera...forgive me. I am so sorry. I... I couldn't protect them.*

"This sword is named 'Fang of the Frumious Maniac Bandersnatch'... I made it from the Beast King's corpse after I killed him. It boasts high resistance to status effects and a strong spirit. If anyone other than me were to hold it, they would be driven mad and lose control."

So the hero had already defeated the Beast King... Damn it! If Todorius were still around, he wouldn't have missed such vital information. I couldn't believe she had defeated Bandersnatch with that human body. If the hero had already gained the Sacred Skill of the Beast King, then our fastest way to attack the hero was lost.

<But...I ask you, Mia the Hero: Why? If you were able to anticipate my attempts to hold the empire hostage, you must have seen through the past battles between me and the Harunae Imperial Army and know that I am a Pandora. If so, what does it matter if you are ahead of me...? Have you already found a way to defeat my curse?>

At this, Mia remained expressionless.

<I have heard that you are a strong and gentle hero. That is wonderful. But if you are the light that shines upon the shadows of this world, then you cannot destroy us. You already know what will happen if my Light of Ruin is activated here, don't you?>

A moment after King Noah finished, Mia disappeared.

<What...?!>

As King Noah's question echoed through my mind, a large hole suddenly opened in his chest, spurting blood. Mia stood atop King Noah's back, holding her disastrous great sword.

"Ghh...?"

I couldn't understand what I was seeing. Mia had stabbed King Noah. It happened so quickly that I could only watch in disbelief.

<Your Majesty...? King Noah? Noah!>

But how? Why...? This cannot be. Noah evolved into Pandora so that Mia would be unable to cut through him at this moment. This is a nightmare. It can't be. No, no! It cannot end like this!

‹My strength is fading. Ahh, I am so tired... O God, great one, the Observer, is this the decision of the Will of the World? But I, I... If this is the role I was meant to play, then...›

King Noah's body collapsed. However, the huge crystal in his chest began to grow in its brilliance. *It's activating...King Noah's skill, Light of Ruin, is activating...*

‹Noooooooo! You fool! Do you have any idea what you've done?!›

"...If the Demon King Noah were allowed to live, further tragedy would have ensued. This is a necessary sacrifice..."

‹You dare call yourself a hero?! You are no savior of humanity, you lunatic!›

"I have known that for a long time. I never wanted to be a savior of humanity. I just wanted to protect those I cared about."

‹Even if it meant destroying your entire country?!› I howled and swung my claws at Mia.

"Yes. Although that...was not my intention." Mia showed no interest in me, instead staring blankly at the intensifying light of King Noah's crystal.

‹Damn you!›

The paw I swung in her direction disappeared, and a deep slash was carved across my body. I didn't even see it coming.

"Grrrraaaaaaaaaagh!"

"The Demon King Noah is dead. After this, many more humans will die as well... I have had enough death for today. Therefore, I will let you live. I hope that you won't kill any more humans in the future... Holy."

My body was enveloped in white light. The same light enveloped Mia.

"With this, we will be able to endure the Demon King's Light of Ruin. This era's war between the monsters and humans is over."

<I... I didn't ask for this...! Now, at the end, I should be with my king...!>

The Light of Ruin spread all throughout the area from the crystal in King Noah's chest. Everything the light touched was turned to sand. In the blink of an eye, mountains were reduced to ash, rivers dried up, and all living beings turned into nothing more than bones. King Noah was no exception: His flesh was stripped from his bones and scattered to the wind.

Only Mia and I remained. But I was blown far, far away, as if repelled by the flash of light. Meanwhile, Mia stood there, looking on.

It was then, as Mia and King Noah grew farther and farther away from me, that they changed. King Noah, who was at this point nothing more than a lump of stripped flesh and bone, suddenly covered Mia.

<Wh-what?! How are you still moving?!> Mia shrieked. I was shocked too—I had thought Noah long dead.

<If my curse will not work on you, then instead I will use my Tainted Blood. Now you will become an Undead and drag your rotten body along with you...>

Those were King Noah's last words. When I came looking for him later, all that was left of him was his carcass, buried in the sand.

All at once, the Harunae Empire was wiped out by King Noah's skill. What remained in its place was the Harunae Desert, where not a single tree nor shrub could grow.

PART 15

. . . .

...**S**O ENDS MY STORY from five hundred years ago. After that, Mia the Hero, who was bathed in the Demon King's blood and thus became a deformed Undead, was abandoned by the humans. She managed to kill Saint Lumira after a long and bitter struggle, battled with human forces around the world, and even came to be called the Demon Queen. By that time, there was no trace of the Mia the Hero of old. And one day, after many repeated and senseless killings, Mia simply vanished. Ha! A miserable ending to her tale.

Ever since the Demon King was cut down, all I could think about was following him to the grave. But then, one day, I heard a revelation from the Will of the World. It said that it would raise the next Demon King, and this time, he would destroy the humans. In order to serve the Will of the World, I am still waiting here on the giant tree island, waiting for the next Demon King to appear.

<...Which is why I must reject your offer to leave this island with you. I will never again leave this place.>

"Hyooo..." The Nomadic Dragon cooed sadly in response.

2

The War Between the Right Head Faction and the Left Head Faction

EVEN AMONG the seemingly equal members of Illusia's party, a power dynamic existed. It was late afternoon on the island at the edge of the world. Allo, Nightmare, and Treant remained in the den they had dug in a tree while Illusia headed off to hunt. Allo and Nightmare were standing face-to-face on a branch just in front of the den.

In terms of appearance, Nightmare—who had evolved from a petit-nightmare and had a total length of over two meters—had the advantage over Allo's small, slender form. Even so, Allo was clearly the more intimidating of the two. If they fought, Allo would have won a hundred battles before Nightmare won a single one. Allo looked up at Nightmare's head, widening her eyes as if she were trying to peer into the depths of its face. Her crimson eyes seethed with magical power.

"Nightmare...why are you always so cold to the Dragon God?"

As Nightmare flinched back, Allo took another step forward. The relationship between the two of them was not particularly bad, but their personalities clashed to no end.

Free-spirited Nightmare's behavior was somewhat incompatible with Allo, who put the Dragon God above all else. They also had different objects of affection. Although they both adored the same two-headed dragon, Allo adored the gentle right head while Nightmare adored the more unfettered left head and treated the right head with a significant amount of contempt.

"Shh...Shhhh..."

Nightmare lowered its head. It was against Nightmare's way of life to change its behavior at the insistence of others. However, Nightmare was not a fool; it knew Allo was much stronger than it was and that Allo was usually quite calm and sensible. However, it also knew that when Ouroboros's right head was involved, Allo's words and actions could get a bit rash. Normally, Allo was quiet in the presence of the Dragon God, but now, the Dragon God's eyes were not watching. If it made it made a mistake here, the worst-case scenario was that Allo would send it tumbling after Gyva, whom she had knocked off the branch with her magic.

"Thank goodness… I'm glad we could agree." Smiling, Allo caressed Nightmare's lowered head with her arm, which she had made huge with her own experimentation.

"Good spider…"

With this, the long struggle between the Right Head Faction and Left Head Faction ended with the complete surrender of the Left Head Faction through armed intimidation by the Right Head Faction. Nightmare breathed a sigh of relief when it saw that Allo had backed down.

Treant, who was watching the scene, was also inwardly relieved.

"Come to think of it… Treant? Which side are you on?"

Allo turned around to look back at Treant, who shivered and shook its trunk. Green leaves fluttered down from its branches. It quickly attempted to mimic an ordinary tree by elongating its body, but trees obviously didn't grow on the branches of the Great Tree.

"I'm just asking. Which side?"

Treant remained silent. It didn't want to say the wrong thing. It didn't like to get involved in pointless disputes, and it didn't like to speak badly of either of Master's heads.

Despite appearances, Treant was a good tree who wanted to be everyone's friend. Not to mention, Treant—a tree monster—couldn't speak. Even if it could, whichever choice it made would cause resentment. Silence was a legitimate position. Therefore, Treant answered with silence.

"C'mon, can't you use Telepathy? The Dragon God was wondering too. Why don't you use it? The truth is, you can, but you don't, right?"

Treant gave up on being silent.

‹...I cannot rank the respect and affection I feel for one master...over the other...›

That was the founding moment of the Treant Neutral Nation. In its mind, Treant bent one of its branches into a fist pump. This way, it could save face with both sides and not spoil Allo's good mood.

"That...is the dumbest thing I've ever heard... You can't just say the first thing that popped into your head! Be reasonable!"

That was the moment that the Treant Neutral Nation collapsed. It didn't last even ten seconds.

‹...The right head, then. The left head is a little harsh on me.›

And that was the moment when the three parties formed the Ouroboros Right Head Alliance.

Then, the next day...

"Gaa! Gaa!"

Ouroboros's left head was delighted to receive a gift from Nightmare: a pillow stuffed with leaves and rolled up in spider silk.

Allo watched the scene idly. Perhaps Nightmare wasn't hitting the right head quite as hard as before due to yesterday's alliance, but that was it. It gave a pillow to the left head but not to the right. But Allo had no intention of confronting Nightmare about this. All she wanted was for Nightmare to change its behavior.

Suddenly, Nightmare hoisted up the web hanging off the side of the branch and pulled up a second pillow. It put the pillow on its back and settled in front of the right head. The right head pulled back in surprise.

<Nightmare? Y-you made one for me too? Really...?>

Nightmare nodded slightly. The right head was ecstatic, repeatedly setting his head on the pillow and poking it with the tip of his nose.

<Thank you, Nightmare! What? You're all shy now? You've got a surprisingly cute side, huh? Admit it!>

The right head put its nose up to Nightmare. Although Nightmare had a flash of murderous intent for a moment, it allowed it.

(I don't know why, but this one kind of disgusts me...)

Allo squinted and glared at the right head's nape for a while, but at no point did he notice her. He just continued nuzzling Nightmare happily for a long time. Allo, who had been quiet long enough, walked up to Ouroboros and called out to him.

"D-Dragon God!"

<Hm? What is it?> The right head looked at her.

"U-um, it's just..."

While Allo was pondering how to respond, Nightmare let out a *"Shh, sh!"* sound. The right head jolted, and then it looked back at Nightmare.

<Yes? What's the matter? You've got a favor to ask me? Ha haaa, I see, you were trying to butter me up, huh, Nightmare? Sure, what is it? I'm in a good mood, so if it isn't too much trouble, I'll do it. A lackey? You want a lackey, is that it? You want another Treant?>

"Um... Dragon King?"

When Allo called out to him, the right head looked back at her apologetically.

<S-sorry, uh, could you give me a second? It's just... Nightmare seems like it wants to say something to me, so I've gotta wait until it puts it all together...okay?>

Allo remained silent.

<N-no? Not okay? Got it. Um, Partner, it seems like Allo wants to say something, so can you listen to her?>

It seemed like he really wanted to prioritize Nightmare. Allo understood. The right head was probably on cloud nine because of Nightmare's sudden friendliness. Allo, on the other hand, spoke to him all the time. It was no surprise that her words were less important to him.

"It's fine..."

<O-oh? You sure? Anyway, Nightmare, you were saying?>

"Shhhh, shh."

Nightmare looked at Allo triumphantly, and Allo knew. It was intentional. Nightmare had given the pillow to the right head as well because it knew this would happen.

Later, after Ouroboros had gone hunting, another meeting was called between the monster and the human.

"...I knew it. You're the same as always, Nightmare." Allo said, puffing out her cheeks and blushing.

"Shh shh shh, shhhh..."

Nightmare laughed and nodded its head slightly. When it came to deviousness, Nightmare was a step ahead of Allo.

If you ask me, they're both scary... Treant thought as it watched the two of them.

Afterword

HELLO, HELLO, this is the author, Necoco. Thank you for purchasing Volume 7 of *Reincarnated as a Dragon Hatchling*! This volume contains the "Island at the Edge of the World" arc.

The island that Illusia and his party have arrived at after leaving the human village is a terrifying place infested with all kinds of strange-looking, high-ranked monsters. Deep within the island, at the root of the Great Tree that towers over even the most massive of dragons, someone is waiting for Illusia and his friends...

As for the contents of the next volume, I would say that this is the first half of the story about the defeat of the Demon King. The main characters in this volume are the strong, fantastical enemies who appear one after another: Eldia, Illusia's dragon father; Lilyxila and her party, who come to scout out the island; and Gyva. Look forward to seeing more of Gyva in the future!

Anyway, with that out of the way...*Reincarnated as a Dragon Hatchling* is finally on its seventh volume. Lucky number seven! To be honest, even including all the stuff I make just for fun, this is the first full-length novel series I've written that's exceeded 500,000 words. I have experience writing 300,000- to 400,000-word novels, but *Reincarnated as a Dragon Hatchling* hasn't just passed 500,000 words—it's over 1,000,000!

Initially, I had guessed that it would be completed in about one million words, but at the current pace, it seems it'll take a little longer... The series may be wrapping up to an end all at once with the next volume. I think I can finally see the finish line, but I wonder how many tens of thousands more words it'll be by then...

It may not be my place to say so, but if any of the readers of this afterword are thinking, "I want to be a novelist!" I recommend that you start by writing short novels of about 50,000 or 70,000 words and get into the habit of completing them.

When I first started writing as a hobby, I remember that I would start out with an idea of nearly one million words and then give up on it after about 20,000 words. This happened over and over again for more than ten works. As those of you who have written before will know, writing requires a lot of power and patience.

Among the countless works I've written and thrown away, there was one that I stopped writing after 50,000 words for the setting and less than 1,000 words of actual text because I got tired of it. I spent much longer thinking about the setting. You may think, "Oh, come on, there's no way that's true, that's ridiculous!" but I think it's quite common for those who have experience in writing.

...Oh? It's just me? That's not true, is it...?

From my own experience, I've found that a novel doesn't connect to its foundations much until it's complete. It's only after you've written the entire plot that you can go back and realize that you should've made the intro shorter or that you need to add more to the rising action and climax to make the conclusion land.

I believe that the ability to structure a story well is what usually makes a story good, but this structure doesn't happen unless you complete the story first and then go back to look at the whole thing.

That's why I don't recommend going "I've worked the plot out to be a million words! All right, let's do this!" As I mentioned earlier, writing takes patience, power, and time.

Some of you may think that I am doing my best, but I believe that the reason I've been able to write *Dragon*

Hatchling up to this point is because of all the readers who have supported me. I definitely could not have come this far on my own. I've truly been blessed.

If it weren't for you, dear readers, I might still only have the outline of a vast plot and 50,000 words written and saved somewhere in the depths of my laptop.

Thank you so much to the readers who have supported *Dragon Hatchling* since its web days and to the readers who support the book version too. Wait, you're reading it on the web? Did you leave comments? And did you buy the book too?! Thank you! Thank you so much! Now, your next step is to review it on your blog, a certain jungle-themed mail-order website, and on the blue bird app, you know the one...heh heh heh.

This volume was released in June 2018, and, what a surprise, a volume of the *Dragon Hatchling* manga was released in the same month! Hooray! A round of applause! It's the manga version of *Dragon Hatchling,* and it's truly wonderful! The comic is full of enjoyable elements in each and every frame, especially the comical antagonistic monsters' movements and Illusia's facial expressions. It's a work that you'll never get tired of no matter how many times you read it! I've already read everything I've been sent ten times over.

There are many things I'd love to point out about the manga version, such as the main character's flippancy, how cute the black lizard is, how ugly the horned rabbit is, and so forth. But because this is only an afterword to the book version, I'll wrap things up here.

—NECOCO

I DREW THIS WHILE THINKING THAT IT MUST BE DIFFICULT TO GO OUT INTO THE CITY AS THE SAINT, AND I PERSONALLY LIKED THE DESIGN.

SO, IF THE RANK F DARKWYRM EVOLVES, THEN...

FIRIN' UP!

Congrats on finishing Volume 7!! That was fast!! I'll be doing my best to keep up with the heat of the original work!

I received a wonderful bonus passage for Volume 1 of the manga, so I drew this scene in return.
—Rio (Manga Illustrator)

AND THERE WAS A HERO AND A SAINT...

MARIELLE... IS SOOOOO CUTE~!

• MARIELLE'S LEGS.

• THIS ILLUSTRATION IS A WORK OF FICTION, ABOUT A WORK OF FICTION, AND MAY DIFFER SLIGHTLY FROM THE ACTUAL NARRATIVE.